Bound By Temptation

(Born in Blood Mafia Chronicles #4)

Cora Reilly

Subscribe to Cora's newsletter to find out about her next books, bonus content and giveaways! (http://corareillyauthor.blogspot.de/p/newsletter.html)

Cover design by Romantic Book Affairs Design

PROLOGUE

Liliana

I knew it was wrong. If someone found out, if *my Father* found out, he'd never let me leave Chicago again. He wouldn't even let me leave the house anymore. It was vastly inappropriate and unladylike. People were still bad-mouthing Gianna after all that time. They'd jump at the chance to find a new victim, and what could be better than another Scuderi sister getting caught in the act?

And deep down I knew that I was exactly like Gianna when it came to resisting temptation. I simply couldn't. Romero's door wasn't locked. I slipped into his bedroom on tiptoes, holding my breath. He wasn't there but I could hear water running in the adjoining bathroom. I crept in that direction. The door was ajar. I peered through the gap.

In the last few days I'd learned that Romero was a creature of habit, so I found him under the shower as expected. But from my vantage point I couldn't see much. I edged the door open and slipped in.

My breath caught at the sight of him. He had his back turned to me and it was a glorious view. The muscles in his shoulders and back flexed as he washed his brown hair. Naturally, my eyes dipped lower to his perfectly shaped backside. I'd never seen a man like this, but I couldn't imagine that anyone could compare to Romero.

3

He began to turn. I should have left then. But I stared in wonder at his body. Was he aroused? He tensed when he spotted me. His eyes captured my gaze before they slid over my nightgown and naked legs. And then I found an answer to my question. He hadn't really been aroused before. *Oh hell.*

My cheeks heated as I watched him grow harder. It was all I could do not to cross the distance between us and touch him.

Romero slid the shower open with unhurried movements and wrapped a towel around his waist. Then he stepped out. The scent of his spicy shower gel wafted into my nose. Slowly he advanced on me. "You know," he said in a strange voice. "If someone found us like this, they might get the wrong idea. An idea that could cost me my life, and you your reputation."

I still couldn't move. I was stone, but my insides seemed to burn, to liquefy into red-hot lava. I couldn't look away. I didn't *want* to.

My eyes lingered on the edge of the towel, on the fine line of dark hairs disappearing beneath it, on the delicious V of his hips. Without my volition, my hand moved, reaching for Romero's chest, needing to feel his skin beneath my fingertips.

Romero caught my wrist before I could touch him, his grip almost painful. My gaze shot up, half embarrassed and half surprised. What I saw on Romero's face made me shiver.

He leaned forward, coming closer and closer. My eyes fluttered shut, but the kiss I wanted never came. Instead I heard the creak of the door. I peered up at Romero. He'd only opened the bathroom door wide. That's why he'd moved closer, not to kiss me. Embarrassment washed over me. How could I have thought he was interested in me?

"You need to leave," he murmured as he straightened. His fingers were still curled around my wrist.

"Then let me go."

He did instantly and took a step back. I stayed where I was. I wanted to touch him, wanted him to touch me in turn. He cursed and then he was upon me, one hand cradling the back of my head, the other on my hip. I could almost taste his lips they were so close. His touch made me feel more alive than anything ever had.

"Leave," he rasped. "Leave before I break my oath." It was half plea, half order.

CHAPTER ONE

Liliana

I still cringed when I thought about my first embarrassing attempt at flirting with Romero. Mother and my sister Aria had always warned me not to provoke men, and I'd never been as daring with anyone as I'd been with Romero that day. He'd seemed safe, like there was no way he could possibly hurt me no matter the provocation. I'd been young and stupid, only fourteen and already convinced I knew everything there was to know about men and love and everything else.

It had been only a few days before Aria's wedding to Luca and he'd sent Romero to protect my sister. It was a big deal to choose a bodyguard for your future wife; only someone who was deserving of your absolute trust could be allowed that close, but that knowledge wasn't even why *I* trusted Romero.

Romero had looked terribly handsome in his white shirt, black slacks and vest that hid his gun holster. And for some reason, his brown eyes had looked kinder than what I was used to from men in our world. I couldn't tear my gaze away from him. I wasn't sure what I'd been thinking, or what I'd expected to achieve, but the moment Romero sat down, I'd settled in his lap. He'd tensed under me, but something in his eyes had made me fall for him that day. Often in the past, when I'd flirted with my father's soldiers, I'd seen in their eyes that they wouldn't hesitate to have their way with me if it wasn't for my father. But with Romero I knew I would never have to worry that he'd take more than what I was willing to give. At least, that's how it had felt that day. He'd seemed like a good guy, like the guys I ever only got to admire from afar because you couldn't find them in the mafia. Like a knight in shining armor, someone dreams of silly girls were made of – girls like me.

Only a few months later, I found out that Romero wasn't who I thought he was, who I wanted him to be and had made him out to be. That day still haunts me after all this time. It could have been the moment that my crush on Romero disappeared for good.

My parents had taken Gianna, Fabiano and me to New York with them to attend Salvatore Vitiello's funeral, even though I didn't know Luca's and Matteo's father. I'd been so very excited to see Aria again. But that trip turned into a nightmare, my first real taste of what it meant to be part of our world.

After the Russians attacked the Vitiello mansion, I was alone with my brother Fabi in a room where Romero had taken us after the Famiglia under Luca's lead had come to our rescue. Someone had given my brother a tranquilizer because he'd completely lost it after he'd seen our bodyguard getting shot in the head. I was oddly calm, almost in trance as I huddled beside him on the bed, staring at nothing and listening for noises. Every time someone walked past our room, I tensed, prepared for another attack. But then Gianna texted, asking me where I was. I'd never moved as fast in my life. It took me less than two seconds to jump off the bed, cross the room and rip the door open. Gianna stood in the corridor, her red hair

7

all over the place. The moment I jumped into her arms, I felt better and safer. Since Aria had moved, Gianna had taken over the role as substitute mother while our own mother was busy taking care of her social responsibilities and catering to Father's every whim.

When Gianna decided to look around downstairs, panic overcame me. I didn't want to be alone right now, and Fabi really wasn't going to wake for another couple of hours, so despite my fear of what we'd find on the first floor, I followed my sister. Most of the furniture in the living room was ruined from the fight with the Russians and blood covered almost every surface. I'd never been very queasy about blood, or anything really. Fabi had always come to me to show me his wounds, especially when there was pus because he hadn't properly cleaned them. And even now, as we strolled past all the red on the white carpets and sofas, it wasn't the blood itself that made my stomach turn. It was the memory of the events. I couldn't even smell blood anymore because the floors had been cleaned with some kind of disinfectant. I was glad when Gianna headed for another part of the house but then I heard the first scream from the basement. I would have turned on my heel and pretended there was nothing. Not Gianna though.

She opened the steel door, which led to a room below the surface. The staircase was dark but from somewhere in the depth of the basement light spilled out. I shivered. "You don't want to go down there, right?" I whispered. I should have known the answer. This was Gianna.

"Yes, but you will stay on the stairs," Gianna said before she started her descent. I hesitated only a second before I went after her. Nobody had ever said I was good at following orders.

Gianna glared. "Stay there. Promise me."

I wanted to argue. I wasn't a little kid anymore. But then someone cried out below us, and the hairs in the back of my neck rose. "Okay. I promise," I said quickly. Gianna turned and moved down the remaining steps. She froze when she reached the last step before she finally stepped into the basement. I could only see part of her back but from the way her muscles tensed I knew she was upset. There was a muffled cry and Gianna flinched. Despite the fear pounding in my temples, I crept downstairs. I needed to know what my sister saw. She wasn't someone who freaked out easily.

Even as I did I knew I'd regret it, but I couldn't resist. I was tired of being left out of everything, of always being too young, of being reminded every day that I needed protection from myself and everything around me.

The moment my feet hit the basement floor, my eyes settled on the center of the room. At first, I couldn't even comprehend what was going on. It was as if my brain was giving me a chance to leave and be none the wiser, but instead of rushing off, I stayed and stared. My mind went into overdrive, soaking in every detail, every *gruesome* detail before me. Details I still remembered vividly years later.

There were two of the Russians who'd attacked us, tied to chairs, and then there was blood. Matteo and another man were beating and cutting them, *hurting* them. My vision tunneled, and terror rose up my throat. And then my gaze settled on Romero, his kind brown eyes, which weren't as kind as I remembered them. His hands, too, were covered in blood. The good guy and knight in shining armor I'd fantasized about, *that guy* he wasn't. A scream ripped from my body, but I could only tell because of the pressure in my chest and throat. I didn't hear anything beyond the rushing in my ears. Everyone stared at me like *I* was the crazy one. I wasn't sure what happened after that. I remembered fragments. Hands grasping me, arms holding tight. Soothing words that did nothing. I remembered a warm chest against my back and the smell of blood. There was a brief burning pain when Matteo injected me with something before my world transformed into eerie calm. The terror was still there, but it was blanketed. My vision was blurry but I could make out Romero kneeling beside me. He picked me up and straightened with me in his arms. The forced calm won out and I relaxed against his chest. Right in front of my eyes a red blotch disfigured his white shirt. Blood from the men that had been tortured. Sluggishly, terror tried to rip through the medication, but it was futile and I gave up the fight. My eyes fluttered shut as I resigned myself to my fate.

***

Romero

As Made Men it was our task to keep those safe that we were sworn to protect: the weak, children, women. I, in particular, had devoted my life to this goal. Many tasks in my job involved hurting others, being brutal and cold, but keeping people safe always made me feel like there was more to me than the bad. Not that it mattered; if Luca asked me, I'd do every bad thing imaginable. It was easy to forget that despite our own ethics and morals and codes, we Made Men were what most people perceived as evil. I was reminded of our real nature, of my real nature when I heard Liliana's scream. The screams of the Russians hadn't moved me. I'd heard those, and worse, before. But that high-pitched, not-ending scream of a girl we were meant to protect was like a fucking stab in the gut.

Her expression and eyes were the worst; they showed me exactly what I was. Maybe a good man would have sworn to be better, but I was good at my job. Most days I *enjoyed* it. Even the terror-stricken face of Liliana didn't make me want to be something other than a Made Man. Back then I hadn't realized that this glimpse of brutality wasn't even the worst way I would fuck up her life.

***

Liliana

I woke to something warm and soft below my body. My mind was sluggish but the memories were clear and focused, more focused than my surroundings when I finally dared to open my eyes.

Movement in the corner attracted my attention. Romero leaned against the wall across from me. I quickly did a check of the room I was in. It was a guest bedroom, and I was *alone* with Romero behind a closed door. Without the lingering effects of whatever Matteo had injected me earlier, I would have started screaming again. Instead I watched mutely as Romero walked toward me. I wasn't sure why I'd ever thought of him as harmless, now his every move screamed danger. When he'd almost reached the bed, I cringed, pressing myself against the pillow. Romero paused, dark eyes softening, but their kindness couldn't fool me anymore, not after what I'd seen. "It's okay. You are safe."

I'd never felt *not safe* in my life – until now. I wanted my blissful ignorance back. I didn't say anything.

Romero took a glass of water from the nightstand and held it out to me. My eyes searched the skin of his hands for blood but he must have cleaned them thoroughly. There wasn't the slightest hint of red, not even between his fingers or under his nails. He probably had a lot of practice cleaning up blood. Bile crept up my throat at the thought.

"You need to drink, kiddo."

My eyes flew up to his face. "I'm not a *kid*."

The ghost of a smile crossed Romero's face. "Of course not, Liliana."

I searched his eyes for mockery, for a hint of the darkness that had been there in the basement, but he looked like the good guy I wanted him to be. I sat up and took the glass from him. My hand shook but I managed not to spill water on myself. After two sips I handed the glass back to Romero.

"You can go to your sisters soon, but first Luca wants to have a word with you about what you saw today," he said calmly.

Fear speared me like a cold blade. I slid out of the bed when someone knocked, and Luca entered a moment later. He closed the door. My eyes darted from him to Romero. I didn't want to break down like I had before, but I could feel another panic attack pushing through the drugs in my bloodstream. I'd never been alone with them, and after today's events, it was too much.

"Nobody will hurt you," Luca said in his deep voice. I tried to believe him. Aria seemed to love him, so he couldn't be bad, and he hadn't been down in the basement torturing Russians. I risked another look at Romero, whose eyes rested on me.

I lowered my face. "I know," I said eventually, which probably sounded as much a lie as it felt. I took a deep breath and leveled my gaze on Luca's chin. "You wanted to talk to me?"

Luca nodded. He didn't come closer, nor did Romero. Maybe my fear was plain as day to them. "You can't tell Aria about what you saw today. She'll be upset."

"I won't tell her," I promised quickly. I'd never intended to talk to her. I didn't want to remember the events, much less to tell anyone about them. If I could, I'd wipe my memory clean of them instantly.

Luca and Romero exchanged a look, then Luca opened the door. "You're much more reasonable than your sister Gianna. You remind me of Aria."

Somehow his words made me feel like a coward. Not because Aria was. She was brave and so was Gianna, both in their own ways. I felt like a coward because I agreed to keep my silence for selfish reasons, because I wanted to forget, and not because I wanted to protect Aria from the truth. I was pretty sure she could have handled it better than I did.

"You can take her to Gianna, but make sure they don't walk around the house again," he said to Romero.

"What about Aria?" I blurted.

Luca tensed. "She's asleep. You can see her later." With that he left.

I wrapped my arms around my waist. "Do my parents know what happened?"

"Yes. Your father will pick you up once he's done with business and then take you back to Chicago. Probably in the morning." Romero waited but I didn't move. For some reason my body bristled at the idea of going closer to him, which was ridiculous considering that not too long ago I'd fantasized about kissing him.

He opened the door wide and stepped back. "I'm sure your sister Gianna is eager to see you."

Taking a deep breath, I forced myself to walk in his direction. His body was relaxed and his face kind, and despite the terror and fear still simmering deep in my body, my stomach fluttered lightly as I brushed past him. Maybe it was shock. I couldn't possibly have a crush on him after today.

CHAPTER TWO

<u>**Liliana**</u>

Whenever I thought I'd gotten over what had happened last September, something would remind me of that day and my stomach would tie itself into a hard knot again. Like today, when Gianna and I headed toward Matteo, Aria and Luca. Father had finally given in and allowed my sister and me to visit New York to celebrate my fifteenth birthday.

"Are you okay?" Gianna asked quietly, startling me out of my rising nervousness. Only being back in New York and seeing Matteo and Luca again was enough to fill my nose with the sweet stench of fresh blood.

"Yeah," I said quickly. I wasn't a little girl anymore who needed her big sisters for protection. "I'm fine."

Aria ran toward us when we'd almost reached them and threw her arms around both of us. "I missed you so much."

Being reunited with my sisters, I couldn't help but smile. I would even have walked straight down into that basement if that meant I could see them again.

Aria gave me a once over. "You're as tall as me now. I still remember when you didn't want to go anywhere without holding my hand."

I quickly looked around, but thankfully nobody was around to overhear her. "Don't say anything like that when Romero is around. Where is he anyway?" I realized a moment too late how idiotic I sounded, and flushed.

Aria laughed. "He's probably in his apartment."

I shrugged, but it was too late. It wasn't that I'd forgotten the blood on Romero's hands but for some reason I wasn't as scared of him as I was of Matteo, or even Luca. And I realized just how much when we walked toward them. My heart sped up and I could feel a panic attack rising up. I hadn't had one in weeks, so I fought it desperately.

"The birthday girl," Matteo said with a smile. How could that charming guy be the same person whom I'd seen covered in blood in the basement?

"Not yet," I said. I could feel my panic already abate. In real life Matteo wasn't as frightening as in my memories. "Unless you have an early present for me."

"I like the way you think," Matteo said with a wink. He took my suitcase, then held out his arm. I glanced at Gianna. "Won't you carry Gianna's luggage?" I didn't want Gianna to think I was flirting with her fiancé even though she didn't seem to like him very much most of the time.

"Luca can take care of it," Matteo said.

Gianna glared at him before she sent me a smile. "Go on."

I accepted Matteo's arm. I wasn't sure why Gianna despised him so much. And it had started before the basement, so it wasn't that. But it wasn't any of my business and Gianna didn't talk about her emotions with me anyway. That was what Aria was for. In their minds I was always too young to get it. But I knew more than they thought.

***

Fifty minutes later, we arrived at Luca's and Aria's apartment building. I checked my reflection in the mirrors of the elevator, making sure my make-up was in place and I didn't have anything between my teeth. It had been months since I'd last seen Romero and I wanted to make a good impression. But when we walked into Aria's and Luca's apartment Romero wasn't there yet. My eyes darted around and eventually Aria leaned toward me, whispering. "Romero's not around because Matteo and Luca are here to protect us."

"I wasn't looking for him," I said quickly, but she didn't buy it. I looked away before she could see my blush.

"Of course," Aria said with a knowing smile. "He'll come over later when Matteo and Luca have to leave for business."

Excitement bubbled up in me, but it was mixed with something queasy and nervous, too. I'd had the occasional nightmare about that night in the basement, not about Romero in particular but I wondered if a live encounter would bring more of the bad stuff up. But that wasn't even the main reason why I was

18

nervous. So far Romero had always ignored me, well not me, but my flirting. He'd treated me like a kid. Maybe he'd finally show more interest, or any interest at all. After all I was turning fifteen and it wasn't as if I hadn't caught many of my father's soldiers checking me out. Maybe I wasn't Romero's type, no matter my age. I didn't even know if he was dating someone or promised to someone.

During dinner I could tell that Aria and Gianna were exchanging the occasional glance. I wasn't sure what it meant. Were they talking about me?

The elevator made a bling sound and started its descent to whoever had called it.

"That's Romero," Aria said. Luca gave her an odd look but I didn't react at all, merely nodded as if I didn't care, but I did, and I was glad for Aria's warning.

"I need to go to the bathroom," I said, trying to sound casual. Gianna rolled her eyes. I snatched my purse from the floor and rushed toward the guest bathroom. When I closed the door, I heard the elevator doors slide open. A moment later Romero's voice rang out. It was deep but not rough. I loved the sound of it.

I faced the mirror and quickly refreshed my make up and fluffed up my dark-blond hair. It wasn't as bright and pretty as Aria's and not as eye-catching as Gianna's red hair but it could have been worse. The others would notice that I'd gone into the bathroom to make myself presentable, my sisters at the very least, but I didn't care. I wanted to look nice for Romero. Trying to look relaxed, I stepped out of the bathroom. Romero had taken a seat at the table and was loading a plate with the remains of our dessert: Tiramisu and Panna Cotta. He was sitting on the chair right beside mine. I glanced at Aria wondering if she had something to do with it. She merely smiled at me, but Gianna didn't even bother hiding her amusement. I really hoped she wasn't going to embarrass me in front of everyone. I strolled over to my chair, hoping I looked grown up and relaxed, but apart from a quick smile Romero didn't pay me any attention. Disappointment settled heavily in my stomach. I sat down beside him and took a sip of my water, more to have something to do than because I was actually thirsty.

If I'd thought Romero's obvious disinterest in me was the full extend of my embarrassment today, I was sorely mistaken. Once Matteo and Luca had left for some kind of business meeting, it became obvious that Gianna and Aria were looking for a chance to be alone. They could have just asked me to leave but apparently they needed to get rid of Romero as well. Aria leaned in to whisper in my ear. "Can you distract Romero for a while? It's important." I didn't get the chance to refuse or ask any questions.

"Romero, why don't you play Scrabble with Lily? She looks like she's bored out of her mind, and Aria and I need a moment for girl talk," Gianna said pointedly.

My face burned in shame. Gianna usually knew better than to embarrass me like that. She made it sound like Romero needed to babysit me while she and Aria discussed important stuff.

Romero walked over from the kitchen where he'd been checking his mobile and stopped beside me at the dining room table. I could barely look at him. What did he think of me now? I peered up through my lashes. He didn't look annoyed but that didn't mean he actually wanted to spend his evening entertaining me. He was a bodyguard, not a babysitter. "Your sister looks like she'd rather spend time with you," he told Gianna. Then his brown eyes settled on me. "Are you sure you want to play Scrabble with me?" he asked, and I couldn't help but smile. Few people ever asked what I wanted; even my sisters occasionally forgot that I was a person with her own opinions and wants.

Aria and Gianna gave me a meaningful look. I needed to convince Romero that I wanted it or I'd ruin things for them. "Yes, I really want to play Scrabble with you. I love that game, please?" I said with a bright smile. I didn't even remember when I'd played it last. Our family had never played board games.

Romero glanced toward my sisters. There was a hint of suspicion on his face. "You could join us," he said.

"I'd rather play alone with you," I said in a flirting tone. Gianna winked at me when Romero wasn't looking. "My sisters hate Scrabble and so does everyone else I know. You are my only hope."

A grin tugged at Romero's lips and he nodded. "All right, but be patient. It's been a while since I played."

Playing Scrabble with Romero was actually a whole lot of fun. It was the first time we really spent time alone together. I looked up from the word I'd just put down, debating if I should ask the question that was burning a hole in my stomach. Romero was busy figuring out his next word. His dark brows were drawn together in an adorable way. I wanted to lean across the board and kiss him. "Do you have a girlfriend?" I blurted when I couldn't hold it in anymore. And then I wanted to die on the spot. Apparently, I didn't need my sisters to embarrass me. I was doing just fine on my own.

Romero glanced up. There was surprise and amusement on his face. I could feel a blush traveling up my neck. *Way to go, Lily.* I'd sounded like a moron. "Is that your way of distracting me from the game so you can win?"

I giggled, glad he wasn't angry with me for asking such a personal question. He returned his attention to the letters in front of him, and my amusement faded when I realized he hadn't answered my question. Did that mean he had a girlfriend? I couldn't ask him again without sounding desperate.

I sank deeper into my chair, annoyed. My eyes darted toward the rooftop terrace where my sisters were having their girl talk.

Aria and Gianna probably thought I wasn't sure they were up to something. They thought I was oblivious to everything going on around me. Just because I was flirting with Romero, however, didn't mean I didn't notice the secretive looks they shared. I didn't ask them because I knew they wouldn't tell me anyway, and I'd feel even more like the fifth wheel. They weren't doing it to be mean but it hurt anyway. Aria looked upset over something Gianna had said. I had to resist the urge to go to them and try my luck.

"It's your turn," Romero's voice made me jump.

I flushed and quickly did a scan of the words on the board, but my concentration was frayed.

"Do you want to stop?" Romero asked after a couple of minutes. He sounded like that was something he wanted. He was probably bored out of his mind.

Pushing my disappointment down, I nodded. "Yeah. I'm going to read in my room a bit." I rose to my feet, hoping my face didn't give my emotions away, but I needn't have worried. Romero gave me a distracted smile and picked up his phone to check his messages. I backed away slowly. He didn't look up again. I needed to figure out a way to get his attention, and not with stupid games.

***

Aria had decorated the entire apartment with balloons for my birthday, as if I was a kindergarten kid. I'd thought we might be allowed to head to one of Luca's clubs but he and even Aria had refused to take me there. The amount of food on the table made it look as if a huge party was planned, but it was only us and Romero's two younger sisters. Aria had asked him to bring them. I felt like the looser kid without friends who needed her big sister to find friends for her. Maybe I should have stayed in Chicago, then at least I could have spent the day with my friends.

When Romero arrived with his sisters, I put on my brightest smile. "Happy birthday, Liliana," he said, handing me an envelope. It was a voucher for a bookstore. "Aria said you love to read."

"Yes, thank you," I said, but somehow I'd hoped for a different gift from Romero. Something personal, something that showed I was special.

"These are my sisters." He pointed at the taller girl with thick brown curls. "This is Tamara, she's fifteen like you." I smiled and so did Tamara but she seemed as embarrassed as I felt. "And this is Keira, she's twelve. I'm sure you'll get along fine." It was obvious that I was supposed to spend time with them because I was still too young to hang with Aria, Luca and the others. It annoyed me, even though Tamara and Keira seemed nice enough, but I hadn't come to New York for a kid party. With another smile, Romero headed for Luca and Matteo, and I led his sisters toward Aria and Gianna, and the buffet.

I tried my best to enjoy the evening and be nice to Romero's sisters but I wanted something special for my birthday, something I'd been dreaming about for a very long time. When I noticed Romero heading out onto the roof terrace for a call, I snuck out as well. The others were hopefully busy enough not to miss me for a couple of minutes. Romero talked on the phone and didn't notice me at first. I followed him quietly and watched as he leaned against the banister. His sleeves were rolled up to his elbows, revealing muscled forearms. I wondered how it would feel to ran my hands over them, to feel his skin and strength.

When his eyes settled on me, his brows drew together in a frown and he straightened. I moved closer and positioned myself beside him. He hung up and put his phone in his pocket. "Shouldn't you be inside with your guests?" he asked with a smile, but I could tell that it wasn't as honest as usual.

I moved a bit closer and smiled up at him. "I needed some fresh air."

Romero's eyes were alert as he watched me. "We should return."

"There's something I want for my birthday," I said quietly. "Something only you can give me." I'd repeated the words in my head countless times but aloud they didn't sound half as flirty as they had in my imagination.

"Lily," Romero began, his body brimming with tension.

I didn't want to hear what he was going to say. I quickly stood on my tiptoes and tried to kiss him. He gripped my shoulders before my lips reached his and held me away from him like I had an infectious sickness.

"What are you doing?" He let me go and took a few steps back. "You are a child, and I'm a soldier of the Famiglia. I'm not a toy you can play with when you're bored."

I hadn't expected that kind of reaction from him. Surprise and shock, yes, but anger? No. "I only wanted to kiss you. I don't want to play games. I like you."

Romero shook his head, then gestured toward the glass door. "Go back inside. Your sisters will start to wonder where you are."

He sounded like a big brother, and that was the last thing I wanted him to be. I whirled around before I walked back in a rush. My heart shriveled in my chest. For some reason I'd never considered a rejection from Romero. I'd fantasized about our first kiss so often that the option of it never happening had never crossed my mind. The rest of the evening, I struggled to keep a happy face, especially whenever I saw Romero. I was actually glad to return to Chicago. I wouldn't get to see Romero for a long time, enough time to get over him and find someone else to crush on.

Romero

I'd known Liliana had a crush on me. Aria had mentioned it before, but I'd never expected the girl to act on her feelings. She was a pretty kid. *A kid.*

I didn't have the slightest interest in her and the sooner she understood the better. She'd looked fucking hurt when I'd lashed out at her, but I had no choice. Even if she weren't still a child, I couldn't have let her kiss me.

When I returned to the living area, Luca walked up to me. "What was that? Why was Liliana outside with you?"

Of course he'd noticed. Luca never missed anything.

"She tried to kiss me."

Luca's eyebrows rose. "I assume you pushed her away."

"Do you really have to ask? She's my sister's age."

"Her age isn't even the main problem. At least in her father's eyes."

"I know." I was a soldier, and girls like Liliana were supposed to stay in their own social circles.

Luca sighed. "That girl will be as much trouble as Gianna, if not worse."

I had a feeling he might be right.

CHAPTER THREE

<u>Liliana</u>

"The nerve of that girl! From the day she's been born she's been nothing but trouble!" Father's words echoed through the house. Fabiano peered up at me as if I knew the answers to his questions. My own mind was a huge question mark. I wasn't exactly sure what had happened but I got the gist of it. Gianna had disappeared while she'd been in New York with Aria. Now everyone was looking for her. No wonder Aria hadn't asked me to visit as well. Not that I would have been too keen on returning to New York after my last embarrassing encounter with Romero four weeks ago. But it still stung that Aria and Gianna had made plans behind my back, behind everyone's back.

I walked down the stairs, motioning for Fabi to stay where he was, and then I inched toward Father's office. Mother was there, crying. Father was on the phone, from his still angry but more restrained tone I assumed with his Boss Cavallaro. Cavallaro was the only person that Father truly respected. Mother spotted me in the doorway and quickly shook her head, but I took another step forward and into the office.

I knew it was better to stay away from Father when he was in a mood like this, even though he'd usually lashed out at Gianna and not me, but my sister was gone now.

Father hung up, then narrowed his eyes at me. "Did I allow you to come in?"

His voice hit me like a whip but I stood my ground. "What happened to Gianna?"

Mother sent me a warning look.

"Your sister ran off. She'll probably get herself knocked up by some idiot, and ruin her and our family's reputation."

"Maybe she'll come back," I suggested. But somehow I knew she wouldn't. This wasn't a spur of the moment thing. She'd planned this, for months probably. That explained all the secrecy with Aria during our last visit in New York. Why hadn't they told me? Didn't they trust me? Did they think I'd run to Father the first chance I got? And then another thought buried itself in my brain. If Gianna was gone, if she didn't marry Matteo, who else would? Fear washed over me. What if Father made me marry Matteo? I'd hoped I could marry for love now that my sisters had already been married off for tactical reasons. Maybe it was a selfish thing to think in a situation like this but I couldn't help it. An image of Romero popped into my head. I knew it was silly to think of him when it came to marriage. Even if Gianna returned and still married Matteo, it would be almost impossible to convince Father to give me to a mere soldier, especially one from New York. And then there was the problem that he didn't even want me and that I'd promised myself to get over him.

I knew all that but that didn't mean I couldn't hope and dream, sometimes it felt like that was all I could do.

"How many men will have had Gianna by then? She'll be worth nothing even if she returns," Father spat. I winced, horrified by his harsh words. Worth nothing? Surely we were more for him than a commodity to sell off. More than a thin piece of flesh between our legs?

Father gripped my shoulders, his eyes burning into me. I shied back but he didn't release me. "Don't think I don't see how you're making eyes at my soldiers. You're too much like Gianna for your own good. I won't have another daughter make a fool out of me."

"I won't," I whispered. Father had never talked to me in that tone before. His expression and words made me feel cheap and unworthy, like I needed to clean myself of my impure thoughts.

"That's right. I don't care if I have to lock you into your room until your marriage day to protect your reputation and honor."

This wasn't about my honor or reputation. I didn't care about it. This was all about my father. It was always about the men in the family, what they wanted and expected.

"Rocco, Lily is a good girl. She won't do anything," Mother said carefully. That wasn't what she usually told me. She always warned me that I was too flirty, too aware of the effect that my body had on men. But I was glad for her support because too often she'd remained silent when Father had attacked Gianna in the same way.

Father let go of me and turned on her. "It was your job to raise decent girls. For your sake, I hope you're right and Liliana won't follow after Gianna." The menace in his voice made me quiver. How could he be so horrible toward his own wife?

Mother blanched. I backed away and nobody tried to stop me. I quickly ran upstairs. Fabi waited for me, his eyes wide and curious. "What happened?" he asked fearfully.

I shook my head in response, not in the mood to recap everything for him, and stormed toward my room.

I'd never been at the center of Father's anger like that. But now that Gianna was gone as well, he'd keep an extra eye on me, making sure I was the perfect lady he wanted his daughters to be. I'd always felt free, never understood why Gianna felt so restrained by our life, but now it started to dawn on me. Things would change now.

***

In the months since Gianna's escape, things at home had been tense at best. Father had lost it over the smallest things. He'd hit me only twice, but Fabi hadn't been as lucky. But worse than the violence was his constant suspicion, the way he watched me like I was another scandal in the making. My golden cage had become a bit smaller, even though that had seemed hardly possible before. I hoped things would change now that Matteo had caught Gianna and was bringing her back to Chicago. Maybe that would appease

Father, although he'd seemed far from appeased when I'd last seen him. I wasn't quite sure what exactly had happened but from what I gathered Gianna had been caught with another man, and that was the worst-case scenario in our world. Father would probably put me in shackles to stop me from doing the same.

"When will they be here?" Fabiano asked for the hundredth time. His voice had a whiny tinge to it and I had to stop myself from lashing out at him in frustration.

Fabiano and I had been waiting on the first floor landing for the last twenty minutes, and my patience was running thin.

"I don't know," I whispered. "Be quiet. If Mother figures out we're not in our rooms, we'll be in trouble."

"But—"

Voices sounded below. I recognized one of them as Luca's. He managed to fill a house with it; no wonder considering how big he was.

"They're here!" Fabiano dashed away and I was close behind him as we stormed down the staircase.

I spotted Gianna immediately. Her hair was brown now and she looked utterly exhausted but apart from that she was the sister I remembered. Father had often made it sound like she would be a new person if she ever returned; a horrible worthless person.

Father sent Fabi and me a glare when he noticed us, but I didn't care. I rushed toward Gianna and wrapped my arms around her. I'd missed her so much. When I'd first heard that she'd been caught by Matteo, I'd worried he'd kill her, so seeing her unharmed was a huge relief.

"Didn't I tell you to keep them upstairs?" Father hissed.

"I'm sorry. They were too quick," Mother said. I peered over my shoulder to see her apologetic face as she came down the staircase. Since Gianna's escape Father had been on edge constantly and often lashed out at her as well. His screams had woken me more than once at night. I wasn't sure when he'd become so violent. I didn't remember him being like that when I was younger, or maybe I'd only been less aware of those things.

"Lily, Fabi, back to your rooms," Father ordered. I let go of Gianna and was about to protest but Fabi beat me to it.

"But Father, we haven't seen Gianna in forever," Fabi grumbled.

Father advanced on us and I tensed. He rarely hit me but he looked furious. He grabbed Fabi and me, and dragged us away from Gianna. Then he pushed us toward the staircase. "Upstairs now."

I stumbled from the force of his push, but when I'd regained my balance I stopped and didn't move. I couldn't believe he wouldn't let us talk to Gianna after we hadn't seen her in so long.

"It's okay," Gianna said but her face told a different story. She looked hurt and sad, and usually Gianna wasn't someone who showed that kind of emotion. "We can talk later."

My eyes were drawn to something behind her: Romero. He stood strong and tall, his eyes firmly focused on my father. I hadn't seen him in seven months and over time I'd thought I'd gotten over my crush, but seeing him now my stomach fluttered with butterflies again.

Father's outburst drew my attention back to him. "No, you can't. I won't have you around them. You are no longer my daughter, and I don't want your rottenness to rub off on Liliana," he thundered. He looked like he would have loved nothing more than to kill Gianna. It scared me. Shouldn't he love us, his children, no matter what? If I ever did something he disapproved of, would he hate me as well?

"That's bullshit," Matteo said.

"Matteo," Luca said. "This isn't our business." My eyes darted between the two, then again toward Romero whose hand was below his vest. A twisted part of me wanted to see him in action. He was probably amazing in fight situations, and an even worse part knew Mother, Fabi and I would be better off if Father was gone.

Mother wrapped her fingers around my wrist and took Fabi's hand. "Come now," she said insistently, tugging us toward the staircase and upstairs.

"That's right. This is my family, and Gianna is still subject to my rule, don't you ever forget that," Father said.

"I thought I wasn't your daughter anymore, so why do I have to listen to a word you say?"

My head whirled around, stunned by the venom in Gianna's voice.

"Careful," Father hissed. "You are still part of the Outfit." He looked like he would have beaten Gianna if it wasn't for Matteo who held her by the waist. Mother tried to pull me along but Romero glanced up that moment and his eyes met mine. His rejection on my birthday was still fresh in my mind, and yet I knew I still wanted to kiss him. Why was it that we sometimes wanted something that was impossible? Something that only led to hurt?

CHAPTER FOUR

Liliana

Sometimes it felt like I had to prove myself to Father every day. He waited for me to mess up like Gianna had, but I wasn't sure how that was even possible; he never let me out of sight. Unless I started something with one of my ancient bodyguards, there was no way I could sully my honor. But Father hadn't forgiven Gianna yet, which was why I hadn't seen her in almost two years. She was forbidden from coming to Chicago, and I wasn't allowed to visit New York. If it wasn't for Aria's sneakiness, I wouldn't even have been able to talk to Gianna on the phone.

Sometimes even I felt anger toward Gianna because her escape had turned my life into hell. Maybe Father would have been less strict if Gianna had played by the rules. And then there were moments when I admired her for her daring. There wasn't a night when I didn't dream of freedom. I didn't really want to run but I wished I could carve myself out more freedom in my life. Freedom to date, freedom to fall in love and be with that person.

I didn't even remember how it felt to be in love. Just like Gianna, I hadn't seen Romero in almost two years. What I'd felt for him back then hadn't been love, not even close. It had been admiration and fascination, I knew that now. But there had been nobody else either. Of course, it was hard to meet someone to fall in love with if you went to an all-girls school and weren't allowed to go anywhere alone.

The sound of glass shattering downstairs tore me from my thoughts. I jumped off my bed and opened my door. "Mother?" I called. She'd been gone all morning. There was no answer but I could hear someone moving in the kitchen.

I crept out of my room and down the stairs. "Mother?" I tried again when I'd almost reached the door to the kitchen. Still no answer. I pushed the door open and stepped inside. A wine bottle lay broken on the floor, red wine spilled around it. Mother was kneeling beside it, her cream-colored skirt slowly soaking up the liquid, but she didn't seem to notice. She was staring down at a shard in her palm as if it held the answer to all her questions. I'd never seen her like that. I walked toward her. "Mom?" I almost never called her that, but it felt like the right choice at the moment.

She looked up, her blue eyes unfocused and teary. "Oh, you are home?"

'Where else would I be?' I wanted to ask, but instead I touched her shoulder and said, "What's the matter? Are you alright?"

She stared down at the broken piece of glass in her hand again, then dropped it to the floor. I helped her to her feet. She wasn't steady on her legs and I could smell alcohol on her breath. It was still early for her to start drinking, and she wasn't really much of a drinker at all.

"I was at the doctor's."

I froze. "Are you sick? What's wrong?"

"Lung cancer," she said with a small shrug. "Stage three."

"But you never smoked! How is that even possible?"

"It can happen," she said. "I'll have to start chemotherapy soon."

I wrapped my arms around her, feeling helpless and small under the weight of that news. "Does Father know?"

"I couldn't reach him. He didn't answer his phone."

Of course not. Why should he answer a call from his wife? He was probably with one of his mistresses. "We need to tell Aria and Gianna. They need to know."

Mother gripped my arm. "No," she said firmly. "It'll ruin their Christmas. I don't want them to know yet. There's no reason to worry them. I haven't spoken to Gianna in a long time anyway, and Aria has enough on her plate as the wife of a Capo."

"But Mom, they'd want to know."

"Promise me you won't tell them," she demanded.

I nodded slowly. What else could I do?

***

Two hours later I heard Father come home and another thirty minutes later, Mother's light steps came upstairs and then the door to the master bedroom closed. She'd been alone. Was Father still downstairs? I left my room and went to his office on the first floor. After a moment of hesitation, I knocked. I needed to talk to him.

Our Christmas party would be in two weeks and now that Mother was sick, Gianna should be invited. She and Mother should get the chance to spend some time together and reconcile.

"Come in," Father said.

I opened the door and poked my head in, half expecting to see him devastated and crying, but he was bent over some papers, working. I walked in, confused. "Has Mother talked to you?" Maybe she hadn't told him about her cancer.

He looked up. "Yes, she did. She'll be starting treatment with the best doctor in Chicago next week."

"Oh, okay." I paused, hoping for something else from Father but he watched me without a hint of emotion on his face. "I was thinking that Mother needs the support of her family now more than ever. Of her whole family."

Father raised his eyebrows. "And?"

"I think we should invite Gianna to our Christmas party. She and Mother haven't seen each other in a long time. I'm sure Mother would be very happy to see Gianna again."

Father's face darkened. "I won't have that whore in my house. Maybe Matteo has forgiven her and even married her despite her transgressions but I'm not that kind."

No, kind definitely wasn't a word I'd use for my father. "But Mother needs every bit of support she can get."

"No, and that's my last word," he growled. "And your mother doesn't want people to know about her sickness. They'd only start to wonder if we invited Gianna. We'll act as if nothing is wrong. You won't even tell your sisters or anyone else, do you understand?"

I nodded. But how could I keep that kind of secret from everyone?

***

The house was decorated beautifully for our Christmas party. Everything was perfect. The scent of roast beef and truffled mashed potatoes carried through the rooms, but I couldn't enjoy it. Mother had spent yesterday and the majority of this morning throwing up because of her treatment. With several layers of make-up, you couldn't tell how pale she was but I knew. Only Father and I knew. Even Fabi didn't have a clue.

Aria and Luca arrived only minutes before the other guests. They stayed in a hotel anyway, so it wasn't too hard to keep Mother's state from them. Aria smiled brightly when she saw me and hugged me. "God, Lily. You look so beautiful."

I smiled tightly. I'd been so excited when I'd found the silver dress a few weeks ago because it made me feel grown-up and accentuated my curves in just the right way, but today my excitement over something like a piece of clothing felt ridiculous.

Aria pulled away and searched my face. "Is everything okay?"

I nodded quickly and turned my attention to Luca who'd waited patiently behind my sister for his turn. He gave me a quick hug. It still felt strange to have him greet me that way. "Father is still in his office and Mother is in the kitchen," I explained. At least I hoped Mother wasn't in the bathroom, throwing up again.

Luca walked past me and my gaze landed on Romero who'd been hidden behind Luca's massive frame. My eyes widened at the sight of him. I hadn't expected him to come. Last year Luca had come alone with Aria. After all, he was more than capable to protect her.

"Hello," I said casually, sounding way more composed than I felt. I hadn't quite gotten over my crush on Romero but I realized with relief that I wasn't a quivering mess around him anymore. The last few months and weeks had changed me.

Romero

Luca had business to conduct with Scuderi and Dante Cavallaro; that was the only reason why I'd come to Chicago with them at all. And now as I stood in the doorway to the Scuderi mansion, staring at Liliana, I wondered if I shouldn't have come up with an excuse. The last time I'd seen Lily she'd been a girl, and while she still wasn't a woman, she'd grown a lot. She was fucking stunning. It was difficult not to look at her. It was easy to forget that there were still a few months until she'd be of age, easy to forget that she was way out of my league.

She tilted her head in greeting and stepped back. Where had the blushing, flirting girl gone? I had to admit I was sad that she wasn't giving me her flirty smile, though it had always bothered me in the past.

I followed Luca and Aria into the house. I could hear Lily's steps close behind me, could smell her flowery perfume and even see her slender frame from the corner of my eye. It took a lot of restraint not to glimpse over my shoulder to get another good look at her.

I spent the next couple of hours watching her discreetly as I pretended to be busy guarding Aria, not that I had much to do anyway. But the more I watched Lily, the more I realized that something was wrong. Whenever she thought nobody was paying attention to her, she seemed to deflate, her smile falling, her shoulders slumping. She was a good actress when she gave it her full attention but her few moments of inattentiveness were enough for me. Over the years as a bodyguard, I'd learned to be aware of even the smallest signs.

When she left the living room and didn't come back, worry overcame me. But she wasn't my responsibility. Aria was. I glanced at Luca's wife. She was deep in conversation with her mother and Valentina Cavallaro. I excused myself. She'd be safe here. Luca was just across the room in what looked like an argument with Dante and Scuderi.

Once I found myself in the lobby, I hesitated. I wasn't sure where Liliana had gone and I could hardly search the entire house for her. If someone found me, they might think I was spying for Luca. A sound from the corridor to my right attracted my attention and after having made sure that I was alone, I followed it until I caught sight of Liliana. She leaned against the wall, her head was thrown back, her eyes closed. I could tell she was trying to keep it together, and yet even like that, she was a sight to behold. Fucking gorgeous. One day a man would be very lucky to be married to her.

The idea didn't sit well with me but I didn't linger on my strange reaction. I walked toward her, making sure to make my steps audible so she knew she wasn't alone anymore. She tensed, her eyes fluttering open but when she spotted me, she relaxed again and turned away. I wasn't sure what to make from her reaction to my presence. I stopped a couple of steps from her. My gaze traveled over her long, lean legs, then I quickly moved on to her face. "Liliana, are you okay? You've been gone for a long time."

"Why do you insist on calling me Liliana when everyone always calls me Lily?" She opened her eyes again and smiled bitterly. She had fucking amazing blue eyes. "Did my sister tell you to watch me?" she asked accusingly.

As if I needed someone to tell me. It had been almost impossible to keep my eyes off Liliana tonight. "No, she didn't," I said simply.

Her blue eyes held confusion, then she turned her face to the side, leaving me to stare at her profile. Her chin wobbled but she swallowed and her expression evened out. "Don't you need to watch Aria?"

"Luca is there," I said. I moved a bit closer, too close. Lily's perfume wafted into my nose, made me want to bury my face in her hair. God, I was losing my freaking mind. "I can tell that something is wrong. Why don't you tell me?"

Lily narrowed her eyes. "Why? I'm not your responsibility. And last time we saw each other you didn't seem to like me very much."

Was she still mad at me for stopping her from kissing me at her birthday more than two years ago? "Maybe I can help you," I said instead.

She sighed, her shoulders slumping a bit more. With that expression of weariness, she looked older somehow, like a grown woman, and I had to remind myself of my promise and oath again. Her eyes brimmed with tears when she peered up at me but they didn't fall.

"Hey," I said softly. I wanted to touch her, brush her hair away from her. Fuck. I wanted much more than that, but I stayed where I was. I couldn't go around touching a daughter of the Outfit's Consigliere. I shouldn't even have been alone with her.

"You can't tell anyone," she said.

I hesitated. Luca was my Capo. There were certain things I couldn't keep from him. "You know I can't promise you that without knowing what you're going to tell me." And then I wondered if maybe she was pregnant, if maybe someone had broken her heart, and the idea made me furious. I wasn't supposed to want her, I shouldn't want her, and yet...

"I know, but it's not about the Outfit or the Famiglia. It's..." She lowered her gaze and swallowed. "God, I'm not supposed to tell anyone. And I hate it. I hate that we're keeping up the charade when things are falling apart."

I waited patiently, giving her the time she obviously needed.

Her shoulders began to shake but she still didn't cry. I wasn't sure how she did it. "My mother has cancer."

That wasn't what I'd expected. Although, now that I thought about it, her mother had looked pale despite the thick layer of make-up on her face.

I touched Lily's bare shoulder and tried to ignore how good it felt, how *smooth* her skin was. "I'm sorry. Why don't you talk to Aria about it? I thought you and her talk about everything."

"Gianna and Aria talk about everything. I'm the little sister, the fifth wheel." She sounded bitter. "Sorry." She released a long breath, obviously trying to get a grip on her emotions. "Father forbade me from telling anyone, even Aria, and here I am telling you."

"I won't tell anyone," I promised before I could really think it through. What was I doing promising that kind of thing to Lily? Luca and the Famiglia were my priority. I had to consider the consequences if the wife of the Consigliere was sick. Would that weaken him and the Outfit? Luca might think so. And not just that, I was supposed to protect Aria. Wasn't it my job to tell her that her mother was sick? That was the problem if you started to think with your dick. Then things always got messed up.

Lily tilted her head to the side with a curious expression. "You won't?"

I leaned against the wall beside her, wondering how I was going to get me out of that corner. "But don't you think you should tell your sister? It's her mother. She deserves to know the truth."

"I know, don't you think I know that?" she whispered desperately. "I want to tell her. I feel so guilty for keeping it a secret. Why do you think I'm hiding in the hallway?"

"Then tell her."

"Father would be furious if he found out. He's been on edge for a long time. Sometimes I think it takes only the smallest incident and he'll put a bullet through my head."

She sounded fucking scared of her own father. And the bastard was scary. I took her hand. "Has he done anything to you? I'm sure Luca could figure out a way to keep you safe." What the fuck was I talking? Scuderi would convince Dante to start a war if Luca took his youngest daughter away from him. You never got involved in other people's family problems. That was one of the most important rules in our world.

"Father wouldn't allow it," she said matter-of-factly. She really wasn't the kid I'd first met. This world took away your innocence far too soon. "And he didn't do anything, but he'd be furious if I went against his direct orders."

"You know your sister, she'd never tell anyone."

"Then she'd have to bear the secret and she wouldn't even be able to talk to Mother about it. Why is everything such a mess? Why can't I have a normal family?"

"We can't choose our family."

"And in my case, not even my future husband," she said. Then she shook her head. "I don't know why I said it. This isn't what I should be worried about now." She looked down at my hand, which was still holding hers. I released her. If Scuderi or one of his men walked in on us, Scuderi would have a new reason to lose his shit.

"You know what? I will tell her," Lily said suddenly. She straightened and gave me a grateful smile. "You are right. Aria deserves to know the truth." Now that she didn't lean against the wall anymore, we were even closer. I should have taken a step back and kept my distance, but instead my eyes were drawn to her lips.

Lily surprised me by walking away. "Thank you for your help." I watched her turn the corner and then she was gone.

Liliana

My heart hammered in my chest, not only because I'd been alone with Romero and had barely managed to leave without kissing him, but because I was determined to go against Father's orders. Maybe Romero had said the truth and he wouldn't tell my sister and Luca about my mother, but really why should he keep a secret for me? We weren't a couple, we weren't even friends. We were nothing to each other. The thought buried itself like a heavy weight in my stomach.

It was better if I told Aria now. She'd find out eventually, and I wanted it to be from me. I found her in the living room, a plate with prosciutto in her hand. She was talking to Valentina. I walked toward them and Valentina noticed me first. There was a flicker of pity in her green eyes before she smiled at me. Did she know?

Of course, she did. Father probably had told his boss Dante right away, and Dante had told his wife. Had Father told other people as well? People he thought more deserving of the truth than his own family? "Hi Val," I said. "Can I steal Aria from you for a moment? I have to talk to her."

Aria gave me a questioning look but Valentina nodded merely. I linked arms with my sister and casually strolled through the room with her. I didn't want Father or Mother to get suspicious. I caught Romero's gaze across the room. He stood beside Luca and Dante but was looking my way. He gave me a small encouraging nod and somehow that small gesture made me feel better. In the last two years I'd convinced myself that the thing with Romero was nothing but a silly crush but now I wasn't so sure anymore.

"Lily, what's going on? You've been acting very odd all evening," Aria whispered as we headed toward the lobby.

"I'm going to tell you in a moment. I want us to be alone."

Aria's face clouded with worry. "Has anything happened? Do you need help?"

I led her upstairs and into my room. When the door had closed behind us, I released Aria and sank down on my bed. Aria sat down beside me.

"It's Mother," I said in a whisper. "She's got lung cancer." Maybe I should have broken it to her in a less direct manner, but it wouldn't have made the news less horrible.

Aria stared at me wide eyes, then she slumped against the wall, releasing a harsh breath. "Oh God. I thought she looked exhausted but I blamed it on another fight with Father."

"They're still fighting and it's making everything worse."

Aria wrapped her arm around me and for a moment we held each other in silence. "Why hasn't she told me herself?"

"Father doesn't want anyone to know. He actually forbade me from telling you."

Aria pulled back. "He forbade you?"

"He wants to keep up appearances. I think he's embarrassed by Mother's sickness." I hesitated. "That's why I didn't tell you right away. I didn't know what to do, but I talked to Romero and he convinced me to tell you."

Aria searched my face. "Romero, hm?"

I shrugged. "Will you tell Gianna when you're back in New York?"

"Of course," Aria said. "I hate that she can't be here." She sighed. "I want to talk to Mother about it. She needs our support but how can we give it to her if we're not supposed to know?"

I didn't know. "I hate how Father's acting. He's so cold toward her. You're so lucky Aria that you have a husband who cares about you."

"I know. One day you'll have that too."

I really hoped she'd be right. Life with someone like my father would be a hell I couldn't survive.

***

Every day, Mother faded a bit more. Sometimes it felt like all I had to do was look away for a moment and her skin had already become a scarier shade of grey and she'd lost even more weight. Even her beautiful hair was gone completely. It was impossible to keep her sickness a secret anymore. Everyone knew. When other people were around Father played the doting and worried husband but at home when we were alone he could barely stand Mother's presence as if he worried that she was infectious. It fell on me to support her while I tried get through my last year in school. Aria, Gianna and I talked on the phone almost every day. Without them I couldn't have survived. And at night when I lay in the dark and couldn't sleep from worry and fear, I remembered the way Romero had looked at me at our Christmas party, as if he saw me for the very first time, really saw me as a woman and not just a stupid child. The look in his brown eyes made me feel warmer even if it was only a memory.

A soft knock made me sit up. "Yes?" I asked quietly. *'Please don't let Mother be throwing up again'*. I wanted one night without the acid smell in my nose. I felt bad for the thought. How could I think something like that?

The door opened and Fabi poked his head through the gap before he slipped in. His dark hair was dishevelled and he was in his pajamas. I hadn't drawn the curtains so I could tell that he'd cried but I didn't mention it. Fabi had turned twelve several months ago and was too proud to admit his feelings to anyone, even me.

"Are you asleep?"

"Do I look like I've been sleeping?" I asked teasingly.

He shook his head, then he put his hands in the pockets of his pajama pants. He was too old to come into bed with me because he was scared of something. Father would have ripped Fabi's head off if he'd found him with tears on his face in my room. Weakness wasn't something Father tolerated in his son, or anyone really.

"Do you want to watch a movie?" I scooted to the side. "I can't sleep anyway."

"You've got only girl movies," he said as if I was asking a huge favor of him but he headed toward my DVD shelf and picked something. Then he sat down beside me with his back against my headboard. The movie started and we watched in silence for a long time.

"Do you think Mom is going to die?" Fabi asked suddenly, his gaze fixed on the screen.

"No," I said with all the conviction I didn't feel.

***

My eighteenth birthday was today, but there would be no party. Mother was too sick. There was no room in our house for celebrations or happiness. Father was hardly home anymore, always gone on business, and recently Fabi had started to accompany him. And so I was left alone with Mother. Of course there was a nurse and our maid, but they weren't family. Mother didn't want them around and so I was the one sitting at her bed after school, reading to her, trying to pretend that her room didn't smell of death and hopelessness. Aria and Gianna had called in the morning to wish me a happy birthday. I knew they'd wanted to visit, but Father had forbidden it. Not even for my birthday he could be nice.

I put the book down that I'd read to Mother. She was asleep. The noise of her respiratory aid, a click and rattling, filled the room. I stood, needing to walk around a bit. My legs and back were stiff from sitting all day.

I walked toward the window and peered out. Life was happening everywhere around me. My phone buzzed in my pocket, startling me from my thoughts. I took it out and found an unknown number on my screen. I pressed it against my ear. "Hello?" I whispered as I walked out into the corridor as not to disturb my mother, even though noises hardly woke her anymore.

"Hello Liliana."

I froze. "Romero?" I couldn't believe he'd called me, and then a horrible idea struck me, and the only explanation for his call. "God, did something happen to my sisters?"

"No, no. I'm sorry, I didn't mean to scare you. I wanted to wish you a happy birthday." His voice was smooth and warm and deep, and it soothed me like honey did with a sore throat.

"Oh," I said. I braced myself against the wall as my pulse slowed again. "Thank you. Did my sister tell you it was my birthday?" I smiled lightly. I could imagine Aria doing that, hoping to cheer me up. She hadn't talked to me about it but I was fairly sure she knew that I still liked Romero after all this time.

"She didn't have to. I know your birthday."

I didn't say anything, didn't know what to say. He remembered my birthday?

"Do you have birthday plans?"

"No. I'll stay at home and take care of my mother," I said tiredly. I couldn't remember the last time I'd slept through the night. If Mother didn't wake me because she threw up or was in pain, then I lay awake staring into nothingness.

Romero was silent on the other end, then in an even gentler voice he said, "Things will get better. I know things look hopeless right now but they won't always be like this."

"You've seen a lot of death in your life. How can you stand it?"

"It's different if it's someone you care for who's dying, or if it's business-related." He had to be careful what he said on the phone, so I regretted having brought it up, but hearing his voice felt too good. "My Father died when I was fourteen. We weren't as close as I'd wanted us to be but his death was the only one that really got me so far."

"Mother and I aren't as close as many of my friends are with their mothers, and now that she's dying I regret it."

"There's still time. Maybe more than you think."

I wanted him to be right but deep down I knew it was only a matter of weeks before Mother would lose her battle. "Thanks, Romero," I said softly. I wanted to see his face, wanted to smell his comforting scent.

"Do something that'll make you happy today, even it's only something small."

"This is making me happy," I admitted.

"That's good," he said. Silence followed.

"I need to go now." Suddenly my admittance embarrassed me. When would I stop putting myself out there? I wasn't someone who was good at hiding her emotions and I hated it.

"Goodbye," Romero said.

I ended the call without another word, then stared at my phone for a long time. Was I reading too much into Romero's call? Maybe he wanted to be polite and call the sister of his boss's wife on her eighteenth birthday to gain some bonus points. But Romero didn't seem to be the type for that. Then why had he called? Had it something to do with the way he'd looked at me at our Christmas party? Was he starting to like me as much as I liked him?

***

Two weeks after my birthday, Mother's health deteriorated even further. Her skin was papery and cold, her eyes glazed from the painkillers. My grip on her was loose, scared of hurting her. She looked so breakable. Deep down I knew it wouldn't be much longer. I wanted to believe a miracle would happen, but I wasn't a small kid anymore. I knew better. Sometimes I wished I were still that naïve girl I used to be.

"Aria?" Mother said in a wispy voice.

I jerked up in my chair and leaned closer. "No, it's me Liliana."

Mother's eyes focused on me and she smiled softly. It looked horribly sad on her worn out face. She'd been so beautiful and proud once, and now she was only a shell of that woman.

"My sweet Lily," she said.

I pressed my lips together. Mother had never been the overly affectionate type. She'd hugged us and read bedtime stories to us and generally tried to be the best mother she knew how to be, but she'd almost never called us nicknames. "Yes, I'm here." At least until Father tried to send me away again. If it was up to him Mother would be locked away from everyone she loved, only cared for by the nurses he'd hired until she finally passed away. I tried to tell myself it was because he wanted to protect her, to let a proud woman be remembered as she used to be and not only for her sickness, but I had a feeling that wasn't his main incentive. Sometimes I wondered if he was embarrassed by her.

"Where are your sisters? And Fabi?" She peered over my head as if she expected to see them there.

I lowered my gaze to her chin, not able to look into her eyes. "Fabi is busy with school." That was a blatant lie. Father made sure Fabi was busy with God-only-knew-what, so he didn't spend too much time with our mother. As if Father worried her sickness would rub off on Fabi if he got too close. "Aria and Gianna will be here soon. They can't wait to see you again."

"Did your Father call them?" Mother asked.

I didn't want to lie to her again. But how could I tell her that Father didn't want them to come visit our dying Mother, that they wouldn't even have known she was close to dying if I hadn't called them. I filled her glass with water and held it up to her lips. "You need to drink."

Mother took a small sip but then she turned her head away. "I'm not thirsty."

My heart broke as I sat the glass back down on her nightstand. I searched for something to talk to my mother about, but the thing I really wanted to tell her about, my crush on Romero, was something I couldn't trust her with. "Do you need anything? I could get you some soup."

She gave a small shake of her head. She was watching me with a strange expression and I was starting to feel uncomfortable. I wasn't even sure why. There was such a look of forlornness and longing in her gaze that it spoke to a dark place deep inside of me.

57

"God, I don't even remember how it is to be young and carefree anymore."

Carefree? I hadn't felt carefree for a very long time.

"There's so much I wanted to do, so many dreams I had. Everything seemed possible." Her voice got stronger as if the memory drew energy from somewhere deep inside of her body.

"You have a beautiful house and many friends and children who love you," I said but even as I did I knew it was the wrong thing to say, and I hated this feeling of always doing the wrong thing, of not being able to help.

"I do," she said with a sad little smile. Slowly it faded. "Friends who don't visit."

I couldn't deny it and I wasn't even sure if Father was why they stayed away or if they'd really never cared about my mother in the first place. I opened my mouth to say something, another lie I'd feel guilty for later, but Mother kept talking. "A house that was paid for with blood money."

Mother had never admitted that Father was doing horrible things for our money and I'd never gotten the impression that she cared much either. Money and luxury were the only things Father had always given freely to her and us. I held my breath, half-curious and half-terrified of what she would say next. Did she regret having had kids? Were we a disappointment for her?

She patted my hand. "And you kids...I should have protected you better. I was always too weak to stand up for you."

"You did everything you could. Father would have never listened to you anyway."

"No, he wouldn't have," she whispered. "But I could have tried harder. There are so many things I regret."

I couldn't deny it. I'd often wished that she would have stood up for us, especially for Gianna, when Father had lost it again. But there was no use in making her feel bad for something that couldn't be changed.

"You only have this one life, Lily. Make the best of it. I wish I had done it and now it's too late. I don't want you to end like me, to look back at a life full of missed opportunities and lost dreams. Don't let life pass you by. You are braver than me, brave enough to fight for your happiness."

I swallowed, stunned by her passionate speech. "What do you mean?"

"Before I married your father, I was in love with a young man who worked in my father's restaurant. He was sweet and charming. He wasn't part of our world."

I glanced toward the door, worried Father would overhear us. As if that could happen. *As if he would actually set foot into this room.* "Did you love him?"

"Maybe. But love is something that develops with time and we never got the chance. I could have loved him very much, I'm sure of it. We kissed behind the dumpsters once. It was cold outside and it smelled of garbage, but it was the most romantic moment of my life." A sweet smile was on her face, an expression I'd never seen on my mother before.

Pity squeezed my heart tightly. Had Father never done anything romantic for her? "What about Father?"

"Your Father..." she trailed off. She took a few shuddering breaths. Even with the help of the oxygen tank, she was struggling to breathe. "He doesn't have time for romance. He never had."

But he had time for whores behind my mother's back. Even I knew about them, and I was usually the last person who got wind of these kinds of things. I'd never heard him say a kind word to Mother. I'd always assumed he could only show affection behind closed doors but now I realized he probably never did. The only nice thing he ever did was to buy her expensive jewelry.

"Don't get me wrong, I respect your father."

"But you don't love him," I finished. I'd always been sure Mother loved Father, even when he didn't return the feeling, but finding out that there was nothing between them somehow felt like a punch in the stomach. Aria and Gianna had made the best of their arranged marriages but now I realized that many weren't as lucky and never loved or even tolerated their husbands. Most women in our world were trapped in a loveless marriage with a cheating and sometimes even violent man.

She sighed, her eyes sliding shut, her skin becoming even paler than before. "I always told myself there was still time to do the things I love, to be happy, and now? Now it's too late."

Would those words always feel like a punch every time she voiced them? "No," I said shakily. "It's not. Don't give up."

She looked at me with a sad smile. "It won't be much longer. For me there's nothing but regret. But you have your whole life ahead of you, Liliana. Promise me you'll live it to the fullest. Try to be happy."

I swallowed hard. All my life my mother had told me to accept my fate, to be a good girl, to be dutiful. "I want to marry for love."

"You should," she whispered.

"Father won't allow it. He'll find someone for me, won't he?"

"Aria and Gianna made good matches. You don't have to marry for tactical reasons. You should be free to fall in love and marry that special boy."

An image of Romero popped into my head, and a swarm of butterflies filled my stomach.

"I remember that look," Mother said softly. "There is someone, hm?"

I blushed. "It's silly. He isn't even interested in me."

"How could he not be? You are beautiful and intelligent and come from a good family. He'd be crazy not to fall for you."

I'd never talked to Mother like this, and I felt incredibly sad that it had taken cancer for us to be this close. I wished she'd been that kind of mother before, and then I felt guilty for thinking something like that. "He's not someone Father would approve of," I said eventually. And that was a huge understatement. "He's just a soldier."

"Oh," Mother whispered. She had trouble keeping her eyes open. "Don't let anyone stop you from achieving happiness." The last few words were barely audible as Mother slowly drifted off to sleep. I slipped my hand out from beneath hers and stood. Her breathing was labored, raspy and flat. I could almost imagine how it would stop any second. I backed out of the room but didn't close the door. I wanted to make sure I would hear it if Mother called for help.

I headed toward the staircase where I almost bumped into Father. "Mother, will be happy to see you," I said. "But she's just fallen asleep, so you will have to wait a bit."

He loosened his tie. "I wasn't going to your mother. I have a few more meetings scheduled."

"Oh, right." That's why he smelled like a perfume shop and why his suit was wrinkled. He'd spent the morning with one of his whores and was probably on his way to the next. "But she'd love to see you later."

Father narrowed his eyes. "Did you call your sister? Luca called me this morning to tell me he and Aria were on their way to Chicago to visit your mother."

"They have a right to say goodbye."

"Do you really think they want to see your mother like this? Your mother was once a proud woman, if she were still in her right mind, she wouldn't want anyone to see her in this pitiful state."

Anger bubbled up. "You're embarrassed by her, that's all!"

He raised a finger in warning. "Careful. Don't take that tone with me. I know you are under a lot of pressure but my patience is running thin at the moment."

I pressed my lips together. "Are Aria and Luca still coming, or did you forbid them from visiting?" I didn't mention that Gianna would be visiting as well. He'd find out soon enough and then Luca would hopefully be there to calm him down.

"They'll be here in the afternoon. That'll give Luca and Dante the chance to discuss business."

That's what he worried about? Business? His wife was dying and he didn't give a shit. I nodded and left without another word. Half an hour later I watched my father leave the house again. There had been a time when I'd looked up to him. When I'd seen him in his black suits and thought he was the most important person in the world. But that hadn't lasted long. The first time he raised his hand against Mother, I knew he wasn't the man I thought he was.

***

Aria, Gianna, and Luca arrived two hours later. Matteo had stayed in New York. Not only because Luca needed someone he trusted there, but because Gianna's encounter with Father would be explosive anyway. If Matteo was there as well, someone would die.

Aria and Gianna hugged me tightly in greeting. "How are you?" Aria asked.

I shrugged. "I don't know. It's hard to see Mother so weak."

"And Father acting like a jerk isn't helping," Gianna muttered.

Luca gave me a small nod. "I'll wait in the kitchen. I still have a few phone calls to make."

I had a feeling he only wanted to give us time alone with our mother and I was grateful for that. I almost asked him about Romero but then I stopped myself.

I led my sisters upstairs. When we stepped into Mother's bedroom, shock flashed across their faces. Even I, who kept her company every day, was shocked every morning when I saw how broken she looked, and the smell was horrible as well. The nurses cleaned the floor and furniture with disinfectant twice a day but the stench of decay and urine still covered everything. It even seemed to cling to my clothes and skin, and clogged my nose when I couldn't sleep at night.

Mother was awake, but it took a moment before recognition shone in her eyes. Then she smiled, and for a moment, despite the tubes disappearing in her nose, she didn't look like death had already marked her as his. Aria immediately walked toward the bed and hugged Mother carefully. Gianna was tense beside me. She and Mother hadn't seen each other in a while, and they hadn't exactly parted on good terms. When Aria stepped back, Mother's gaze settled on Gianna and she started crying. "Oh Gianna," she whispered.

Gianna rushed toward our mother and embraced her as well. It almost broke my heart that this reunion had such a horrible reason. I wished we'd come together like this long before today. I pulled two more chairs toward the bed and put them next to the one I'd spent countless hours in. We all sat down and Mother looked at peace for the first time in a while. I let Aria and Gianna talk and listened. Gianna leaned over to me when Aria told Mother about a new exhibition in New York. "Where's Fabi? Shouldn't he be home?"

"Father always has someone pick him up from school and then I don't see Fabi until dinner."

"Is he inducting Fabi already? Fabi's way too young for that bullshit."

"I don't know. It's difficult to talk to Fabi about it. He doesn't tell me everything like he used to. He's changed a lot since Mother got sick. Sometimes I don't recognize him."

"The mob changes them all. It sucks the good out of them," Gianna murmured.

"Look at Matteo and Luca, and Romero they aren't all bad."

Gianna sighed. "They aren't good either. Far from it. With Fabi, I know how he used to be before the rottenness wormed its way into him, but with Luca and Matteo I always only knew them as Made Men, so it's different." Gianna narrowed her eyes in contemplation. "Are you still crushing on Romero? Shouldn't you have moved on to a new target by now?"

I flushed, but didn't reply. Luckily, Aria involved Gianna in the conversation and I could relax again.

    ***

Gianna, Aria and I fell asleep in our chairs. Two hours later we were woken by Father's sharp voice. "What is she doing here?"

I sat up, taking a few seconds to get my bearings. Father stood in the doorway and was glaring daggers at Gianna. He still hadn't forgiven her for what she'd done. He'd probably take his wrath into the grave with him.

"I'm not here to see you, believe me," Gianna muttered.

Aria rose from her chair and went over to Father to give him a quick hug. Usually his mood always brightened when she was around but he didn't even look at her.

"I don't want you in my house," he said to Gianna.

I spotted Fabi a couple of steps behind him, obviously unsure how to react. I knew he'd missed Gianna very much and had always been eager to talk to her on the phone, but Father's influence on him had grown in the last few months and it was clear that my little brother wasn't sure which side to choose.

I stood, chancing a worried look at Mother. She was still out from her meds. I didn't want her to witness this. "Please, let's discuss this outside," I whispered.

Father turned on his heel and stepped out into the corridor without a single glance at Mother. The rest of us followed. Gianna didn't give Fabi a chance to make up his mind, she hugged him and after a moment he hugged her back. Father glowered at my brother. I couldn't believe he wasn't able to let his stupid pride take a backseat for once. Mother needed us in her last days, but he didn't give a damn. He didn't even wait for me to close the door before he went off again.

"I forbade you from stepping foot into this house," he snarled.

I slid the door shut and leaned against it. My legs felt shaky.

"It's also Mother's house and she asked to see me," Gianna said. It was true. I'd lost count of the many times Mother had asked about Gianna.

"I paid for this house and my word is law."

"Don't you have any respect for the wishes of your dying wife?" Gianna hissed.

I was pretty sure Father would have hit Gianna, even though she was Matteo's wife, but Luca came upstairs in that moment. It didn't stop Father from saying more nasty things and Gianna from firing right back at him. I couldn't take it anymore. I rushed past them. Their fighting followed me down the corridor and even downstairs I could still hear their shouting. I stormed into the kitchen, threw the door shut and leaned against it before I buried my face in my hands. The tears I'd been fighting for so long, pressed against my eyeballs. I couldn't hold them back.

A noise made me look up. Romero stood at the kitchen counter and was watching me over his coffee cup. I cringed in embarrassment and quickly tried to wipe my cheeks clean. "I'm sorry," I said. "I didn't know someone was in here." I didn't even know Romero was here at all, but I shouldn't have been surprised. Since Matteo had stayed in New York, Luca needed someone who could keep an eye on my sisters when he was busy.

"This is your home," he said simply. His eyes were kind and understanding. I had to look away or I'd really start bawling, snot and sobs and all, and that was the last thing I wanted.

"It used to be," I whispered. I knew I needed to keep my mouth shut but the words kept coming. "But now it feels like I'm trapped. There's nothing good. Anywhere I look there is just darkness, just sickness, and hate and fear." I fell silent, shocked by my outburst.

Romero set down his coffee. "When was the last time you left the house?"

I didn't even know. I shrugged.

"Let's take a walk. We can get a coffee. It's really warm outside."

Euphoria burst through the dark cloud that had been my emotions in the last few weeks. "Are you sure that's okay?"

"I'll check with Luca but I don't see why it should be a problem. Just a sec."

I stepped aside so he could walk by. His delicious aftershave entered my nose as he passed me and I wanted to press my nose into his shirt to find solace in his scent. My eyes followed him, traced his broad shoulders and narrow hips. Mother's words shot through my mind again. Maybe happiness wasn't as far away as I thought.

Romero

I shouldn't even consider being alone with Lily, not now, not ever. Not when I couldn't stop noticing how grown up she looked. She wasn't the little girl I'd first met. She was a woman in marriageable age now, but she was out of my league. At least by her father's standard. I was one of the best fighters in New York, only

Luca and Matteo were as good with the knife or the gun, and I wasn't exactly penniless, but I definitely wasn't mob royalty and couldn't afford a penthouse like Luca's. I wasn't even sure why the fuck I was thinking about those kinds of things now. I wasn't going to ask for Lily's hand, not now, not ever, and at this time there were more important things to take care of.

I climbed the stairs, following the sound of arguing. Gianna and her father were at it again and Luca seemed to try to keep them from ripping their heads off. Only problem was that he looked like he was close to losing his own shit. I walked toward them and Luca gave me an exasperated look. Scuderi was a pain in the ass, and Luca wasn't the most patient person on this planet. A bad combination. He came toward me. "I'm going to lose my fucking mind if Gianna and her old man don't stop fighting."

"Lily is taking it badly. She's had to witness her mother's deterioration for months now. I want to take her out for a walk and a coffee to take her mind off things."

Luca scanned my face with an expression I didn't like one bit. "Sure, but I really don't need any more problems. Things between New York and Chicago are already shaky."

"I won't do anything that'll hurt our relationship to Chicago."

Luca nodded but he didn't look convinced. He glanced back to Scuderi and his two daughters. "I better get back. Be back before dinner, then Scuderi doesn't have to know Liliana ever left the

70

house. The bastard hardly pays attention to anything, least of all that girl."

I turned on my heel, leaving Luca to his shitty task of mediating between Scuderi and Gianna. Lily sat at the kitchen table when I entered the room but quickly rose, a hopeful expression on her pretty face. Pretty? What the fuck, Romero? I couldn't start thinking like that when I was around her. Lines easily got blurry, and Luca was right. We didn't need any more shit on our plate.

"So? Can we go out?" Lily asked with that same hopeful smile on her face.

I stopped more than an arm-length away. "Yes, but we need to get back before dinner."

That left a little more than two hours.

A hint of disappointment flickered in her eyes but it was gone quickly. "Then let's go."

We stepped out of the house and Lily stopped on the sidewalk and tilted her head up with a blissful expression. Sunrays cast her face in a soft glow. "This feels so good," she said softly.

I know so many things that feel even better.

How would her face look in the throes of passion? It was something I'd probably never find out. I didn't say anything, only watched her as she soaked in the sun.

She blinked up at me with an embarrassed smile. "Sorry. I'm wasting time. We were supposed to have coffee and not stand on the sidewalk all day."

"This is about you. If you'd rather stay here and enjoy the sun, we can do that too. I don't mind." Not one fucking bit. Watching Lily was something I could do all day.

She shook her head. Her blonde hair settled in soft waves on her shoulders and I had to stop myself from reaching out and letting a strand of it glide through my fingers. For some reason I didn't know, I held out my arm for her. She hooked her arm through mine without hesitation, a grin twisting her lips as she peered up at me. Damn it. I led her down the street. "Do you know a nice café? I've been in Chicago plenty of times in the last few years but I'm not that familiar with the culinary scene."

"Just a ten minute walk away is a small café with fantastic coffee and delicious cupcakes. We could go there. I usually only order everything to-go but we could sit down, if you want?" There were many things I wanted, most of them involved Lily naked in my bed.

"That sounds good. Lead the way."

"You know what I like about you? You are so easy-going and relaxed. You seem like the guy next door. Nice and kind."

"Lily, I'm a Made Man. Don't make me into a hero that I'm not. I'm not kind or nice."

"You are to me," she said lightly. Her blue eyes were far too trusting. She didn't know the things I'd been thinking about her, most of them hadn't been nice. I wanted to do so many dirty things to her, she wouldn't even understand half of them, and that was why I needed to keep my distance. Maybe she looked grown-up, but she was still too young, too innocent.

I only smiled. "I'm trying."

"You're doing good," she said teasingly. The sadness and hopelessness were gone from her face for the moment, and that was all the encouragement I needed.

Liliana

Romero smirked. "Thanks." I could have kissed him then. He looked so handsome and sexy.

"You're very welcome," I said. We strolled down the street toward the small café that looked like it belonged in a cobblestone street in Paris and not in Chicago. It was strange walking with a man who wasn't twice my age like my father's bodyguards. Only when we stopped at the counter did Romero release my arm, but until then we'd walked close like lovers. How would it feel if it were the truth? If he wasn't just trying to distract me from my sick mother, if we were really a couple?

"Everything okay?" Romero asked in a low voice.

I had been staring. I quickly turned my attention to the girl behind the counter who was waiting for our order. "A cappuccino and a Red Velvet Cupcake," I said distractedly. It was my standard order and my mind was too frazzled to check the blackboard for the daily specials.

"The same for me," Romero said and took his wallet out to pay for us both.

"You didn't have to pay for me," I whispered when we walked toward a free table near the window.

Romero raised one dark eyebrow. "A woman never pays when she's with me."

"Oh?" I said curiously. Romero looked like he already regretted his comment but it was too late. He'd piqued my curiosity. "How many girlfriends have you had?"

It was a very personal question.

Romero chuckled. "That's not something I'm going to tell you."

"That means many," I said with a laugh. The server brought our order, giving Romero time to compose himself. The moment she was out of earshot I said, "I know how things are with our men. You have a lot of women."

"So you know all of us?" Romero asked. He leaned back in his chair like he didn't have a care in the world.

I took a sip from my cappuccino. "Women talk and from what I hear most Made Men don't say no to the whorehouses of the Outfit. For most of them it's some kind of hobby to have as many women as possible."

"Many men do, but not all of them."

"So you are the exception?" I asked doubtfully. I wanted it to be true, but I was realistic.

Romero took a bite from his cupcake, obviously considering what to tell me. "I've had wild days when I was younger, eighteen or nineteen maybe."

"And now? Do you have a girlfriend? A fiancée?" I'd always put the thought out of my mind but the way Romero had talked it was a valid option. I sipped at my coffee, glad for the feel of the cup in my hands. It gave me something to focus on.

Romero shook his head with an unreadable look on his face. "No, I've had girlfriends in the last few years but it's difficult to have a steady relationship if work always comes first. I'm a soldier. The Famiglia will always be my top priority. Most women can't bear it."

"Most women don't get asked if they want this life or not. What about an arranged marriage?"

"I don't like the idea of someone telling me who I should marry."

"So your family never tried to set you up with someone?"

Romero grinned. I could have jumped over the table and crawled onto his lap. "Of course they have. We're Italian, it's in our bloodstream to meddle with our children's lives."

"But you never liked any of the girls they suggested?"

"I liked some of them well enough but either they weren't interested in me or I couldn't see myself spending the rest of my life with them."

"And nobody ever tried to force you into marriage?"

"How would they force me?"

I nodded. Yes, how? He was a Made Man, not a stupid girl. "You're right. You can make your own decisions."

Romero set down his cup. "Luca could ask me to marry for political reasons. I probably wouldn't refuse him."

"But he wouldn't do that," I said.

"Maybe you'll get to choose for yourself as well. You might meet the perfect guy soon and he might be worthy in your father's eyes."

The perfect guy sat in front of me. It stung that Romero suggested I'd find someone else. Didn't he realize I had feelings for him? I didn't want to find some guy my father would approve of. I wanted the man in front of me.

After that, we talked about random things, nothing of importance, and far too soon we had to make our way back to my home. This time we didn't link arms. I tried not to be disappointed, but it was hard. When we stepped into the entrance hall of the house, I could feel the weight of the lingering sadness return to my shoulders.

Romero lightly touched my arm. My eyes traced his strong jaw with the hint of dark stubble, his worried browns eyes, his prominent cheekbones. And then I did what I'd promised myself not to do again but right in this moment, in this cold, hopeless house he was the light and I was the moth. I pushed to my toes and kissed him. The touch was the briefest contact, hardly there but it made me long for more. Romero grasped my arms and pushed me away. "Liliana, don't."

I untangled myself from his hold and left without another word. Mother had said I should take risks for my happiness, and I was doing just that.

Romero

I stormed into the kitchen. I needed another coffee. The door smashed shut behind me with too much force. I wanted to tear something into tiny pieces. My lips still tingled from that ridiculous kiss. You couldn't even really call it that. It had been over too quickly. Because I'd acted like the dutiful soldier I was supposed to be. Fuck it.

I made myself a coffee and emptied it in one gulp, then put the cup down with a loud clang.

The door to the kitchen swung open and Luca leaned in the doorway with a questioning look on his face. "You realize this isn't your home, right? I don't think Scuderi appreciates you destroying his expensive marble counter." The corners of his mouth twitched in an almost smile.

I relaxed against the kitchen island. "I don't think Scuderi even knows where his kitchen is. Where is he anyway? It's suspiciously quiet in the house. I thought he and Gianna would never stop fighting."

Luca's expression darkened. "They would still be at it, but Scuderi left for a meeting, which I'll have to do soon as well. Dante and I are going to discuss the Russians tonight at some Italian restaurant he loves."

"I assume I'll stay here to keep an eye on the women," I said tightly. The idea of being around Lily all evening worried me.

Luca came up to me. "Do I have to worry what went on between you and Liliana while you were gone for coffee? Do I even want to know?"

I glared. "Nothing happened, Luca. You know me, I'm a good soldier."

"You are also a guy with a dick and Liliana is a gorgeous girl who's been flirting with you for years. Sometimes that can lead to unfortunate accidents."

I released a long breath.

"Fuck," Luca muttered. "I was joking. Don't tell me there's really something been going on."

"Liliana kissed me but you could hardly call it that. Our lips barely touched and I pushed her away, so you have nothing to worry about."

"Oh, but I have to worry considering the look of regret on your face when you said that your lips barely touched. You want her."

"Yes, I want her," I muttered, starting to get annoyed by his interrogation. Luca used to be the guy who couldn't keep it in his pants and now he was acting all high and mighty. "But I'm not going to act on it. I can control myself. I'd never do anything to hurt the Famiglia."

Luca clapped my shoulder. "I know that. And if you're ever at risk of following your dick instead of your brain, just remember that Liliana is going through a lot. She's probably only looking for a distraction. She's vulnerable and young. I know you won't allow her to ruin her life."

That was a guilt trip if I'd ever seen one. I nodded, because the words waiting on the tip of my tongue were too harsh for my Capo.

Aria walked into the kitchen in that moment, but she stopped when she saw us. "Am I interrupting anything?" She glanced between Luca and me. "I thought we should start dinner. Father

79

gave our maid the day off because he doesn't want anyone in the house right now. That means we have to cook."

"Let's order pizza," Luca said. He walked toward his wife and pulled her against him before kissing the top of her head. In the first few years of working for Luca, I'd have bet everything that he wasn't capable of that kind of affection.

"Did your conversation have something to do with Lily?" Aria asked casually as she rifled through several flyers from pizza delivery services.

I didn't say anything, and Luca shrugged. "Why do you ask?" he said.

Aria shook her head. "I'm not blind. Lily has been acting odd ever since she returned from her walk with Romero." She fixed me with a warning stare. "I don't want her alone with you."

Luca's eyebrows shot up. I knew I had to look pretty shocked too.

"Don't give me that look. You know I like you Romero, but Lily has been going through so much recently and when it comes to you her brain stops working. I don't want to have to worry about her."

"So now you're protecting her virtue?" I asked sarcastically.

"Hey," Luca said sharply. "Don't take that tone with her."

Aria shook her head. "No, it's okay. I'm not protecting her virtue. I just don't want her to get hurt. You have younger sisters, don't you want to keep them safe?"

"I do," I said. "And I would never do anything that'll hurt Lily. But I respect your wish. I won't be alone with Lily from now on." With a curt nod in Luca's direction, I headed out of the kitchen. Aria's words didn't sit well with me. Luca had trusted me with her, though he was a possessive bastard, but Aria didn't trust me with her sister. Of course, truth was I'd never been remotely interested in Aria. I wasn't blind. She was beautiful, and definitely sexy, but I'd never fantasized about her, and not just because I knew Luca would cut my dick off if I made a move. Lily was a different matter. I'd imagined her naked body beneath me more than once and when I was close to her I wanted to press her against the wall and have my fucking way with her. That was a major problem. Maybe it was for the best that Aria's orders were now another barrier between Lily and me.

CHAPTER FIVE

Liliana

Someone was shaking me. I opened my eyes but at first everything was blurry.

"Lily, get up. I think Mom's going to die," Aria said in a panicky voice. I jerked upright, my head spinning.

Aria was already on her way out of my room, probably to wake the others. One of us had always sat at Mother's bed to make sure she was never alone. Tonight it had been Aria's turn. I untangled myself from my blankets, slipped out of bed and hurried toward the bedroom at the end of the corridor. The smell of antiseptic and disinfectant greeted me even before I entered but my nose had grown used to the biting stench by now. Gianna was already inside, perched on the edge of the bed. Mother's eyes were closed and for a moment I was sure I was too late and she'd already died. Then I saw the slow rise and fall of her chest. I approached the bed hesitantly. Gianna barely glanced my way. She was glowering at her lap. I wrapped my arms around her shoulders from behind and pressed our cheeks together.

"I hate this," Gianna whispered.

"Where's the nurse?"

"She left so we could say goodbye in peace. She gave Mother another dose of morphine so she could go without pain."

Aria and Fabi came into the room. Fabi was wearing his brave face, and damn it, he looked so grown up. He was taller than Aria already. Luca stood in the corridor but didn't come in, instead he closed the door, giving us privacy.

Mother's breathing was low, barely noticeable. Her eyes flickered back and forth under her lids as if she was watching a movie in her head. It wouldn't be much longer. Fabi grabbed the foot of the bed, his knuckles turning white. There were tears in his eyes but his face was like stone. I knew that look, *that posture*.

I turned away from him. Aria walked up to us. "How is she?"

I wasn't sure how to answer that question.

Gianna glared. "Where's Father? He should be here!" She'd spoken quietly but Aria and I still chanced a worried glance toward Mother. She didn't need to get upset in the last moments of her life. My stomach constricted painfully and for a second I was sure I'd have to rush to the bathroom to throw up. Death was part of our life, especially when you grew up in our world. I'd attended countless funerals in the last few years but almost all of them had been for people I'd barely known.

"I don't know," Aria admitted. "I knocked at his door and even walked in but it didn't look like he'd slept in his bed at all."

Gianna and I exchanged a look. Was he really with one of his whores tonight? Mother had been feeling very weak yesterday so it didn't come as a surprise that tonight could be the night. He should have stayed home to be there for her.

"Do you know where he is? You've been acting like his best buddy the last few days," Gianna muttered with a scowl in Fabi's direction.

He stiffened. "He doesn't tell me where he goes. And I'm not his best buddy, but as his only son I have responsibilities."

Gianna stood, and I had no choice but to let her go. "Oh my god, what kind of bullshit is that. I can't believe it," she hissed.

"Gianna," Aria said in warning. "It's enough. Not here, not right now."

"It doesn't matter that Father's not here," I said firmly. "We are here for her. We are the most important people in her life, not him."

That was the last time we mentioned Father that night. Hours passed with Mother's state staying the same, and occasionally my eyes fell shut, but then her breathing changed.

I sat up in my chair and took her hand. "Mom?" I asked.

Aria was holding her other hand. Gianna didn't move from her spot in the armchair in the corner. Her legs were pressed up against her chest, her chin resting on her knees. Fabi had fallen asleep with his cheek on the wooden foot of the bed. I reached out and nudged him. He jerked up in his chair.

Mother's eyelids fluttered like she was going to open them. I held my breath, hoping she'd look at us once more, maybe even say something but then her breathing slowed even more.

I wasn't sure how much longer it took. I lost any sense of time as I monitored Mother's chest, the way it barely moved, until it stopped altogether. Fabi ran out to get the nurse, but I didn't need her to tell me what I already knew; our mother was gone. The nurse moved around us, and then with a sad nod, she disappeared again.

I let go of Mother's hand, stood from my chair and stepped back. Aria didn't move, still clutching Mother's hand. One moment Mother was there and the next she was gone. Just like that a life ended, and with it the dreams and hopes of that person. Life was so short, any moment could be your last. Mother had told me to be happy, but in our world happiness wasn't something that came by easily.

Aria rested her head on the edge of the bed, sobbing without a sound. Just like me, Fabi stood back. He looked like he couldn't comprehend what had happened. Gianna walked up to Aria, for the first time in hours moving closer to the bed and put her hand on Aria's shoulder. She didn't even glance Mother's way, and I got it. Gianna's relationship with our mother had always been difficult and only gotten worse when Mother had accepted how horrible Father had treated Gianna after she'd run away. In the days since her arrival here, Gianna's feelings had often changed from one second to the other.

After a moment, Aria stood and pressed a kiss to Mother's forehead. To my surprise, Gianna did the same, though she quickly stepped back from the bed again. I could only stare. I knew I should kiss Mother's forehead as well as a last goodbye, but I couldn't bring myself to touch this lifeless corpse. That wasn't her anymore. That was something empty and lifeless.

I staggered out of the room. My throat was cording up and my eyes were burning. I wanted to run and never stop but in the corridor I bumped into Romero. If he hadn't grabbed my shoulders, I would have toppled over. I gasped for breath. Panic was slowly tightening around my body like a vice.

"Take her away," Luca ordered. I hadn't even noticed him.

"What about Aria's order?"

"I don't give a damn."

Romero wrapped an arm around my waist and steered me down the hallway. I was still trying to suck air into my lungs but it was futile. My legs buckled.

"Hey," Romero said in a soothing voice. "Sit down." He guided me to the floor and helped me put my head between my legs while he drew calming circles on my back. The feel of his warm hand steadied me.

"Just breathe," he murmured. "It's okay."

His voice pulled me out of the black hole that wanted to consume me and eventually my breathing returned to normal. "She's dead," I whispered when I was sure I could speak.

Romero halted in his stroking of my back. "I'm sorry."

I nodded, fighting back new tears. "Father wasn't there. I don't know where he is. He should have been there for her in her last moments!" The anger felt good, better than the sadness.

"Yes, he should have. Maybe Dante called him away."

I glowered up at Romero. "Dante wouldn't have done it, not in the middle of the night, not when he knows that our mother is so sick. No, Father didn't want to be here when Mother died. He barely visited her since she got worse. He's a selfish bastard and is probably screwing one of his whores right this moment."

Romero smiled darkly. "I sometimes forget that you're an adult now and know the ugly sides of our world."

"You better not forget," I said. "I know more than all of you think."

"I don't doubt it," he said. For an instant we only stared at each other. I felt calmer now.

"Thanks," I said simply. Romero pulled his hand away from my back. I wished he hadn't. His touch had felt good. He straightened and held out his hand. I took it and he pulled me to my feet. The door to Mother's room opened and Aria stepped out, her eyes zooming in on Romero and me. He let go of my hand, gave me an encouraging smile before he went to Aria to tell her how sorry he was about Mother's death. Aria nodded but then her eyes darted to me again. Her cheeks were wet with tears. I walked toward her and wrapped my arms around her. Romero took that as his cue to leave but before he turned the corner he glanced over his shoulder and our gazes met. The cold and empty feeling in my chest eased and something warm and more hopeful took its place. Then he disappeared from my view. I almost went after him, but my sisters needed me now. Steps sounded behind us and then Luca was heading our way, lowering his phone from his ear.

"He doesn't answer his phone? Did you try to send him a message?" Aria asked as she pulled back from me and hurried toward her husband.

Luca grimaced. "Yes, I sent him two messages, but he hasn't replied yet, and he doesn't answer my calls. I doubt he'll be back any time soon."

I returned into Mother's bedroom even though my body bristled at the mere idea, but Aria needed some time with her husband. I'd only be the fifth wheel. Before I closed the door, I saw Luca cradling my sister's face and kissing her eyelids. That was love and devotion. He wouldn't have left her side if she'd been dying. He wasn't a good man, but he was a good husband. I prayed that I'd be as lucky one day. I couldn't live the life my mother had, with a cold husband who didn't care about me. I knew Romero wouldn't be like that. But it wasn't like Father would choose him for my husband.

Gianna was back in her armchair but she was talking on the phone in low voices, probably with Matteo. She, too, had found someone.

Fabi was gone. I didn't want to interrupt Gianna so I went in search of my little brother. I found him in his room, sitting at his desk and polishing one of his many combat knives. They were shiny already.

"Do you want to talk?" I asked.

He didn't even look up, only pressed his lips together.

I waited, then I nodded. "Okay. But if you change your mind, I'm in my room."

Romero waited outside. He nodded toward my brother. "Do you want me to talk to him? Maybe he needs someone who isn't family."

"You mean who isn't female," I said bitterly, but then I swallowed my emotions. "You're probably right. He'd rather talk to you than me."

Romero looked like he wanted to say more but then he walked past me and toward my brother. "Do you need help polishing your collection?"

Fabi's head shot up. Admiration flickered across his pale face. He didn't say anything but he handed Romero a cloth. Romero perched on the edge of the desk and unsheathed his own knife from its holster. A long, curved blade that looked absolutely deadly. Fabi's eyes lit up and he rose from his chair to take a closer look. "Wow," he breathed.

"I should probably polish it first. Your knives are in a much better condition."

"That's because they are only for show," Fabi said. "But yours is a weapon, it's real. How many have you killed with it?"

I closed the door quickly. I'd had enough death for one night. I didn't want to know how many Romero had caused in his lifetime. I glanced down toward the bedroom where Mother's corpse waited to be taken away, then I turned around and headed toward my room. Aria had Luca, Gianna had Matteo, and for the moment even Fabi had Romero, but I'd deal with this alone. I'd been doing it for weeks and months now.

Romero

I wanted to be there for Lily, wanted to console her, but I respected Aria's wishes. She too had gone through enough shit and didn't need the additional grief of worrying about her sister.

Instead I showed Fabiano how to handle my knife, how to unsheathe a long blade as quickly as a short one. It was easy to distract him from his sadness. But damn it, he wasn't the one who needed me most.

Needed you? Goddammit, if I started thinking like that now, I'd get myself in huge trouble. Lily wasn't my responsibility, and she definitely didn't need me.

Fabi drew his knife from the holster I'd lent him and grinned at how fast he'd done it. I'd been like that once, eager to learn everything there was about fighting, about winning. Eager to prove myself. My father had been a low debt collector, someone who never got to talk to the Capo directly. I'd wanted to be better, to prove my worth to him and myself. Fabiano had huge expectations resting on his shoulders, he had plenty of ways to fail, but very few options to excel.

"I need to go to Luca now," I said eventually. Fabi nodded, and settled back on his chair. He picked up a cloth and polished the same knife again. I guessed he'd spent all night like that and maybe even the next few days.

I walked out and headed for the stairs but stopped in front of Liliana's door, listening for a sound. Maybe I wanted to hear crying so I could storm in and console her, be her knight in fucking armor.

I moved on.

CHAPTER SIX

Liliana

I looked deathly pale in mourning. Aria, Gianna and I wore the same modest black dress and ballet flats, our hair pinned up in a bun. I didn't wear make-up, even though the shadows beneath my eyes were scary. Father had organized a huge funeral; expensive oak coffin, a sea of beautiful flowers, only the best food for the feast afterwards. He acted like the devastated widower everyone expected to see. It was a marvelous show. He should have been there for Mother when she really needed him. This was only to impress people and maybe to make him feel better. Even a man like him had to feel guilty for abandoning his dying wife.

The funeral was a big affair in our world. Father was an important man, and so Mother's death was a social event. Everyone wanted to attend, and everyone was crying crocodile's tears, as they said their condolences. My eyes were dry as sand. I could see people glancing my way, waiting for me to cry over my mother, to show the reaction they all expected from me. But I couldn't cry. I didn't want to cry, not surrounded by so many people with their fake tears. They pretended they'd cared for my mother, that they'd known her but none of these people had visited her when she was bound to the house. She'd been dead to them long before her death. The moment she hadn't been the glitzy society lady they'd ditched her like a dirty rag. They made me sick, all of them.

Father put his arms around Fabi's and my shoulder as he led us toward the coffin. I shuddered under his touch. I didn't think he realized it was revulsion for his closeness that had caused my reaction because he actually squeezed my shoulder. It took incredible self-control for me to stay where I was and not rip away from him.

The priest started his prayer as the coffin was slowly lowered into the hole. I peered up through my lashes and caught Romero's eyes over the grave. Unlike Luca and Matteo, who'd flown in for the funeral, Romero wasn't allowed to stand on this side with our family. His expression was solemn as we watched each other but then he lowered his gaze back to the coffin. He'd been avoiding me in the last few days. When I entered the room he was in, he usually left with a stupid excuse. It was obvious he couldn't stand my presence and didn't know how to tell me. Everyone was walking on eggshells around my siblings and me now. I wished he'd tell me the truth. I could handle it. Father led us back toward the other mourners, away from Mother's grave and finally let go of me. I released a quiet breath, glad to be out of the spotlight and away from my father.

The moment people started to head for the coffin to say their last goodbye, I backed away. Nobody stopped me. Nobody even seemed to notice. They were busy putting on their show. I turned and didn't look back. I rushed down the path, away from the grave, sending pebbles flying as my feet pounded the ground. I wasn't even sure where I was going. The graveyard was huge, there were plenty of places to find peace and silence. I reached a part that was even more opulent than where mother had been buried. Rows over rows of old family vaults surrounded me. Most of them were locked but one of the iron gates was ajar. I headed that way, and after having made sure nobody was watching me, I opened it and slipped inside. It was cool in the vault and the smell of mildew drifted into my nose. Everything was made from gray marble. I sank down slowly and sat with my back against the cold wall.

In moments like this I understood why Gianna had run away. I'd never had the urge to leave this life behind forever, but sometimes I wanted to escape at least for a little while.

I knew eventually someone would notice I was missing and come looking for me, but I didn't even care that Father would lose his shit on me.

It took less than an hour before I heard someone call my name in the distance. I opened my lips to reply but not a sound came out. I rested my head against the marble, and peered out through the bars of the iron gate. So often in my life I'd felt like I was surrounded by invisible bars, and now I sought shelter behind them. A bitter smile twisted my lips. Steps crunched outside of the vault. I held my breath as someone came into view outside the gate.

A tall form with a familiar frame loomed in front of it. Romero. He hadn't seen me yet but his eyes scanned their surroundings. They passed right over the spot I was hiding and he was about to turn away. I could have stayed hidden, alone with my anger and misery and sadness, but suddenly I didn't want this. For some reason, I wanted Romero to find me. He hadn't faked tears and he wasn't family; he was safe. I cleared my throat quietly but of course a man like Romero didn't miss it. He turned and his eyes zoomed in on me. He headed for me, opened the gate and stepped in with a bent head because he was too tall to stand. He held out his hand for me. I searched his eyes for the pity I hated so much, but he looked merely concerned and maybe even like he cared. I wasn't sure what to make of his concern when not too long ago he'd done his utmost to stay away from me.

I slipped my hand into his and his fingers closed around me before he pulled me to my feet. The momentum of the movement catapulted me straight into Romero's arms. I should have pulled back. He should have pushed me back. We didn't.

It felt good to be so close to someone, to feel his warmth, something my life had seemed so devoid of recently. He slowly backed out of the vault, taking me with him, still holding me close.

"We've been looking for you for almost an hour," Romero said quietly, worriedly, but all I could focus on was how close his lips were and how good he smelled. "Your father will be glad to know you're safe."

My father. Anger surged up in me at how he'd acted in the last few months. I was so tired of being angry, of not knowing where to go with my anger. I stepped onto my toes, closed my eyes and pressed my lips against Romero's. This was the third time I did this.

It seemed I never learned, but I wasn't even scared of being rejected anymore. I was so numb inside, there was no way anything could hurt me again.

Romero's hand came up to my shoulders as if he was going to shove me away, but then he merely rested them there, warm and strong. He didn't try to deepen the kiss but our lips moved against each other. There was only the barest touch and even that was over too quickly. Something trailed down my cheeks and caught on my lips. I'd never imagined my first real kiss would taste of tears. I sank back down onto my heels and my eyes fluttered open. I was too drained, too sad, too angry, to be embarrassed about my actions.

Romero searched my face, his dark brows drawn together. "Lily," he began, but then I started crying for real, fat tears rolling down my cheeks. I buried my face against Romero's chest. He cupped the back of my head and let me sob. In the safety of Romero's arms I dared to give my sadness room, didn't fear it would swallow me whole. I knew Romero wouldn't let it. Maybe it was a ridiculous notion but I believed Romero would keep me safe from everything. I'd tried to forget him, had tried to move on, find someone new to focus my crush on but they all fell short.

"We should return. Your father will be worried sick by now."

"He isn't worried about me. He's only worried about how I make him look bad," I said quietly, pulling back. I wiped my cheeks. Romero brushed a strand away that stuck to my wet skin. We still stood close but now that I had a better grip on my emotions I stepped back, ashamed by the way I'd thrown myself at Romero. *Again.* I was glad I couldn't read his mind. I didn't want to know what he thought of me now.

Romero's phone rang and after an apologetic smile at me, he picked up. "Yes, I have her. We'll be there in a moment."

I stared off toward an elderly man who stood before a grave. His lips were moving and he was leaning heavily on a walking stick. I had a feeling he was talking to his deceased wife, telling her how his days had been, how much he wanted to be reunited with her again. That would never be my father. He seemed to have gotten over Mother's death already.

Romero touched my shoulder lightly and I almost flew back into his arms, but this time I was strong. "Are you ready to head back?"

Ready? No. I didn't want to see Father or the fake mourning. I didn't want to hear one more word of pity. "Yes."

Neither of us mentioned the kiss as we walked back toward my mother's grave. Romero had kissed me, or let me kiss him out of pity, that was the harsh truth of the situation. Luca and Aria were the only people waiting for us.

Aria rushed toward me and wrapped me into a tight hug. "Are you okay?"

I felt bad instantly. She too had lost our Mother. She too was sad, and now she'd had to worry about me on top of everything. "Yes, I just needed a moment alone."

Aria nodded with understanding. "Father and the other guests have moved on to the house for the funeral feast. We should head there too, or Father will get even angrier."

I nodded. Aria shot Romero a look I had trouble deciphering. Then she led me toward the car, her arms tightly wrapped around my shoulders. Luca and Romero trailed behind. I didn't look back at Mother's grave again, knew it would have been too much for me.

"What was that look you gave Romero?" I asked quietly as we settled on the backseat.

Aria made an innocent face but I didn't buy it. I knew her too well even if we weren't as close as we used to be, due to the distance between us. She sighed. "I told him to stay away from you."

"You did what?" I hissed. Luca glanced over his shoulder at us, and I lowered my voice even further. I hoped he hadn't heard what I'd said. Romero seemed busy finding a good radio station.

"Why did you do that?" I asked in a bare whisper.

"Lily, I don't want you to get hurt. You think Romero will make you feel happier and help with the sadness, but it'll only make things worse. Maybe you think you've fallen for him but you shouldn't mistake loneliness for something else."

I stared at my sister incredulously. "I'm not an idiot. I know my own feelings."

Aria took my hand. "Please don't be mad, Lily. I only want to protect you."

Everyone always said they wanted to protect me. I wondered from what. Life?

***

Two days later, Aria, Gianna, Matteo, Romero and Luca left for New York. I wasn't sure when I'd see them again. Aria had asked Father if I could visit them for a couple of weeks in the summer but he'd refused with a not so veiled look in Gianna's direction. I'd put on a brave face, told them I'd be busy spending time with my friends and taking care of Fabi. Romero hadn't even hugged me goodbye, and he and I never got the chance for a private talk. Maybe it was for the best that I couldn't ask him about the kiss.

Aria called the same evening, trying to make sure I was really okay. I wasn't but I didn't tell her.

Instead I learned to go through the motions, trying to pretend things were going well. But my friends were either on vacation or busy with family matters, and I spent my days alone in our house with only the maid and my ancient bodyguard for company. Father and Fabi were gone almost all the time, and when they returned they shared new secrets they couldn't talk to me about, and even in their presence I felt alone. The loneliness you felt when you were surrounded by people was the worst kind.

I often spent hours sitting in the chair next to the bed where mother died, thinking about her last words and wondering how I was supposed to keep my promise. Father didn't allow me to go to college, didn't allow me to visit New York, didn't want me to party with my friends. All I could do was wait for something to happen, for life to happen. Maybe if Mother hadn't died Father would have spent the summer introducing me to potential husbands and I would have a wedding to plan in the near future. Even that seemed preferable to the way my life unfolded now, without anything to look forward to.

Romero

Luca, Matteo and I played cards when Aria's cellphone rang. She sat on the sofa with Gianna, drinking wine and laughing.

The moment Aria started talking I knew something was wrong. Luca put his cards down as well.

"Why didn't you call before? You should have send her with us right away!"

Luca got up.

"You can talk to me, too," Aria said, then she glanced toward Luca. "My Father wants to talk to you." She held out the phone for him and Luca took it with a worried glance at his wife.

Gianna crossed the room toward her sister. "What's going on?"

I had a bad feeling.

"Lily's passed out today. Apparently she hasn't been eating much since the funeral."

I rose from my chair. "Is she alright?"

Aria nodded. "Physically, yes. Father called a doctor and he said she needs to eat and drink more. But it's more than that. From what Father said Lily's been alone almost the entire time since we left. Nobody took care of her. I can't believe I let Father talk me into leaving her there. I should have taken her to New York with me right away."

"By my honor, no harm will come to Liliana when she's here. She'll be well protected. I will make sure of that," Luca said. Then he listened to whatever Scuderi had to say on the other end. "I'm aware of that. Believe me, Liliana will be just as safe as she's in Chicago." He listened again and then he hung up.

Aria rushed toward him. "And? Will he allow her to come here?"

Luca smiled tightly. "He agreed to let her spend the entire summer here, maybe even beyond that. He seemed really worried about her."

"Really? That's great!" Aria said, beaming.

"I doubt he's doing it because he's worried but who cares as long as he allows her to stay with us," Gianna said.

"When will she arrive?" I asked, trying to sound casual, as if I was merely a concerned soldier making sure he could fulfill his bodyguard duties.

Luca's expression made it clear he didn't buy it for one second but Aria was too wrapped up in her euphoria to pay attention. "Tomorrow afternoon."

"She'll be staying in our apartment, right?" Aria asked.

Luca nodded. "I told your father I'd personally make sure that she'd be safe."

"You mean that she doesn't go around having fun or god forbid sully her purity," Gianna muttered.

"Yes, that," Luca said matter-of-factly. "And since war with the Outfit might be the outcome if I don't keep my promise I'll do everything in my power to make sure she has only very limited fun." Again his eyes found me and I had to suppress a curse. He didn't even know about the kiss Lily and I had shared in the graveyard. I wondered how much worse it would be if he actually knew.

"We could spend the summer in the Hamptons. It's too hot and stuffy in the city and we're using the mansion not often enough anyway." Aria touched Luca's forearm and fixed him with one of her looks that always got him. "Please, Luca? I don't want Lily to be stuck in the apartment. In the Hamptons we can lie at the pool and swim in the ocean and take trips with our boat."

"Okay, okay," Luca said with a resigned look. "But Matteo and I can't stay with you the entire time. We have a lot to deal with at the moment. Romero and Sandro will have to keep you safe while we're gone."

Aria chanced a glance in my direction. She probably wondered if it was a good idea to have me around her sister, and to be honest I wondered the same thing.

CHAPTER SEVEN

<u>Liliana</u>

I hadn't even realized how much I'd neglected myself in the last two weeks since Mother's funeral. I hadn't been hungry and rarely thirsty, so I hadn't eaten much.

Of course, I was happy that my fainting had changed Father's mind. Sending me to New York was the greatest gift he could have given me. In the last two weeks I'd wanted nothing more than to be finally out of this house.

When I landed in New York, Aria and Luca were waiting for me. After a brief moment of disappointment that Romero wasn't there, I allowed myself to be happy that I was here at all. Aria hugged me tightly. When she pulled back, her eyes wandered over my body. "How could Father not have noticed something before. God, you've lost so much weight, Lily."

"It's only a few pounds and I'll gain it back in no time," I said with a smile.

"You better," Luca said, giving me a one-arm hug. "I will have you force-fed if necessary. I promised your father to take good care of you."

I rolled my eyes. "I don't even understand why Father cares. He hardly paid attention to me and now he's suddenly worried sick over me? What is that all about?"

A look of worry passed Aria's face and I was about to ask her about it, when Luca nudged me and her toward the exit. "Let's get going. I hate this place."

"So what are we going to do today?" I asked as we headed toward the car. After weeks of doing nothing, of feeling nothing, I needed to get out, needed to *feel alive* again.

"Nothing," Aria said apologetically.

My face fell and Aria hurried to add, "But only because we're leaving for the Hamptons early in the morning. We'll be spending the summer at the beach."

"Really?" I asked.

Aria smiled brightly, and suddenly the dark cloud over my head burst open.

Romero

I was good at keeping a straight face even in difficult situations, but when I first saw Lily as she walked into the penthouse, I wasn't sure I could hide my fury. Fury toward her Father for letting his own daughter drown in her sadness while he was busy furthering his position in the Outfit by inducting his too young son.

Lily had lost weight, enough that her collarbones and shoulder blades stood out. She looked breakable, but still so goddamn beautiful. I wanted to protect her from everything.

Her eyes met mine, and the longing in them almost compelled me to cross the room, to wrap her in my arms, but I stayed where I was, not only because of the look Aria sent me. Luca had given his promise to Scuderi. We, the Famiglia, would keep Liliana safe, and that included her honor. Considering that most of my dreams included Lily in some state of undress I definitely needed to keep my distance, and I would.

In the last few weeks, I'd fucked several girls in the hopes that they'd dispel Lily from my mind, but seeing her now, I realized that it had been completely in vain. Of course, it hadn't really helped that I'd imagined it was Lily every time I'd been with a woman.

I was completely screwed.

Luca came up to me as I leaned against the kitchen counter and watched the reunion of the three sisters. "Is this going to be a problem, you being in a mansion with Liliana?"

"No," I said firmly.

"You sure, because that look on your face a moment ago told me a different story."

"I'm sure. Liliana is a pretty girl like you said, but I've been with pretty girls. I've been with prettier girls even. I won't risk Scuderi's wrath."

It was a fucking lie. None of the girls I'd been with could compete with Lily's beauty, but thankfully Luca couldn't read minds even though he tried to make the stupider soldiers believe he had some sort of sixth sense like that just to keep them in line.

"Not just Scuderi's wrath," Luca said. "This is fucking serious. I mean it, Romero."

Was that a warning?

I had to bite back a comment and nodded. Luca was a good Capo and I'd never had a problem following his rules but for some reason this didn't sit well with me. Lily tried to catch my eye during dinner but I made sure to keep my attention on Matteo and Luca. I didn't want Lily to get her hopes up.

And what was more important, I needed to get my own fucking urges in check.

Liliana

Romero was still ignoring me. Though ignoring wasn't quite the right word. He treated me with polite detachment, always friendly, but never too warm. If I hadn't known what Aria had told him, I'd have taken it harder but as it was I was fairly sure that he was interested in me.

The first day at the mansion, the sun was shining brightly and we decided to have dinner outside on the beach. I decided to wear my pink beach dress. It was low-cut, backless and hugged my curves. Well, at least it usually did, now it was slightly loose in certain places but it looked still very nice. When my sisters and I headed for the table that the men had set up, Romero looked up from the barbecue that he was manning and the look in his eyes when he spotted me was all the encouragement I needed. That was far from the polite detachment of the last twenty-four hours.

He tore his gaze away from me and returned to his task of turning the steaks. He looked amazing too, the way the sinking sun caught on his brown hair, the way his forearms flexed when he moved. I loved the way he'd rolled up the white sleeves and had opened the upper two buttons of his shirt, revealing a sliver of tanned chest.

"You're drooling," Gianna whispered in my ear.

I flushed and jerked my gaze away from Romero, then glared at my sister who sank down at the table with a sneaky grin on her face.

I took the chair beside her. "Did you tell Romero to stay away from me as well?"

Gianna took the bottle of white wine out of the cooler and filled our glasses. "Me? No. You know me. I'm all for the naughty and forbidden. If you want to have a piece of Romero, then do it. Life is too short."

I paused with the wine glass against my lips. Mother's words crashed into my mind, almost the same words. "Aria disagrees," I said, then I downed half of the wine.

"Aria's trying to act like a mother hen, but you have to decide what you want."

"Are you trying to get me in trouble?" I asked, feeling my stomach warm from the wine. I finished my glass in another long gulp.

"I don't think you need me for that, to be honest," Gianna said with raised her red eyebrows. "But do me a favor and slow down with the wine."

"I thought you wanted me to have fun."

"Yeah, but I want you to be sober enough to realize what you want. And I don't think Romero will take you seriously if you're shitfaced."

"You're right. He's too much of a gentleman to take advantage of a drunk girl."

Gianna snorted. "Wow, now I know why Aria's worried." She watched Romero for a while. He was laughing about something Matteo had said. "I wouldn't put too much trust in his gentlemanliness, if I were you. Stay in control when you're with him. He's still a Made Man. Don't make me have to kill him, okay?"

"I thought you weren't a mother hen?"

"I'm not. I'm the angry mother bear who's going to tear his dick off if he hurts you."

I burst into laughter. Aria joined us at the table in that moment and mustered us with suspicion. "I don't know if I like you two alone together. It smells like trouble if you ask me."

"You don't want me alone with anyone it seems," I said, only half teasing.

Aria groaned and took a glass of wine for herself. "Are you still mad at me?"

"I'm not mad at you." I was only going to ignore Aria's orders, and I'd do my best to convince Romero to ignore them as well.

Aria glanced at Gianna who made an innocent face, then at me. "I don't like this. Promise me you two aren't getting into trouble."

"I've had enough trouble, thank you very much," Gianna said with a grin.

Aria fixed me with her older sister look.

"I'll behave, I promise," I said eventually. Then I poured myself more wine, trying to come up with a plan to get some alone time with Romero. I knew Aria would do her best to be my constant shadow.

***

During the day it was pretty much impossible to shake Aria off. She watched me, and particularly Romero like a hawk. When had she turned into such a killjoy? The nights and the early mornings were the only options I had. Since I barely slept anyway, that wouldn't prove too much of a problem. For some reason the darkness made me afraid of falling asleep, so I spent the nights fantasizing about Romero and making plans on how to seduce him while I caught the occasional hour of sleep when my sisters and I were sunbathing in the afternoon.

It had taken me a few days to gather my courage for my next move. I knew how to put on a brave face but this wasn't something I'd ever done before. I had no experience with men, except for the harmless flirting I'd done with Father's soldiers over the years.

I wasn't as worried about Romero's rejection as I used to be. I'd caught him watching me too often in the last few days when he thought nobody was paying attention. When the sun came up, the first hesitant rays brushing my face, I slipped out of bed and crept toward my window facing the beach. Like every other morning in the last few days, I spotted a lonely figure jogging along the beach in shorts and without a shirt. This was the highlight of my day. I wasn't sure where Romero took the discipline to get up before sunrise every morning to work out, and I really hoped he wouldn't show that much self-control when it came to me. I watched him jog uphill toward the mansion and pressed myself closer to the wall so he wouldn't find me spying on him. After he'd disappeared from view, I waited another five minutes before I headed out of my room. It was deadly silent at this hour, barely six o'clock. My sisters were still asleep; they never got up this early, and Matteo and Luca had left for New York yesterday and wouldn't be back until tonight, so the only person who could have crossed my path was the other guard

Sandro. When I passed Sandro's door I made sure to be extra quiet, but there was no sound coming from his room. I picked up my pace the closer I got to Romero's room.

I knew it was wrong. If someone found out, if *my Father* found out, he'd never let me leave Chicago again. He wouldn't even let me leave the house anymore. It was vastly inappropriate, and unladylike. People were still bad-mouthing Gianna after all that time. They'd jump at the chance to find a new victim, and what could be better than another Scuderi sister getting caught in the act and with a soldier no less?

And deep down I knew that I was exactly like Gianna when it came to resisting temptation. I simply couldn't. Romero's door wasn't locked. I slipped into his bedroom on tiptoes, holding my breath. He wasn't there but I could hear water running in the adjoining bathroom. I crept in that direction. The door was ajar. I peered through the gap.

In the last few days I'd learned that Romero was a creature of habit, so I found him under the shower as expected. But from my vantage point I couldn't see much. I edged the door open and slipped in.

My breath caught at the sight of him. He had his back turned to me and it was a glorious view. The muscles in his shoulders and back flexed as he washed his brown hair. There was a cross wrapped in barb-wire inked into the skin over his spine. Naturally, my eyes dipped lower to his perfectly shaped backside. I'd never seen a man like this, but I couldn't imagine that anyone could compare to Romero. Even the fantasy-Romero from my dreams couldn't compare.

He began to turn. I should have left then. But I stared in wonder at his body. Was he aroused? He tensed when he spotted me. There was another tattoo over his heart, the motto of the Famiglia.

His eyes captured my gaze before they slid over my nightgown and naked legs. And then I found an answer to my question. He hadn't really been aroused before. *Oh hell.*

My cheeks heated as I watched him grow harder. It was all I could do not to cross the distance between us and touch him. I'd never understood the concept of wanting something so badly, it hurt; I did now.

Romero slid the shower open with unhurried movements and wrapped a towel around his waist. Then he stepped out. The scent of his spicy shower gel wafted into my nose. Slowly he advanced on me. "You know," he said in a strange voice. "If someone found us like this, they might get the wrong idea. An idea that could cost me my life, and you your reputation."

I still couldn't move. I was stone, but my insides seemed to burn, to liquefy into red-hot lava. I couldn't look away. I'd spent hours going over the things I wanted to say once I had him cornered, but now I was speechless.

My eyes lingered on the edge of the towel, on the fine line of dark hairs disappearing beneath it, on the delicious V of his hips. Without my volition, my hand moved, reaching for Romero's chest, needing to feel his skin beneath my fingertips. I had no impulse control when it came to him. Maybe it should have terrified me. Girls weren't supposed to be like that.

Romero caught my wrist before I could touch him, his grip almost painful. My gaze shot up, half embarrassed and half surprised. What I saw on Romero's face made me shiver.

He leaned forward, coming closer and closer. My eyes fluttered shut, but the kiss I wanted never came. Instead I heard the creak of the door. I peered up at Romero. He'd opened the bathroom door wide. That's why he'd moved closer, not to kiss me. Embarrassment washed over me. How could I have thought he was interested in me?

"You need to leave," he murmured as he straightened. His fingers were still curled around my wrist.

"Then let me go."

He did instantly and took a step back. I stayed where I was. I wanted to touch him, wanted him to touch me in turn. He cursed and then he was upon me, one hand cradling the back of my head, the other on my hip. I could almost taste his lips they were so close. His touch made me feel more alive than anything ever had, and I wanted more of this feeling, wanted to drown in it.

"Leave," he rasped. "Leave before I break my oath." It was half plea, half order.

I wanted him to break his oath, wanted nothing more, but something in his gaze made me back away a few steps. I was brave but I wasn't stupid. Letting my gaze travel the length of him one last time, I quickly rushed outside and crossed the bedroom, only stopping to check the corridor before I left. There was nobody around so I stepped out and hurried toward my room. I'd almost reached my door when Gianna showed up, still dressed in pajamas and cup of hot chocolate in her hands. She halted, eyes narrowing in suspicion. "What are you doing sneaking around the corridor in your nightgown?"

Why did she have today to get up early?

"Nothing," I said a bit too fast. I could feel heat creep up into my cheeks. When would my body ever stop betraying me in situations like this?

"Nothing," Gianna repeated, crossing her arms in front of her chest and taking a casual sip from her cup. "Right. Isn't Romero's room in that direction?"

I shrugged. "Maybe. It's not like he's ever invited me over."

"Doesn't mean you haven't been there."

"Are you done with your interrogation? I don't know why you suddenly try to sound like Father. It's not like you've always been playing by the rules."

"Easy, tiger. I was just curious. For all I care you can visit Romero and whoever else you want as often as you like, but you know how things are. If the servants catch you, rumors will spread like wildfire. You have to be clever about it and running around the house like a chicken without its head isn't going to help. If Aria had caught you like this, you'd have a lot of explaining to do."

"I did nothing wrong," I said stubbornly.

Gianna smiled bitterly. "I know, but that doesn't mean they won't punish you for it. Just be careful." She handed me her cup of hot chocolate. "I think you need it more than me."

I'd thought I was being careful, but at least my sisters seemed to see right through me. I could only hope they would keep my secret from their husbands. Both Romero and I would get in huge trouble if people started to believe something was going on between us, even if there wasn't. Nobody cared about the truth. I wished there was something to talk about, wished Romero had kissed me like I'd wanted him, wished he hadn't stopped at kissing.

Romero

I almost chased after Liliana to drag her back into my room and have my way with her. Damn it. She'd wanted me. It had been written all over her face plain as day. The first moment I'd turned around and seen her standing there with huge blue eyes, I'd thought I was imagining it. After all, I'd been thinking about her during my shower. She was on my mind way too often. If Luca knew how

116

hard it was for me to concentrate at the moment, he'd have someone else protect Aria, and he'd definitely have me sent back to New York, far away from Lily. If I was a good soldier, I'd ask him to do it, but I didn't want to go anywhere. I wanted to stay near Lily.

I ran a hand through my wet hair as I glared at the bathroom door. Why had I sent her away? She'd wanted me to kiss her. She'd wanted more than that. Why did I have to listen to my fucking conscience then?

But it wasn't even morals that kept me from kissing Lily. It went against my oath, my duty, but that wasn't the main reason. Even though she wasn't really mine to protect, I still *wanted* to protect Lily, even from herself. She couldn't possibly realize the consequences of flirting with me like that. In our world a girl's entire worth was based on her reputation, her pureness, that was true in particular for girls from high-ranking Made Men. But even among soldiers only very few women were allowed to date someone they chose. We still followed the same rules from more than a century ago and I doubted that would change any time soon. If I let Lily close, if I let this thing between us unfold, if I took her the way I wanted her, then she'd be ruined in our society's eyes.

Of course, there were plenty of things we could do that wouldn't destroy her virginity. So many things, damn it.

That was a very dangerous thing to consider because if I really started to think of all the ways I could have Lily without ruining her, the likelier it got that I actually acted on those ideas, and I wasn't sure if I was strong enough to stop at a certain point. At least, not if Lily didn't ask me to, and I had a feeling she wouldn't.

During breakfast, I acted as if nothing had happened. Aria was already too attentive. And Gianna seemed to know more than she should as well.

Lily met my gaze when her sisters weren't looking and the look in her eyes made my cock twitch. Today I'd given her an opening. She knew now that I wanted her.

I'd spent my life for others, always putting my own needs second. Would it really be so bad if I took what I wanted for once? Never in my life had I wanted anything more than the girl across from me.

Why should I deny myself this?

CHAPTER EIGHT

<u>Liliana</u>

I stared up at the ceiling, or rather where I knew it was. The darkness was impenetrable, I couldn't even make out my own hand. Sometimes it felt like darkness was all there was in my life. A long tunnel without an end. Especially at night Mother's words haunted me. I'd promised her I'd be happy, but I wasn't even sure how to do it. A deep loneliness filled me, had taken hold of me ever since Mother had died. We'd never been as close as some daughters were with their mothers, but she'd been there, a constant presence. And now it seemed like I was all alone. Of course there was Fabi, but he was young and would soon be involved in mob business, and Father...Right now, being here in the Hamptons made me happy but it was a temporary thing.

My sisters, they were always there for me, but they had their own lives, they had husbands, and one day they'd have their own families. They'd still love me, and still take care of me, but I wanted my own happiness, separate from them. I wanted what they had. And I knew the only person I wanted that kind of happiness with was Romero.

He had been watching me differently this summer. In the past years, his expression had made it clear that I was nothing but a girl to him, someone to protect. But recently something had changed. I wasn't an expert when it came to men, of course, but his gaze had held a hint of something I often saw on Luca's face when he watched my sister Aria.

At least, I was quite certain. I pushed my blanket off my body and sat up. I didn't bother turning on the lights from fear of attracting attention and instead felt my way toward the door. I inched the handle down and slipped into the corridor. It was silent and dark, but at least here I could make out schemes. Not that I needed to see something to find Romero's room. I knew exactly where it was. I had lost count of the times I'd imagined going there. But so far reason had stopped me. Tonight I was tired of listening to reason, of playing it safe. I didn't want to be alone, didn't want to spend all night staring into the darkness, being lonely and sad. I crept down the corridor, careful not to make a sound, hardly daring to breathe. When I reached the door to Romero's room, I stood there for a long time. It was silent inside. Of course; it was already way past midnight and he always got up early for his run.

My fingers shook with nerves when I gripped the door handle and pushed it down. The door opened without a sound. I snuck in and closed it again, then I didn't move for a long time, only stared toward the bed and the contours of Romero's body. His curtains weren't drawn, so the moonlight provided some light. His back was turned toward me and the blanket only reached his waist. My eyes traced his muscled shoulders and arms. I moved closer, one hesitant step after the other. This was so wrong. Romero had caught me in his room before, and worse, he'd caught me spying on him in the shower, but this felt more intimate. He was in bed, and if things

120

went my way, I'd soon join him. What if he sent me away? Or worse, what if he got angry and told Luca? What if they sent me back to Chicago into that dark and hopeless house with my father who didn't miss my mother at all?

I froze a couple of steps from the bed. My breathing had quickened as if I'd exerted myself and my hands were clammy. Maybe I was losing my mind. I was trying to tell myself that I was doing this because Mother had wanted me to be happy, but maybe I was only using that as an excuse for my insanity. I'd wanted Romero long before Mother had ever said anything, and had even tried to kiss him long before her death.

I shook my head, getting mad at myself for overthinking everything. There had been a time when I'd done whatever I wanted as long as I felt like it. I took another step toward the bed but I must have made a sound without noticing it because Romero's breathing changed and his body tensed. Oh no. There was no going back now.

He rolled onto his back in one fluid move, then his eyes settled on me. He relaxed but quickly tensed again. "Liliana?"

I didn't reply. My tongue seemed to be stuck to the roof of my mouth. What had I been thinking?

Romero swung his legs out of the bed and sat on the edge for a moment, silently watching me. Could he see my face? I probably looked like a mouse trapped by a cat, but I wasn't afraid. Not one bit. If anything, I was embarrassed, and strangely excited. I was a twisted and sick mouse, that much was sure. He stood, and of course my eyes did a quick scan of his body. He was only wearing boxer shorts. He looked too good to be true. Like he'd stepped right out of my dreams. It was embarrassing to think how often I'd dreamed of Romero and all the things I wanted to do with him.

"Lily, what are you doing here? Is everything okay?" There was worry in his voice, but there was also something else. Something I'd heard when he'd caught me spying on him in the shower. It was something darker and almost eager.

My stomach fluttered with butterflies and I took a step in his direction. I wanted to fly into his arms, wanted to kiss him, and so much more.

"Can I sleep with you?" The words shot out, just like that, and once they were out I couldn't believe I'd said them. Especially since they could easily be taken the wrong way.

Romero froze. Silence stretched out between us. I was sure it would crush me any second. I took another step in his direction. I was almost in arm's reach now.

The sound of Romero's breathing was incredibly loud. I could see his chest heaving. Was he angry?

"This isn't something you should joke about," he said quietly. "It's not funny." He was angry. Maybe I should have taken the hint and turned on my heel to leave his room, but like Gianna I had never been very clever in situations like this.

"I wasn't joking, and I didn't mean it like that," I whispered. "I want to sleep in your bed, just sleep." For now. I wanted more than that, eventually.

"Liliana," Romero murmured. "Have you lost your mind? Do you even realize what you're saying?"

Fury rose up. Everyone always thought I was too young, too naïve, too female to make decisions. "I know exactly what I'm saying."

"I doubt it."

I bridged the distance between us until our chests were almost pressed against each other. Romero didn't back away but he braced himself. "Every night I feel like darkness is swallowing me whole, like my life is spiraling out of control, like there's nothing good in my life. But when I think of you those feelings disappear. I feel safe when I'm with you."

"You shouldn't. I'm not a good man, not by any standards."

"I don't care about good. I grew up in this world. I know how things are, and I'm fine with it."

"You don't even know half of it. And if you really know how things are, then you should realize what could happen if someone found you in my room at night."

"I'm tired of hearing what I can't do. Can't I decide for myself? It's my life, so why can't I make decisions?"

Romero was quiet for a moment before he said, "Of course, it's your life, but your father has certain expectations of you. And not only that, Luca gave him and Dante Cavallaro his word that he'd take good care of you and keep you safe. That includes your reputation. If someone told them you were in my room right now, that could mean war between the Outfit and New York. This isn't a game. This is too serious for you to play around."

"I'm not playing around. I'm so lonely, Romero," I whispered. "And I like you. I really like you." That was an understatement. "I only want to be close to you. You kissed me back and I know how you've been looking at me. I know you are interested in me."

He didn't say anything.

Doubt wormed its way into my brain. Had I been imagining the looks he'd given me? "If you don't like me, then tell me. It's okay." It wasn't. I'd be crushed, but maybe it would be for the best. I'd move on with my life somehow.

"Fuck," he murmured, turning away from me and leaving me to stare at his back. "If I was a good guy, I'd tell you exactly that. I'd fucking lie to you for your own good. But I'm not good, Lily."

Relief flooded me. He hadn't said he didn't like me. I'd read the signs right. God, I could have screamed with joy. I rested my palms against his bare shoulder blades. His skin was soft except for a few small scars, but they made him only more desirable to me. They flexed under my touch but he didn't step away. "So you are interested in me? And you like me?"

124

Romero let out a harsh laugh. "This is crazy."

"Just tell me. Do you find me attractive?"

He turned around. I wasn't quick enough to pull my hands away so they now rested against his chest. That felt even better. I had to stop myself from running my hands up and down his body. Even in the half-dark I could see the fire in his eyes. He scanned me from head to toe. I was only wearing pajama shorts and a tank top, but I wasn't even embarrassed. I wanted Romero to see me like that, wanted to get a reaction from him.

"Lily, you are stunning. Of course I find you attractive. Look at you, you are too fucking beautiful for words."

My lips parted. That was more than I'd dared to hope for. I moved even closer and peered up at him. "Then why do you keep pushing me away?"

"Because it's the right thing to do, and because I know the risks."

"Isn't it worth the risk?"

Romero stared down at me with such intensity that I couldn't help but shiver. He didn't reply. He gripped my hips and pulled me against him before his lips came down on mine. I opened up without hesitation, eager for that kiss, eager for his closeness. His tongue plunged into my mouth. There was no flicker of hesitation or doubt in his kiss. I moaned. This was so different from our first kiss, more intense. He cupped the back of my head, guiding me the way he wanted it. I could hardly keep up. I stepped on my tiptoes and leaned against him as I gripped onto his shoulders for balance. The kiss consumed me, stirred a fire in my belly and made me long for much more.

Romero jerked away and I tried to follow him but he kept me at arm's length. His breathing was harsh and there was a wild look in his eyes. "Give me a second," he rasped.

He squeezed his eyes shut as if he was in pain. All I could think about was to kiss him again, to have his hands on my body. I wanted nothing more. But I did as he asked and gave him a few seconds to get control over himself. Eventually he opened his eyes again. The wild look was gone and was replaced by something more controlled. His grip on my shoulders relaxed and his thumbs lightly stroked my skin. I wasn't even sure he noticed. The light touch raised goose-bumps of delight all over my skin. I waited for him to say something, but also feared what he would say. One of his hands traveled up to my cheek. "You should leave now," he said quietly.

I froze. "You're sending me away?"

Hesitation flickered across his face. "It's for the best, Lily, believe me."

I took a step back. I wasn't going to beg him. If he didn't want me to spend the night, then I'd have to accept it. "Okay. Good night." I turned around and hurried out of the room. I hardly paid attention as I crossed the corridor toward my room. I'd put myself out there today, had risked everything to get what I wanted. I wouldn't do that again. I had a huge crush on Romero but I also still had my pride. If he didn't want to risk this, then I'd accept it.

I closed the door and crept back into my bed. Like before the darkness closed in on me. It was too silent in my room, too lonely and empty. Even the memory of the kiss Romero and I had shared couldn't cheer me up. Not when it was probably the last time I'd kissed Romero. It took a long time for me to fall asleep and then Mother's pale unhappy face haunted my dreams.

***

Romero and I barely looked at each other the next morning. I didn't seek his closeness like usual. I tried to avoid his eyes as much as possible but a few times I caught him stealing glances my way. I wasn't sure what they meant, but I was glad that he and I didn't get to spend time alone together. Of course he was almost always around. It was difficult to avoid your bodyguard, but I did my best to focus entirely on my sisters, to enjoy my time with them.

Romero

It was way midnight when I headed for my room. Luca, Matteo and I had played cards until an hour ago, a distraction I fucking needed, and afterward when they had joined their wives in bed, I'd sat on the terrace, and wondered why I couldn't have the same.

A noise made me pause. My hand went to my gun as I followed the sound toward Lily's door. She sounded like she was in distress, mumbling in her sleep and crying. I checked the corridor, but I was alone. Everyone was long asleep or at least busy behind closed bedroom doors. I pushed the door open and slipped in. It took my eyes a moment to get used to the darkness, which was worse than in the rest of the house. The curtains didn't let any light in. I kept the door ajar and moved further into the room. I knew what I should do, and it definitely wasn't being alone in Lily's bedroom with her at night. On my list of things to avoid that was really at the top.

She was in obvious distress and I'd vowed to protect her but a nightmare wouldn't harm her. There was no reason for me to be here. I could have called Aria or Gianna, or just let Lily sleep through her nightmare, but I was a stupid fucker.

When she'd come to my room two days ago, it had taken every fucking ounce of self-control to send her away. I'd wanted her in my bed, and not just for sleep. When I'd first heard her question if she could sleep with me, I'd almost gotten a hard-on. I knew she didn't mean it that way, but I'd never wanted to misunderstand someone more than that night.

This was messed up. I'd always put my job and the Famiglia first. All the women in my life so far had been a nice distraction, but they'd never even come close to interfering with my duty. Lily was different. I wasn't sure how she'd done it, but I couldn't get her out of my freaking head. I glanced between the open door and Lily's bed, then I walked toward her. I left the door ajar, even though part of me wanted to close it and have total privacy, but if I wanted any chance at keeping my promise I needed the risk of someone walking by and looking into the room.

As I stood over Lily, I watched her for a moment. She lay on her back, her blonde hair spread out on her pillow, and her brows drawn together. Even in the throes of a nightmare she was fucking beautiful. Damn it. What had I gotten myself into? I touched her shoulder. She was dressed in only a tank-top and my fingers brushed the naked skin of her shoulders, and the touch sent a freaking shiver all the way to my cock. Her fucking shoulder, not her boob or her butt or her pussy. I almost got a fucking hard-on from touching a shoulder for God's sake. This was pathetic on a whole new level. "Liliana?" Somehow it felt safer to use her normal name instead of her nickname.

Her eyes moved under eyelids and she stirred under my hand but still didn't wake. I gently touched the side of her neck, feeling her pulse flutter under my fingertips. "Lily," I said a bit louder.

She jerked and her eyes flew open, staring straight at me. "Romero?" she whispered in a voice still heavy with sleep. I wanted to kiss her so badly.

Liliana

Someone touched my throat, tearing me from sleep. I opened my eyes but it took a few seconds before my brain registered what was before me: Romero.

"Romero?" Maybe I was still dreaming. It was definitely an improvement over my previous dream about my Mother who had talked to me with lifeless eyes about happiness.

"It's okay," Romero said in his deep voice.

I looked around. "You are in my room." I sounded like a moron. But I was stunned. After all, he'd as good as thrown me out of his room two days ago and now he stood in my own. A bit of a twist I hadn't expected. Not that I minded.

Romero's lips twitched as if he wanted to smile but then he became serious again. Sometimes I thought he tried to keep in his smiles because he worried that if he allowed that kind of emotion, all of them would come up. "You had a nightmare. I decided to wake you."

I nodded. He stood beside my bed, half bent over me. If I'd reached out I could have grabbed his neck and pulled him down. My fingers itched to do just that, but I hadn't forgotten his rejection not too long ago. He needed to make the next step and I wasn't sure if coming into my room to wake me from a nightmare counted as one. I wanted it to. I sat up and my blankets fell down to my hips. I wore only a flimsy camisole. Romero's eyes followed the movement, and lingered on my chest.

"Thanks for waking me. I had a dream about my mother." I wasn't sure why I said it. My nightmare was the last thing I wanted to think, much less talk to Romero about. His eyes returned to my face. Sometimes I thought I could drown in them. When he was around I felt so happy and light. Somehow I knew he was the one, the person I was meant to be with. I'd known it pretty much from the beginning. If there was something like fate, then this was it.

Romero brushed a strand of hair from my forehead and I leaned into the touch. Somehow he was closer now. "You miss her."

I nodded. I did, but her last words haunted me more than her death. Her sadness over the things she'd missed, the longing in her eyes – I didn't think I could ever forget that. Romero and I locked gazes and just stared at each other. In the dim light spilling from the corridor I could see the conflict in Romero's eyes. I wanted to lean forward but I stopped myself. I had to be strong, had to have some self-respect.

I was about to say something, anything, to stop the mounting tension but then Romero leaned down and kissed me. I hadn't expected him to and gasped against his lips, but my surprise lasted only a couple of seconds, then I wrapped my arms around his neck and kissed him back with everything I had. He put one knee down on my bed beside me and cradled my head. His kiss banished the last of my tiredness and the lingering sadness from my dream. I wasn't sure how long we kissed, Romero kneeling on the bed and I half-sitting, but I came more alive with every second. Eventually I pulled back, my breathing harsh. There was an insistent pounding between my legs but I knew it would have been wrong to take things further tonight.

Romero stroked my cheek and was about to straighten but I caught his arm. "I don't want to be alone tonight."

I waited for protest but it didn't come. My heart dropped when he walked toward the door. Would he leave without a word? Instead he closed the door silently before he returned to the bed. With every step that he took in my direction, my heart seemed to swell with emotion. Romero removed his gun holster and put it down on the nightstand, then slipped out of his shoes. I scooted to the other side of my bed to make room for him, excitement fluttering in my chest. He didn't slip under the covers with me as I'd hoped, instead he stretched out on top of it. I peered over my shoulder at him. He looked tired, even more tired than I felt. He smiled. It looked almost resigned, with a hint of regret. He snuck his arm around my waist and hugged me to his body, my back pressed against his chest, with the blankets between us. I wanted that barrier gone but decided to let him have his way for tonight. I'd won a small battle, the war could wait. Despite the material bunched between us I was fairly sure I could feel how much our kiss had affected Romero. Smiling to myself, I closed my eyes. "Thanks for staying with me."

Romero kissed the back of my head. "Get some sleep. I'll keep the nightmares away."

"I know you will," I whispered.

***

When my alarm woke me the next morning, I was alone in bed. I sat up and pressed the button that let the curtains glide open. Blinding light greeted me and I quickly squeezed my eyes shut. When I'd finally grown used to the brightness I looked around in my room for a sign of Romero's sleepover but there was nothing. It might as well have been a dream. For a heart-stopping moment I considered just that. I pressed my nose into the pillow and caught his scent. Not a dream. I slipped out of bed. Of course he didn't stay until the morning. Romero was cautious, one of us had to be. If one of my sisters walked in without knocking, which had happened before, then we could have been in huge trouble. Still it felt like a small rejection that he had left me alone without a word.

Get a grip, Lily.

We had to be careful or I'd be sent home and then we wouldn't get to spend any time at all together. This was a good beginning.

A beginning for what? I wasn't that naïve to believe that my father would accept Romero as a potential candidate for marriage. I wasn't even sure if Romero considered me as someone he'd want to marry. But I was getting ahead of myself. I wanted to take risks, enjoy life and be happy. This night with Romero was a step in the right direction.

I rushed through my shower but took extra care with my make-up and hair. Then I headed downstairs. I could hear my sisters already laughing in the kitchen and followed the sound. They stood at the kitchen counter, coffee cups in their hands. Nobody else was there but the big wooden table was set for six people, so the men would hopefully join us later. Trying to hide my disappointment that Romero wasn't there yet, I walked toward them. Aria poured me a cup of coffee and handed it to me with a worried look. "Didn't you sleep again last night?"

I paused with the cup against my lips, my pulse quickening. Had they seen Romero walking into my room? Or maybe even leaving it in the morning? "Why?" I asked hesitantly.

Gianna snorted. "Because you look fucking tired. There are dark shadows under your eyes."

I thought I'd put enough concealer on it. Damn it. "I'm fine. I dreamed of Mother, but it wasn't bad."

Aria wrapped her arm around my shoulders. "Still about what she said to you?"

"Yeah," I said evasively. "I can't get her words out of my head."

"Don't take everything she said too much to heart. She was sick. It's not your job to undo her mistakes. She was unhappy at the end but it was her own fault," Gianna said.

"Gianna," Aria said in warning.

"It's not like Mother tried to guilt me into anything. She only wanted me to be happy."

"And you're going to be happy. We'll make sure of it," Aria said, squeezing my shoulder lightly before stepping back. "Let's start to eat. Who knows when the men will show up. They had something to discuss."

"Oh?" I asked nervously as we went over to the table and sat down. "Business?" If I was already a nervous wreck when Romero and I hadn't even really done anything yet, how much worse would it be once there really was something going on?

Aria gave me an odd look. "I suppose. It's all they ever talk about."

"You're acting kind of odd," Gianna said as she grabbed a Danish from the bread basket. She scanned my face. "Did anything happen?"

"No," I said too quickly. I grabbed a bowl and some cereal and milk. Luckily the men arrived at that time. I froze as my eyes settled on Romero. His gaze barely brushed me as he, Luca and Matteo headed for the table. Despite knowing that we had to act normal and not draw any suspicions toward us, his blatant refusal to look my way sent a stab of worry through me. I grabbed my spoon and started eating my cereal. I could feel my sisters' eyes on me. They knew me too well but I wouldn't give them a chance to suspect anything. I didn't want them to have to keep a secret from their husbands, especially not that kind of secret. The rest of breakfast I made sure to keep my eyes away from Romero and instead talked to my sisters.

After breakfast, Aria and Gianna decided to head to the pool again. I went to my bedroom to change into a bikini, a cute pink thing with white dots. When I stepped out, I almost bumped into a hard chest. I gasped, not having expected someone to be in front of my door. "God, you startled me," I said with a small laugh.

Romero didn't say anything. His eyes roamed my body. "You look breathtaking."

I couldn't hold back a jibe. "You didn't seem to notice at breakfast."

Romero met my gaze. "I did notice, believe me. It's impossible not to," he said quietly. We were alone in the corridor and standing close enough that I could smell his aftershave. "I didn't want to ignore you, but we don't have a choice. This has to stay a secret."

"This?" I asked. "What exactly is this?" We had hardly done anything yet. We'd kissed three times but that was it.

"I don't know. Maybe nothing. But I want you Lily. I can't get you out of my head. No matter what I do there's always you."

I exhaled. It felt as if a huge rock had dropped off my shoulders. So it wasn't just me. "I want you too. So what are we going to do now?" I took a step closer. Romero's eyes travelled the length of my body again and it made me tingle all over. How would it feel if he touched every spot his eyes had wandered?

Romero moved closer and I dipped my head back to stare up into his face. He didn't touch me, even though I wanted him to. "What I want to do is take you into your bedroom and rip off your bikini, then taste every inch of your skin. I know you'll taste absolutely perfect."

"Why don't you find out?" I whispered.

"Damn," Romero muttered. He cupped the back of my head and tilted it to the side, then he bent down and pressed an open-mouthed kiss over my pulse-point before he traced my jugular with his tongue. I let out an embarrassing moan as my core tightened with arousal. I tipped my head further to the side, giving him better access, but he had moved on from my throat and kissed my lips. I pressed myself against him. His shirt felt cool against my naked skin. A noise from somewhere in the house made us jump apart. There was no one in the corridor but it was a good reminder that we needed to be careful. After another glance down the corridor, Romero cupped my cheek again. "You do taste as perfect as I thought."

I smiled. "You haven't even tasted all of me." My cheeks flamed when I realized what I'd said and how Romero would understand it.

Romero's eyes darkened with what I suspected was desire. "I intend to, trust me."

I shivered. "You do?"

"God yes." He sighed, then took a step back. "But we need to be careful. This is a dangerous path we're on."

"I know but I don't care. I want this."

Romero kissed me again. He shook his head. "I don't know how you did it but I can't get you out of my fucking mind. And now this." He gestured at my bikini. "You're lucky you can't read my mind, you'd be shocked."

"Not as shocked as you, if you could read my mind," I said with what I hoped was a seductive smile. I turned around and walked away, making sure I swung my hips.

Romero

As I watched Lily prance away, I almost groaned. Her tiny bikini barely covered her perfect butt cheeks and her long legs drove me just as wild. I wanted to read her mind, wanted to find out what she desired and give to her.

Her earlier comment about tasting her had filled my head with images of my mouth on her pussy. I couldn't wait to find out

138

if it was as pink and perfect as I imagined it. I wanted to lick her until she begged for mercy.

My pants became uncomfortable and I had to shift to give my cock a bit more room. How would I be able to restrain myself if I kept thinking about tasting her? It had already been difficult enough to lie in her bed at night without those images in my head, torturing me. I knew Lily would visit me again at night. Now that she knew how much I wanted her, she would use her chance.

But I also knew that I needed to establish certain boundaries. Flirting and kissing was still tolerable, though I was fairly sure that Luca and Aria, and most definitely Scuderi, would disagree. Taking things further was something I couldn't risk. I'd given Luca a promise and I should at least try to keep it to some extent.

CHAPTER NINE

<u>Liliana</u>

That night I crept into Romero's bedroom again. The lights were out but he was sitting with his back against his headboard. He didn't say anything as I approached the bed and suddenly I was nervous.

"Hey," I whispered, then yawned because it had been a long day and as usual sleep evaded me. "Can I come into your bed?"

Romero lifted his blankets. I quickly slipped under them but didn't snuggle against him, suddenly shy. Romero peered down at me, then he reached out and brushed a few strands from my forehead. I braced myself on my elbows to kiss him, but he shook his head. I froze.

"I don't think we should be kissing when we're in bed together."

"You don't want to kiss me anymore?" Was I that horrible?

"No, I still want to kiss you and I'm going to kiss you but not when we're in bed. There are certain boundaries we shouldn't cross, Lily."

"Okay," I said slowly. Maybe he was right. Kissing in bed was only a small step away from doing much more, and some things simply couldn't be undone. "But can we snuggle?"

Romero chuckled. "I should probably say no," he murmured. "But I'm screwed anyway."

He lay down and opened his arms. I inched toward him and put my head down on his upper arm. I wasn't sure why I felt so comfortable in his presence. I wasn't someone who liked physical contact with people I didn't know, but with Romero I'd always wanted closeness.

I closed my eyes but I didn't fall asleep immediately. "Have you ever regretted working for Luca? As the son of a soldier, you would have had the option not to become part of the Famiglia. You could have lived a normal life."

"No. This was all I ever wanted," Romero said. His fingers ran up and down my forearm in a very distracting way but I wasn't sure if he even realized what he was doing. "I've known Luca and Matteo long before I was inducted. I always looked up to Luca because he was older and strong as a bear, and Matteo and I always got in trouble together."

"I bet Matteo got in trouble and you had to save his ass."

Romero let out a laugh. "Yeah, that's more like it. When Luca became a Made Man and when I heard the story of how he killed his first man at eleven, I wanted nothing more than to be like him."

"You were only eight then. Shouldn't you have been playing with matchbox cars instead?"

"I always knew I wanted to become a member of the Famiglia. I wanted to be their best fighter. I often practiced with Matteo and in the beginning even with Luca. They wiped the ground with me. But I was a quick learner, and when I was inducted a few years later, only a handful could see eye to eye with me in a knife fight, and I got only better with time. I worked hard."

I could tell he was proud of what he'd achieved. "What did your family want? Did they try to keep you away from the mob?"

"My father didn't want his life for me. As a debt collector he had to do many horrible things. But he and my mother trusted me to decide for myself."

How would it be to have people trust you to make your own decisions?

"This life, does it make you happy?" I asked softly. Sometimes I wished there was an easy definition for what made me happy.

"At times, but nobody can always be happy." He was silent for a moment. "What makes you happy?"

"I don't know. This, but I know it's fleeting."

Romero's chest rose and fell under my cheek until I was sure he'd fallen asleep. "Happiness often is. That doesn't mean you can't enjoy it while it lasts."

***

Deep down I knew I needed to stop this madness. If someone caught us, both our lives would be ruined. But I couldn't.

142

Whenever I was near Romero the sorrow that had rested so heavily on me in the last few weeks seemed bearable. Everything seemed lighter and more hopeful.

I eased the door open. As usual the lights were out but the curtains weren't drawn so the moonlight illuminated the contours of the furniture and showed me my path toward the bed. I closed the door without a sound and tiptoed across the room. Romero wasn't asleep. I could feel his eyes following me as I slipped under the covers. He lay on his back, his arms propped up behind his head. I couldn't make out his expression. He waited for me to put my head on his chest so he could wrap his arm around me. He'd never made the first move but tonight I didn't just want to fall asleep beside him. I wasn't exactly sure what I wanted, but definitely more. I was glad for the dark when I got up on my knees and straddled his hips.

Romero tensed beneath me and sat up, his palms flat against my shoulder blades. "What are you doing?" he murmured, a quality to his voice I'd never heard before.

"I don't know," I whispered before I lightly brushed my lips over his. I wasn't sure what kind of reaction I'd expected, definitely not the one I got. He flipped us over so my back was pressed into the mattress and he was hovering over me. He wasn't holding me down but his body caged me in, his knees between my legs, his arms beside my head, his upper body over me. Romero everywhere. God, and it felt good. Maybe there should have been anxiety and trepidation. We were alone in his bedroom, and if I called for help I'd get in more trouble than when I let him do whatever he

143

wanted. But I wasn't scared of Romero. Maybe I was stupid not to be. I knew what he was capable of. He was a killer. And he was a grown man, who'd had many women before me who delivered when they offered their body to him. Everyone always told me that playing games would get me in trouble one day. Maybe tonight they'd be proven right.

Despite this my body reacted to Romero's closeness. My center tightened in anticipation, of what I wasn't even entirely sure, and heat pooled in my belly. For a long time the only sound in the dark was our rapid breathing. "Lily," he said quietly, imploringly. "I pride myself on my self-control, but I'm a man, and not a good one either. So far I've tried to be a gentleman. I know you're sad and lonely, and I didn't want to take advantage of you. But if you go the next step and offer more, then you can't expect me not to take you up on that offer."

"Maybe I want you to." My heart pounded in my chest as the words left my mouth.

Romero brushed his lips over my temple, the barest touch that made me tingle. "Do you even know what you're offering, Lily?"

I hesitated.

Romero released a long breath, kissed my forehead and began to pull back.

I gripped his shoulders, even through his t-shirt his heat seemed to scorch me. "Sometimes when I'm alone I try to imagine how it would feel if you touched me."

"Fuck," he breathed. And then he kissed me gently before pulling back again. Even my hands couldn't stop him this time.

"Why are you pulling away?"

"Lights."

"Lights?" I said nervously.

"I need to see your face." The lights came on and I blinked against the sudden brightness. He lay down beside me but he kept one arm around my waist. "When you imagine my touch, do you ever caress yourself?" he asked in a low voice.

My eyes widened a fraction and heat crept into my face. Romero cupped my cheek and traced the blush there. "Tell me," he said.

I lowered my gaze to his chin. "Yes," I admitted in barely a whisper. What would he think of me now?

Romero pressed his nose into my hair. "Fuck."

"You said that already."

He didn't laugh like I'd expected him to. He was very quiet. His hand on my waist tightened when he raised his head and fixed me with a hungry gaze. He brought his mouth down on mine and I parted my lips for him. His tongue slipped in and everything around me seemed to fade to nothingness as I tasted him. It wasn't our first kiss but it felt like something else entirely, with me in bed with him, with nothing to stop us. His kiss was fiercer. There was no hesitation or surprise this time. He sucked my lower lip into his

145

mouth, then my tongue. He sucked it lightly, and I wasn't sure how it was possible that I felt the motion all the way between my legs.

"Is this okay?" he murmured against my throat and all I could do was nod. Aria and Gianna always called me a chatterbox but with Romero words so often failed me. His lips lightly traced the skin over my collarbone, then his tongue slid out to taste me. His mouth moved even lower to the edge of my camisole. His fingers traced the fabric and his lips followed the same path. I arched my back, wanting him to move even lower, to do more.

"You told me I should find out how you taste everywhere. I'm very tempted to do it," he murmured. He peered up. His eyes had a predatory look on his face. The only expression that had ever come close was when he'd been down in the basement with the Russians. There was something dark and unhinged in his brown eyes, but this time I wasn't afraid. "What do you want?" he asked roughly.

If only I knew. "More," I said softly.

Romero lowered his gaze to my chest. My nipples strained against the thin material of my camisole, hard and aching for attention. Romero lightly traced his thumb over one nub and I gasped.

"Like this?" he asked.

I nodded furiously. "More."

Romero chuckled, and the sound made me ache even more for his touch. He took both of my nipples between his thumbs and forefingers, and lightly twisted them back and forth through the silk. I squeezed my eyes shut at the sensation between my legs. I pressed my thighs together, desperate for some kind of relief. Romero cupped my nipple with his lips, sucking it gently into his mouth. For some reason the fabric seemed to heighten the sensations even more. I was close to exploding. His hand brushed my hipbone before it moved under the hem of my camisole and softly traced my stomach. Goose-bumps covered my skin at the light touch. He released my nipple but the wet fabric of my camisole stuck to it. I couldn't believe this was finally happening.

Romero moved onto my other nipple and repeated the same procedure. I rubbed my thighs together. The tension between them was almost unbearable. Romero's eyes followed the movement before they darted up to my face. "Do you want me to touch you there?"

I nodded quickly. Romero smiled. He trailed his hand down my side until he reached my thigh. He stroked the outer side lightly, his eyes never leaving my face, making sure I was okay. His strokes moved closer to my inner thigh until I wanted nothing more than to grasp his hand and push it into my panties. As if he could feel my impatience, Romero tugged lightly at my shorts. I opened my legs without even thinking about it, a silent invitation. Was I being too forward? I didn't care.

He slid his hand into the leg of my shorts and then his fingers traced the sensitive skin at the edge of my panties. He watched my face closely when he inched his index finger under the fabric and brushed my folds. I gasped and he groaned. I was already so wet that his finger slid over me easily. His lips claimed mine with less restraint than before, and I didn't mind. "Is this okay?" he rasped between kisses as his finger kept lightly tracing my folds. Sparks seemed to soar through my core. It felt so much more intense than when I touched myself.

"Yes," I whispered.

His finger moved up between my folds, spreading my wetness up to my nub. He started to rub back and forth, the barest touch that felt incredible. My hips jerked up from the intense sensation. I moaned into his mouth, my legs opening wider to give him better access. He kissed my neck, then he sucked my nipple into his mouth again, soaking my camisole even more. His fingers between my legs drove me higher and higher.

"You feel so good, Lily. So soft and wet and warm," he murmured.

I whimpered in response. Hearing him say those words made me relax further under his touch. He was gentle and unhurried. I ran my hands over his back and hair, wanting to feel as much of him as possible, wanting to have him closer in every way possible. I'd always wanted him and my sisters had often told me that feeling would cease with time, but my want had only grown. I didn't think it would ever stop, not that I wanted it to.

Romero's other hand moved to the edge of my pajama top and inched it down, freeing my breast. I had to fight the urge to cover myself up. For some reason it was more difficult to bare myself to his eyes than to have him touch me in my most private place. Embarrassment flew out the window when Romero lowered his head and captured my nipple between his lips. At the same time his finger on my clit started moving faster. I shivered and buried my face in the crook of Romero's neck. His tongue licked my nipple lightly and it felt even better without the fabric as a barrier. My embarrassing moans and breathless sighs couldn't be stifled against his skin. I pressed my lips together, trying to hold the sounds in, but everything Romero did felt so good.

Romero released my nipple. "I wish I could hear your moans. I love the sound."

I lifted my head. "Really?"

Romero smiled a smile I'd never seen before. It was darker, more dangerous, and indescribably sexy. "Really. Can't you feel how much I love this?"

He pressed a bit tighter against me and something hard and hot dug into my leg. I couldn't believe I'd done this to him. Romero kissed my mouth, then the spot beneath my chin, my throat until he'd worked his way back down to my nipple. He trailed his tongue around it, then moved on to my other breast. "I've been wanting to do this for so long. Fuck, I don't care that it's wrong, that it goes against my promise, I can't resist you."

Hearing him say that felt like ultimate triumph and when he sucked my nipple back into his mouth I fell apart. I stifled my cries in the pillow, knowing we had to be careful.

Romero kissed my throat and I smiled at him. "Wow."

"Yes, wow. Watching you was fucking amazing."

I raised myself on my elbows, my eyes moving down to the bulge in his boxer shorts. I'd been wanting to see him naked again ever since I watched him shower. I rested my palm against his erection. Even through his boxers he felt incredibly hot.

"I'm not sure that's a good idea," Romero said in warning, but he grew even harder beneath my touch.

"I want to do it," I said.

Romero didn't protest. He lifted his hips and pulled down his boxers. His erection sprang free.

I curled my fingers around the base, surprised at how wide it was. Romero sucked in a deep breath and dropped back on the bed, his hands flat on the mattress. I stroked lightly up and down, ran my fingers over his tip and back down to his balls. I couldn't stop exploring him, curious and excited at the same time.

Romero cupped my cheek and I turned to look at him but didn't stop my explorations. "Damn it, Lily, you're driving me crazy."

"How do you want me to touch you?" I asked quietly. I wanted to make him feel as good as he'd made me feel. I'd overheard Gianna say something about blowjobs to Aria once, and that those brought any man to his knees, but I wasn't sure I could pull it off in a satisfactory way. Maybe I should have asked Gianna for instructions…

"You're doing good."

I didn't want to do good. I wanted to be amazing. Pushing my worries aside, I bent over him and took him into my mouth.

Romero jerked under me in surprise and gripped the back of my head. "You don't have to do that."

It wasn't said with conviction. I licked from his base up to the top. He didn't taste of anything, except for the tip where a few droplets had gathered. I licked them away without thinking.

Romero cursed, raking his hand through my hair.

"Am I doing this right?" I asked after a couple of minutes.

"Fuck yes. You don't even know how hard it is not to thrust into your mouth."

"If that's what you want, you can do it."

"No, not today. Take your time and do what you like. I'll enjoy it all, trust me," he said in a low voice. And so I did. I licked around his tip and took him into my mouth, trailed my tongue along his length over and over again. Romero didn't make a lot of sounds but his hand in my hair tightened and he sucked in his breath every now and then.

"I'm going to come," he warned. I sucked harder, gripping his thighs to find better leverage, and then Romero came with a low groan. I kept him in my mouth, waiting for him to go soft, but he didn't. He wasn't as hard as he'd been but he definitely wasn't soft.

"I meant that as a warning. You didn't have to swallow, Lily," Romero said. He pulled me toward him and kissed me. "Are you okay? Or was it terrible for you?"

"Terrible? No, why? I wanted to make you feel good. I don't mind it when you come in my mouth."

Romero let out a breathless laugh. "Don't say those things to me. I won't be able to focus anymore."

I grinned, then my gaze flitted down to Romero's erection again. "Why isn't it going soft?"

I could see Romero's confusion, then realization set in and his mouth twisted in a grin that bordered on proud. "Only because I've come doesn't mean I'm not still turned on. It takes more than one orgasm to *make me go soft.*"

"Really?" I asked wickedly.

Romero shook his head. "Not tonight. It's late. You can't stay that long."

Disappointment banished my excitement. "I know."

Romero stroked my cheek. "We have to be careful. Believe me I'd love to spend all night with you."

I nodded and put my head back down on his chest. I wanted to catch a couple of hours of sleep before I had to sneak back to my room. *Enjoy the moment,* I told myself before I fell asleep.

CHAPTER TEN

<u>Romero</u>

After Lily had given me that blowjob, I spent the next day thinking about nothing but returning the favor with my tongue. It was a good thing that the mansion wasn't the most dangerous place, because my focus was gone. I didn't think I'd have done a good job protecting anyone if someone had attacked.

My cock was so hard it almost hurt as I waited in my bed that night for Lily to come over. When midnight rolled around and she wasn't there yet, I almost went in search for her. I couldn't remember the last time I'd been that horny.

When my door finally opened and Lily walked in, I had to stop myself from shoving her up against the wall and bury myself in her. That was the one thing I couldn't do. Many borders had already been crossed but that was where I had to draw the line.

Lily hopped into bed and kissed me eagerly. It seemed I wasn't the only one who'd waited for this. "Gianna and Matteo were in the corridor, so I had to wait," she said, her fingers already slipping below my shirt.

I loved her touch, but it was my turn. I grabbed her and flipped her on her back. She gasped in surprise. I hooked my hands in her waistband and slid her panties down her legs, then I paused.

This was still new for Lily. I couldn't treat her like the woman I'd been with before. "Is this okay?"

She lifted her legs to help me pull her panties over her feet. She nodded quickly. There was only need in her eyes. I smiled. I positioned myself between her legs and a hint of embarrassment showed on her beautiful face, but I didn't give her time to think about it. I lowered myself to my stomach, pushed her legs farther apart and took a long lick.

And damn it, she tasted even better than I'd imagined.

Liliana

I'd heard girls talk about boys going down on them in school but I'd never been able to imagine how it would feel to have someone's mouth on me like that. Would it be strange? Wet? Disgusting? Awkward?

It was none of those things. It was mind-blowingly wonderful. Or maybe that was only because Romero knew exactly what to do, how to nibble and suck and lick until my fingers dug into the mattress because I couldn't take the pleasure anymore. And it seemed to get better every time we did it. Weeks past and every night Romero pleasured me with his mouth. He seemed to enjoy it as much as I enjoyed going down on him.

Tonight, he was taking his time and I had no mind to rush him. It felt too good. Romero's stubble scratched me lightly at times and that intensified the sensations even more. He lifted his head and I huffed in protest.

He chuckled, but didn't lower his mouth. "Tell me when you're coming, okay? I want to know."

"Okay," I said, then moaned when Romero closed his lips over my clit and continued where he'd left off.

I could feel myself getting closer. My thighs began to quiver. "I'm coming," I gasped, too caught up in my pleasure to be embarrassed about it.

Romero's finger brushed my opening and then he slid it in. I arched off the mattress. There was a flicker of pain but for some reason it made me come even harder.

Eventually I lay motionless on the bed, trying to catch my breath.

Romero blew out a harsh breath. "Goddammit. You're so tight."

I couldn't say anything in response, too overwhelmed by the feeling of him in me. He moved his finger slowly, stroking the inside of my walls, tripling the sensations in my body. He curled his finger and my hips bucked off the mattress as I gasped in surprise and another orgasm rocked through me. He pulled his finger out and actually put it in his mouth. I could only stare, strangely turned on by the sight.

Romero crawled back up to me.

A question burned in my mind. What if the brief pain had meant Romero had broken my hymen? It was ridiculous that I even had to worry about something like that.

Romero smoothed my brows. "Hey, did I hurt you?"

"No, I...I only wondered if..." I felt embarrassed to voice my worries.

Romero seemed to puzzle it together on his own though. "You're scared that you aren't a virgin anymore because I put my finger in you." I couldn't decipher the emotion in his voice. Was he angry? Annoyed?

He cupped the back of my head. "I wouldn't do that to you, Lily. I wouldn't just take your virginity without permission, and even then..." He shook his head. "I shouldn't even think about taking your virginity. But you don't have to worry. My finger isn't wide enough and I didn't go deep enough to do any damage. You're safe."

"I wasn't scared, I just..." Yes, what? I had been worried. There was no denying it. It wasn't that I didn't want Romero. I did. But that was a huge step, one I couldn't take back.

"It's okay. You should be scared about that. Your life would be ruined if you lost your virginity before your wedding night," he said in a strange tone. He wrapped his arms around me, so I couldn't

157

look at his face anymore. "I want you to be the one, you know?" I whispered into the dark.

"But I cannot do it," Romero said, his fingers tightening on my arm.

"Why not?"

"Lily," Romero said almost angrily. "You know why not. So far we've been lucky that we didn't get caught. Your sisters and Luca are already suspicious as it is. Right now we could still deny everything and nobody would be able to prove the opposite, but if we slept with each other, then there would be evidence."

"Evidence?" I huffed. "We aren't planning to commit a crime."

"In our world it is. We don't play by the rules of the outside world and you know it."

"We only want to be together because we love each other. Is that so bad?" I snapped my mouth shut when I realized what I'd said. I'd practically put the words "I love you" into Romero's words when he'd never said them. I hadn't either but I knew I loved him. Did he love me as well?

He'd become motionless and for a moment even stopped breathing altogether. "Fuck," Romero whispered harshly. He pressed a kiss against my temple. "This is spinning out of control."

"I meant it, Romero. I love you," I said.

He was quiet. "You shouldn't. We don't have a future, Lily."

My heart ached from his words. I didn't want to believe them to be true. "You don't know that."

"You're right," Romero said eventually. He kissed my temple again and then neither of us said anything.

***

Mother had died with longing in her eyes and regret on her lips. This wasn't how I wanted to end. I didn't want to have a pile of 'what if's' and 'how could it have been' in my head during the last hours of my existence. I wanted to look back and not wonder how wonderful life could have been. I wanted Romero. I wanted Romero to be my first, wanted to share everything with him. Right in this moment, I wanted nothing more, and I knew that even if I'd come to regret it, that regret could never be as torturous as the one I'd feel if I didn't do it, the one where I'd always be left wondering how it would be to become one with the person I loved. Sometimes you had to risk something to live, and Romero was a risk I was willing to take. That was all I could think about as I relished the last few moments of my orgasm.

Romero climbed up my body and brushed a kiss across my lips. He was about to lie down beside me, as he always did after he'd taken care of me, but I held onto his shoulders. "I don't want to stop tonight."

He became very still. His dark eyes traced every contour of my face as if he was hoping for a hint of regret somewhere, but I knew he wouldn't find any. I'd spent too many nights longing and wondering and wishing, and tonight I'd finally get what I wanted. Of course, I needed Romero's cooperation but I had a feeling he wouldn't refuse me. He was dutiful and responsible, but he was also a man, and he wanted me. I could see it in his eyes, and his erection pressed up against my hipbone was a pretty good indicator as well. "Lily," Romero rasped, then cleared his throat. I had to stifle a smile. "That's something that can't be undone. Everything we've done so far is easy to hide, but beyond this point, there are ways to prove our...transgressions."

I laughed softly. "Transgressions?" I lifted my head and kissed him. "How can this be wrong?" Of course, I knew that Father and many other people in our world could have written a novel on all the ways, but I didn't care. There was no part in me that thought what we were doing was wrong, and that was all that mattered.

"We discussed this already. I shouldn't do this. For God's sake, I made a promise to Luca to protect you. How is ruining your life protecting you?"

"You aren't ruining my life. I want this, doesn't that count for anything?"

"Of course it does."

I pressed myself against him and grasped his cock through his boxers. "I want you. Only you. I want you to be my first." I wanted him to be my only one. "Don't you want to be my first?"

Romero exhaled a laugh and kissed the corner of my mouth, then my cheek before his eyes burned into mine again. "You know how much I want you. I can hardly think of anything else."

I curled my fingers tighter around his erection. "I know."

He released a harsh breath, then let out a quiet laugh. "You've got me in your hands in every possible way. That's not how it's supposed to be."

I smiled. It felt good to know that I had that kind of power over someone like Romero. But he held just as much power over me, and my heart. It was a scary thing, knowing that someone else had the power to crush your heart with a few words. Love was scary. "I want you to be the one, Romero. I don't want anyone else. Please."

He kissed me again, fiercer this time, and lightly thrust into my hand. He felt hot and hard, and I couldn't wait to feel him in me. "Are you sure?" he asked, but there was hardly any vehemence behind the words.

"Yes. I want you."

Romero nodded. Excitement and nerves burst in my body. I'd half expected him to be more against it, but I was glad he hadn't tried to talk me out of it. Today I'd finally become his.

Romero

I was supposed to be the voice of reason, the one to protect Lily from herself and from me, but I wasn't as strong as everyone thought I was. Luca believed in me, trusted in my dutifulness and restraint. He didn't know me well enough. Trust and longing filled Lily's beautiful blue eyes. She wanted me, and damn it, I wanted her more than anything. Every fucking time I'd fucked her with my finger, I'd imagined how it would be to have my cock in her, to feel her hot walls around me. I couldn't deny her. Maybe if there had been a flicker of doubt on her face but there was none. I tasted her mouth once more. She was sweet and soft and irresistible. Her fingers around my cock tightened and she bucked her hips lightly – an invitation I understood only too well, and longed to accept. I pulled away from her lips. "Not yet."

"But," she started. I slipped my hand between her legs and entered her with my middle finger. She let out a low breath and opened a bit wider for me. I loved how fucking responsive she was. Always so wet for me. There had been plenty of moments in my life when I had felt powerful but giving Lily pleasure beat them all. She didn't say anything else, only closed her eyes and relaxed, trusting me to make her feel good. I kissed her breast, then nibbled on her nipple as I slowly slipped my finger in and out. Her breathing quickened but I kept a steady rhythm. I moved lower and positioned myself between her thighs. I let myself enjoy the sight of my finger as it entered her perfect pink pussy. Everything about her was beautiful. I leaned forward, not able to resist a moment longer. I closed my mouth over her bundle of nerves and teased her with my lips and tongue while my finger kept thrusting into her, deeper and harder now. I could feel her hymen every time I pushed in. I pressed my tongue against her clit, and slipped another finger into her. I'd never tried it before and her walls clamped around me tightly. Her breathing hitched in surprise and she tensed under me. I circled her lightly with my tongue the way she loved it, then took her between my lips and suckled. The tension left her body and a new wave of wetness followed, making it easier for my fingers to enter her. I found a slow rhythm as I listened to the sweet moans and sighs coming from her lips. I could have listened to her forever. I never got tired of giving her pleasure. There was just no better feeling in the world than making Lily explode with pleasure, and the knowledge that I was the only one doing it to her. A darker emotion filled me. She wasn't really mine, might never be. One day she might have to marry someone her father chose for her and then that man would see her like this. Unreasonable fury surged through me, but I pushed the feeling aside. This wasn't the moment to think about those kinds of things. I didn't want to lose control only because I let my thoughts stray to dangerous places. I wanted to enjoy every fucking second of this, especially because I didn't know how many more chances we would get together.

I focused on Lily's sweetness, until she finally came apart, stifling her moans in my pillow. I wished I could hear her cry out without restraint, without the fear of getting caught. One day. One day, I'd really make her mine. I'd figure out a way.

I pulled my fingers out and sat back, relishing the sight of her heaving chest as she enjoyed the aftermath of her orgasm. Slowly her eyes opened and she smiled. Damn it. That smile got me every time. I bent over her and kissed her, then I reached for the drawer in my nightstand and grabbed a condom.

Lily watched me, and the briefest flicker of nervousness crossed her face.

I paused. "Are you sure you want to do this?" I wanted to shoot myself for asking. I wanted nothing more than to be in her, to make her mine, to feel her walls around my cock. Why did I have to act all noble? Who was I kidding?

She licked her lips in the most torturous way possible and whispered, "Yes, I want you."

Thank God. I kissed her lips again. I slid off the bed and got out of my underwear. My cock strained to attention. I quickly rolled the condom over it before I climbed back on the back. This wasn't the first time Lily had seen me naked, but today there was a flicker of anxiety on her face when she watched my cock. I moved between her legs, letting my fingers trace the soft skin of her thighs.

There was only trust in her eyes. I didn't deserve that much trust from her, and yet I fucking loved seeing it on her face. I supported my weight on my elbows and started kissing her gently. The tip of my cock rested lightly against her wet heat. I wanted to bury myself in her and it took every ounce of self-control to stay still and wait for her to relax under me. I hooked my hand under her thigh and pulled her legs a bit father apart. I looked deeply into her eyes, then I shifted my hips and started to push into her. I didn't take my eyes off her as I inched into her tight heat. She felt so fucking amazing. Tight, and warm and wet, and I just wanted to push into her to the hilt. Instead I focused on Lily's eyes, on the way she trusted me to make this good for her, to take care of her and be careful. Her face flashed with discomfort when I wasn't even halfway in. I paused but her fingers on my shoulders tightened. "Don't stop," she said quickly.

"I won't," I promised. Stopping was the last thing I wanted to do. I traced my lips over her temple, then I pushed further into her until I reached her barrier. I didn't tell her it would hurt. She'd only tense. I pushed the rest of the way into her. Her walls squeezed my cock tightly. I didn't move.

Lily's face was contorted in pain.

"It's okay," I murmured. "This was the worst part." At least, I hoped it had been. She felt so tight around me, I was worried if I started moving, I'd make things only worse for her, but I couldn't stay in her like that forever. And I really wanted to move, wanted to lose myself in her. "Lily?"

She gave me a shaky smile. "I'm okay. It's not as bad as it was."

That wasn't really something a guy wanted to hear from the girl he was with. I wanted to make her feel good but I knew it would be difficult during her first time. Even though I wanted nothing more than to move, I decided to stay as I was and kiss her for a while. My cock screamed in protest.

"You can really move," she whispered. And that was everything it took. I withdrew almost all the way before I slowly slid back into her.

She exhaled, fingers digging into my back. I slowed even further and tried to go not quite as deep and soon Lily's body loosened under me. I made love to her like that for a long time, and when she responded with the first hesitant moan, I wanted to fucking scream in triumph. But I couldn't last forever, not with the way her walls clamped around me and I had a feeling she wasn't going to come. Next time she would. And there would be a next time, I knew that now. When it came to Lily, I couldn't resist temptation.

I sped up even more until I felt my cock tighten and released into her. I held Lily tightly as I rocked my hips desperately, then I stilled.

She closed her eyes and rested her forehead against my chest.

"Are you okay?" I murmured.

She nodded, but didn't say anything. I pulled back slightly and tilted her face up, worried she was crying. But she merely looked exhausted, and happy.

Relief washed over me. I pulled out of her slowly and removed the condom. Before I thrust it into the trash bin, I caught sight of the blood smeared on the condom.

For some reason it took that image to let reality set in. Fuck. What had I done?

"Romero?" Lily whispered. I lay down beside her and pulled her into my arms. She didn't need to know my thoughts. I didn't want her to worry.

It didn't take long for her to fall asleep but I lay awake for hours. Eventually I slipped out of bed and walked toward the window. I stayed out toward the ocean for a long time. Regret wasn't a useful emotion. You couldn't undo the past. I turned back to the bed.

Lily lay curled up under the blanket, only her beautiful hair and peaceful face peeking out. She was deep asleep. I needed to wake her soon, so she could return to her own room. The sky outside the window was already starting to turn grey. Soon people would get up and it would be too risky if Lily was still in my room then. I should have sent her away immediately afterward for her own safety, but I didn't have the heart to do it, and I didn't want to see her go either so soon after what we'd done.

"Fuck," I muttered. So far everything Lily and I had done had been risky but untraceable. But this, this could destroy Lily's reputation and even start a war. Taking Lily's virginity was a selfish thing to do. I knew better. I'd learned to make reasonable decisions over the years, to make decisions that were good for the Famiglia. But today I'd ignored my duty and my promise to Luca.

Lily sighed in her sleep and turned around. The blankets moved with her and the pink spot on the sheets became visible. I closed my eyes. *Fuck.* This was supposed to happen in her wedding night. But I knew that Rocco Scuderi would never give Lily's hand to me in marriage. I was only a fucking soldier. Respected and honorable, but a soldier nevertheless. Despite my guilt over having taken Lily's virginity, I knew I would do it again. I'd wanted to make her mine for so long, and this was the only way I could. At least now a part of her belonged to me, at least she'd never forget our night together, but I also knew it wasn't enough. I didn't want Lily to have only the memory of our shared night for the rest of her days, I wanted to remind her of the pleasure I could give her every night, I wanted to taste her, smell her, feel her every fucking night. I wanted to have her fall asleep in my arms and wake up next to me in the morning. I wanted to make her mine for everyone to know, but there was no way in hell I could do this without betraying Luca and the Famiglia. Luca treated me like a brother but if I did this, if I went against the Outfit by claiming Lily officially, he'd have to put me down like a rabid dog for the good of the Famiglia.

With a sigh, I walked toward the bed and bent over Lily. I brushed her hair away from her face. "Lily, you need to wake up," I whispered.

Her eyelids fluttered and she turned on her back. The blankets slipped away, revealing her perfect breasts. Her nipples

168

puckered at the cool air in the room. My cock stirred in response. I leaned over her. She even still smelled like me. Fuck. I was already getting hard again. She opened her eyes and gave me a sleepy smile. Happiness and trust shone on her face. Didn't she realize that I'd destroyed her life last night?

A light blush appeared on her cheeks. I kissed her forehead. "You need to leave," I said.

She froze, eyes filling with insecurity. "Did I do something wrong last night?"

Good Lord. I wanted to stab myself with my fucking knife. I was such an asshole. I should have never let it come this. Lily was a good girl and I'd ruined her. I kissed the spot below her ear, then her cheek. "No, you did nothing wrong, honey."

She relaxed. She lifted her hand to the back of my head, looking hopeful. "Can we snuggle a bit?"

She sounded fucking vulnerable. Of course she wanted closeness after last night, and I wanted it too, but it was getting light outside. But the way she was looking at me I couldn't tell her 'no'. I slipped under the blankets and she pressed up against me. Her naked skin brushed mine, and all of my senses sprang to life. I pushed my lust down. This wasn't the time. I stroked her hair. "Are you okay?"

She nodded against my shoulder. "I'm a bit sore." She sounded embarrassed.

I pressed a kiss against her temple. And I wasn't sure why I said it because it definitely didn't make things easier but it slipped out, "I love you."

She sucked in breath before whispering, "I love you too."

I was digging my grave and hers too, only because I couldn't control my dick, my heart and my mouth.

She let out a small happy breath. She didn't seem to realize in how much trouble we were. I couldn't stop feeling guilty. I wished I could say I would have acted differently if I got the chance, but I knew I'd sleep with her again. I'd wanted her, still wanted her.

CHAPTER ELEVEN

Liliana

I couldn't believe Romero and I had actually slept together. I didn't feel regret. Maybe it would come at some point but I couldn't imagine it.

It had been painful and yet it was the happiest moment in my life so far. And afterwards when Romero had admitted he loved me, I'd wanted to tell everyone about it. Let them get angry, let them call me names, what did I care? I was happy, and that was all that mattered. But I knew better. Romero and I needed to keep it a secret. Maybe one day we'd figure out a way to make it official without causing a war, but right now I only wanted to enjoy our time together. The summer was drawing to a close but Father didn't seem to want me back. Maybe he'd forget I existed and I could move to New York for good.

The first time I'd faced Aria and Gianna after losing my virginity, I'd worried they'd see something was different, but of course they hadn't. Nobody suspected anything.

Maybe that realization was why I got more daring.

It was almost noon and I could hardly keep my eyes open. Romero and I had made love until the early morning hours, and once I'd been back in my room I'd only managed two hours of sleep before I had to get up for breakfast again.

"Why don't you rest on the sofa for a while? You look tired," Aria said when I yawned again. We'd been rifling through a brochure that detailed events in the Hamptons for something to do in the next few days. Sunbathing and swimming were getting old.

Gianna wiggled her eyebrows behind Aria's back. "She does. She doesn't seem to get enough sleep at night."

Romero glanced over from where he stood with Luca and Matteo, but he didn't seem worried. I decided to ignore Gianna's comment. I stood from the table. "You're probably right, Aria. I'll lie down for a bit."

Aria set the brochure aside and peered down at her watch before she looked over to Luca. "If we want to head out for lunch, we should leave soon."

Luca nodded.

I walked toward the sofa, stretched out and closed my eyes. I almost immediately drifted off into a light slumber, only interrupted by the sound of Aria and Luca leaving, followed a few minutes later by Gianna's and Matteo's laughter as they headed for the beach. In the following silence, I felt my mind drift off again.

"I'm wearing you out," Romero said from close-by.

I opened my eyes to find him standing over me with a smirk. Slowly my own lips curled into a grin and my sleepiness began to disappear. I hooked my leg behind his knee in an attempt to make him fall forward and preferably land on top of me, but Romero was too strong. After a quick glance toward the terrace door he leaned down, though, and gave me a kiss. When he was about to pull back again, I wrapped my arms around his neck and my legs around his waist.

"Aria and Luca are out for lunch, and Gianna and Matteo will spend the day on the boat. That leaves the house to us."

Romero looked conflicted but when I pressed my core against his crotch, I knew I had him. He was already hard. With a growl, he lowered himself on top of me. Our lips eagerly found each other. After a few minutes of heated kissing and roaming hands, Romero drew back. "It's too risky to have sex out here."

"I know, but there are other things we can do," I said, before I pulled Romero's head back down for another kiss. He didn't protest again, which might have also had something to do with the fact that I was rubbing his erection through his pants.

For some reason making out with Romero in the middle of the living room made things seem more real between us, like we could maybe be an official couple, and not just something that needed to happen in the secrecy of darkness.

My lips were raw from Romero's kiss, but I loved it. Romero slipped his hand under my shirt and sneaked his fingers under my bra cup, finding my nipple. I gasped and arched off the sofa. Romero kissed me even harder. I swung my leg over his lower back, pulling him even tighter against me. I couldn't wait to feel him without the clothes between us. Maybe I could convince him to risk a quickie in the living room.

A door banged and steps rang out, but there was no time to react before Aria appeared in the living area. "Lily, I--" She snapped her lips shut and froze, so did Romero and I. Romero pulled his hand out from under my shirt and sat back quickly. He held his arms in a way that was supposed to hide his erection, but I doubted he was fooling Aria. My eyes searched the area behind her back but Luca wasn't there. That was the only good things about our situation.

Nobody said anything for a long time. I tried to reposition my bra and straighten my hair but I wasn't doing a good job because my hands were shaking. "This isn't how it looks," I said, but stopped when I realized how stupid that sounded.

Aria raised her eyebrows as if she thought exactly the same thing. "That's why I didn't want you alone with her, Romero. I knew this would happen!"

"You make it sound like I had nothing to do with it. It wasn't only Romero's doing," I said, but Aria hardly paid me attention. She was glaring at Romero. "Why are you back anyway? Shouldn't you be having lunch with your husband?"

"Are you blaming me for this?" Aria asked incredulously. "Luca got a call that there was trouble in one of the clubs. Something with one of the Russian underbosses, so he dropped me off in the driveway and headed straight to New York. You're lucky he didn't come in."

"If you tell Luca," Romero began but Aria interrupted him. "I won't tell him," she said.

Romero helped me to my feet. "He's your husband. You owe him the truth."

What was he doing? He'd be in big trouble if Luca found out, and what if Luca told my father? I gave Romero a confused look but he didn't react. Then another thought struck me. Maybe he wanted people to find out. Maybe he hoped Luca would approve and would figure out a way for my father to agree on a union between Romero and me. Hope flared up in me.

"Lily, can I talk to you in private, please?" Aria asked.

I nodded, even though my stomach turned from anxiety. Aria was my sister. I loved her and trusted her, but Romero was right. She was also the wife of the Capo, and I wasn't sure where her loyalties lay. I followed her toward the dining room and then into the kitchen. She didn't say anything until we'd both settled on bar stools.

"How long has this been going on?" she asked. God, she even sounded like the wife of a Capo, so grown up and responsible.

"A while. Almost since I came to New York," I admitted. There was really no use in lying any more. And I actually wanted to talk to her about it. Romero and I had been keeping this a secret for close to three months.

Aria nodded slowly, her eyes full of worry. "I should have known. Sometimes I thought I saw you exchanging those secretive looks only lovers do, but I didn't want to believe it."

I wasn't sure what to say, if she even expected me to say anything. "We tried to hide it."

"Of course, you did!" Aria whispered harshly. "Oh Lily. This is bad, you know that, right? If Dad finds out all hell will break lose. You'll be in major trouble, and not only that. Father might very well start war over this. After all, Luca promised to keep you safe while you were in New York and having one of his men have an affair with you is definitely a breach of that promise."

"Affair?" I said offended. What Romero and I had was so much more than that. "You make it sound like it's just about sex."

Aria's eyes widened. "I didn't mean it like that, but...wait a second. Please tell me you haven't slept with him yet." Her expression was so pleading and anxious, I almost considered lying to her.

I bit my lip. "I really love him, Aria."

"So you did sleep with him," she said quietly. She made it sound like it was the end of the world.

I nodded. "And I don't regret it." I was so glad that I got to share that moment with Romero. I wanted to share so much more with him. Every time I'd slept with him in the last few weeks, I'd grown closer to him, though I didn't think that was possible.

Aria leaned back and released a long breath. "Father will kill you if he finds out. After the thing with Gianna, he'll completely lose it."

"Mother told me to be happy shortly before she died. And Romero makes me happy. I want to be with him."

"Lily, Father won't allow it. No matter what any of us says, he won't let you marry a mere soldier from New York. He can't gain anything from such a union, not when I'm already married to the Capo and Gianna to the Consigliere."

"I know," I said in a whisper. "But...I..." I trailed off. I knew Aria was right. I'd known it pretty much from the beginning. I hated that I had to apologize for loving someone, for wanting to be with that someone. It shouldn't be like that.

Aria took my hand and linked our fingers. "Some women manage to fake their virginity on their wedding night. Maybe you can do that too. And it's not like Father has already set up a wedding for you, so we can figure something out until then."

"Aria, I don't want to marry anyone else. I only want Romero. I mean it, I love him."

Aria looked into my eyes for a very long time. I wasn't sure what she was hoping to find there but I gave her time. "You do, don't you?" she said, resigned. "What about him? Does he love you?"

"He said it after we made love for the first time." I'd hoped he would say it again after our first night together but so far he hadn't. Maybe he wasn't the type to say it out loud very often.

"Are you sure he's serious about you?"

"Of course, didn't you hear what I told you?" I said, but even I could hear the flicker of uncertainty in my voice and I wasn't sure where it was coming from.

"Some men say things they don't mean after sex because they feel guilty."

My eyes widened. "He wouldn't do that. And if you're saying he only tried to get in my pants, that's ridiculous. You know Romero, he wouldn't use me like that."

"No, you're right. Romero isn't the type and he wouldn't risk so much for sex. He must care about you if he goes against Luca's orders."

"You won't tell him, right?"

"I told you, I won't. He's got enough on his plate already, I don't want him to worry about this as well. We'll figure something out. But until then, please be more careful. I'm not going to tell you to stay away from Romero because I suspect you'd just go behind my back, but if someone else finds out, things could really get out of hand."

"I know," I said. "Romero and I will be careful."

Aria pressed her lips together. "And there's really no way that you'd consider breaking things off with Romero?"

"No," I said without hesitation.

She smiled sadly and hopped off the bar stool. "I want to talk to Romero now."

I pushed to my feet and grabbed her arm. "Why? Will you try to talk him into leaving me?"

"Do you really think I'd do that to you?" Aria asked in a hurt tone.

I felt bad instantly but Aria had changed over the years. Maybe it was because she'd taken more responsibilities as Luca's wife, but sometimes I thought she acted too much like a meddling mother when it came to me. I didn't doubt she always wanted what she thought was the best for me, only problem was I wasn't sure if we both agreed on what that was. "No. But why do you want to talk to Romero?"

"I just do," she said stubbornly. "Please stay here while I go talk to Romero. Do me that favor."

"Aria, please don't make a bigger deal out of this than it is."

"Oh Lily, this is a much bigger deal than you think." she said before she walked off.

Romero

I wanted to tear my hair out in frustration. We should have been more careful. I usually never let my guard down. I always anticipated possible risks. Today I'd failed on so many levels, it was pitiful.

Aria advanced on me. She looked royally pissed. And I couldn't blame her. She stopped right in front of me, her blue eyes blazing with anger. "How could you do that? What were you thinking?" she hissed. "But you probably weren't thinking, at least not with your head." She made a gesture in the general direction of my crotch.

My eyebrows shot up. This was so unlike Aria. "This isn't only about sex."

"Lily said the same thing, but what is it then? You know the rules, for God's sake. It's ironic that I have to remind you."

"I know the rules," I said tersely, getting angry. But Aria was the last person I should be mad at. She was right.

"Lily said you slept with her." Aria shook her head. "God, Romero, if someone finds out, Lily will be ruined. Or do you intend to marry her?"

"I can't. You know that. Your father would never allow it, and if we went against his wishes that would mean war."

"I *know*. So why did you do it?"

"I didn't push Lily if that's what you think," I said. Did she think I'd forced her sister somehow? "Lily wanted it too."

"I don't doubt it. I see how she's looking at you. She loves you. Of course she wants to sleep with you, but you should have known better!"

"I know. What do you want me to say? That I'm sorry?"

"You'd be lying," Aria muttered.

Indignation shot through me but she was right. I wasn't sorry that I'd slept with Lily, at least not enough that I wouldn't do it again. "Are you going to tell me to stay away from her now?"

"You'd be going behind my back. And Lily would hate me if I tried to get between you and her. You've slept with her already, so it's not like it matters if you do it again as long as you are careful not to get caught and not to get my sister pregnant."

"Are you going to give me the talk?" I said in amusement.

"I'm serious. If Lily gets pregnant, then things will get really bad."

"We're careful."

"As careful as you were when I caught you on the sofa?"

"I mean it. Lily won't get pregnant."

Aria covered her face with her hands. "God, I can't believe we're having this discussion. I wanted Lily in New York so she'd have some fun, but not that kind of fun."

I wasn't sure what to say. Guilt weighed heavily on my shoulders, but like Aria had said it was too late now.

"Would you stay away from her if I threatened to tell Luca?" Aria asked as she lowered her hands.

"No," I said without hesitation.

"Good," she said, throwing me off track. "At least that means you're serious about her. Maybe we can find a solution for you and my sister. Let me think about it."

"I've been thinking about it for a long time but maybe you are more lucky than me. Unless we want war, we'd have to convince your father to agree on a union between Lily and me."

"Gianna and I married for political reasons. Why should Lily not be allowed to marry someone she wants?"

"If I was more than a soldier, then maybe your father would consider it."

Aria's eyes lit up. "You could become a Captain with your own group of soldiers. You've been working for Luca for so long and he always says you're his best soldier. The only reason why he hasn't already promoted you is because he trusts you with me and doesn't want anyone else as my guard."

I stared at her. Usually the position of Captain was handed down from father to son. Soldiers rarely received the honor of becoming Captain.

"Father still hasn't found a husband for Lily. That's a good sign. Gianna and I were long engaged when we were Lily's age, so maybe he's open for suggestions and it would be a good move to improve relations between New York and Chicago again."

"You'd make a good Capo too," I said with a smile.

"I'm married to a good Capo, that's all."

"You are," I said. "But I don't want to become Captain only because you talk Luca into it. I haven't worked this hard for a pity promotion."

"I won't have to talk him into it, and Luca never does anything because of pity. You should know that."

I nodded. She had a point. "Once you tell him, there's no going back. He might not take it so well. I went against his direct orders after all. That's still a crime."

"Yeah, you did," Aria said. "But he loves you like a brother. He'll forgive you. I'll just have to figure out a way to break it to him."

"I could talk to him. I have to own up to my actions."

Aria shook her head. "No, I can be more convincing than you, and he can't stay mad at me for long."

I laughed. "You Scuderi women have a way with men."

Aria smiled for the first time since she'd found Lily and me on the sofa. I took that as a good sign, even though I wasn't so naïve to think that I'd become Captain tomorrow and then Scuderi would gladly accept me as his future son-in-law. This would be a difficult battle.

CHAPTER TWELVE

Liliana

I nervously paced the kitchen. What took Aria so long? I didn't even want to know what she was saying to Romero. What if she convinced him to break things off with me? She'd promised not to do something like that but I wasn't sure. If she thought she had to protect me from harm, she'd play dirty if she had to.

The door opened and Romero stepped in. He looked almost relaxed. I hurried toward him. "What did she say?"

"That we should be careful."

"That's all? She's not going to tell Luca about it?"

"No, not right now."

"What does that mean?"

A slow smile curled his lips. "There might be a way for us to be together."

"You mean officially?" I asked excitedly.

"Yes, but first Aria needs to figure out a way to talk to Luca, and then we'll go from there."

I tried to hold back my joy, but it was difficult. I wanted nothing more than a real future with Romero.

I stood on my tiptoes and kissed him, but after only a few seconds Romero pulled back with a pained look. "We need to be more careful. Aria will rip my head off if she catches us kissing out in the open like that again."

"Probably not only your head," I said with a wicked grin, cupping him through his pants.

Romero groaned, gripped my wrist and pulled my hand away. "Lily, stop torturing me."

"I thought you like it when I torture you."

Romero leaned down, his lips brushing my ear. "I do, when we are *alone*."

"Then how about we head to my room?"

"There's nothing I'd rather do, but we shouldn't risk it during the day," Romero said regretfully. "And I really need to call Luca and ask about the problem with the Russian underboss."

I pouted playfully. "I hate it when you're being reasonable. Tonight is too far away. I want you now."

"Fuck," Romero muttered. Then he gave me a dangerous grin. "Go ahead. I'll come after you in a few minutes."

I dashed off toward my room, already feeling my core tighten with anticipation.

***

The next day, Luca returned from New York. He was on edge, so our confession would have to wait. During dinner that evening,

Aria, Romero and I acted as if nothing had ever happened. I really hoped Aria would figure out a way to talk to Luca soon so we could all find a way to make a future for Romero and me possible.

Gianna kept chancing look at Aria and me as if she could smell that something was going on. Gianna had always been drawn to trouble so it was really no surprise.

Halfway through the main course, Luca's phone started buzzing. "What now?" he growled as he dropped his fork. Today definitely wasn't the day to tell him about Romero and me. I hadn't seen him in such a bad mood in a while. He got up, pulled the phone out of his pants pocket and answered it.

"Rocco, I didn't expect your call," he said.

We all turned toward the conversation.

Luca glanced in my direction. "Liliana is doing well."

My Father had only called once the entire summer to ask how I was. For some reason I worried about the true reasons for his check-in.

"Tomorrow? That's short-notice. Has something happened?"

I put my fork down, my stomach tightening with anxiety.

"Of course. She'll be there," Luca said with a frown. He hung up and returned to the table, lowering his large frame into the chair.

"What's going on?" Aria asked before I could even utter a word. She looked as worried as I felt. Did she think Father had found out something about Romero and me? If that were the case, the call wouldn't have gone over so peacefully, that much was sure. And who should have told them? Nobody in this house would.

"Your father wants Liliana to come home tomorrow," Luca said thoughtfully.

"What?" I said, shocked. Romero didn't quite manage to hide his surprise either. I had to force myself to tear my gaze away from him quickly before Luca got suspicious. "That soon?"

Matteo laughed. "You've been here for three months."

Gianna rammed her elbow into his side and he rubbed the spot with a smirk.

"I was joking, damn it. Why do you have to be so violent?" he asked.

I wasn't in the mood for jokes. I felt like the rug had been pulled out under my feet. I'd always known I'd have to return eventually but now that I was being faced with my Father's order, I felt heartbroken.

"He wants you on the earliest flight. He booked the ticket already," Luca continued as if his brother and Gianna weren't still bickering.

"Did he say why?" I asked.

"He said something about social responsibilities. Apparently there are a few parties he wants you to attend, but he wasn't very forthcoming with information."

My eyes darted to Romero again, but then I focused on Luca. "Did he say how long I had to stay in Chicago?"

Luca narrowed his eyes. "No. Chicago is your home, so I had no right to ask."

"Lily is of age, she could simply refuse to return," Gianna said matter-of-factly. Matteo had his arm wrapped around her shoulder. As usual their fighting hadn't lasted very long. They'd probably soon go to their room to make up.

"Then I'd drag her into that plane if necessary. If her father wants her to come home, she'll go. I won't risk a conflict over something as ridiculous as this."

I bit my lip. "It's okay. I'll go. I'll survive a few parties, and I'm excited about seeing Fabi again. I missed him. I'll plead Father to let me return to New York as soon as possible."

I didn't talk for the rest of dinner and was glad when I could finally get up. It was ridiculous of me to be so nervous about going home; because despite everything Chicago was still supposed to be *my home*. I headed out toward the terrace and wrapped my arms around myself, feeling inexplicably cold even though it was still warm.

The door slid open behind me again and Aria walked up beside me, giving me an understanding smile. "I'll call Father and ask him to send you back for another visit soon. It's not like he needs you in Chicago. You'll be back before you know it."

"You're probably glad I'll be gone because that means I can't see Romero for a while," I snapped. I felt instantly bad for lashing out at my sister. Closing my eyes, I said, "Sorry."

Aria touched my shoulder lightly. "Don't worry. And I really don't want you to leave, please believe me."

I nodded. "I've gotten used to life here. I've been happy. I don't even remember the last time I was happy in Chicago."

"This is only a temporary thing. You'll be back here in no time, and while you're in Chicago I'll talk to Luca about Romero. Maybe when you're back we've made a plan on how to convince Father to accept Romero as your husband."

Hope flared up in me. I looked at my sister. "You're right. I should see it as a short vacation. Maybe soon I'll be able to call New York my home for good."

We didn't say anything after that, only stood beside each other and watched the boisterous ocean. What I really wanted to do was talk to Romero, be in his arms and convince myself that this thing between us was meant to last, but it was way too early to retire to bed and we couldn't risk anything with everyone still awake.

When the breeze picked up, Aria and I returned into the living room. Romero caught my eyes from across the room. I couldn't wait to be alone with him tonight, to feel his body sliding against mine. I'd never needed him more.

***

Earlier than usual I crept out of my room and headed for Romero's. I wanted to spend as much time with him as possible. He didn't look surprised when I slipped in.

He was sitting on the edge of his bed, arms braced on his knees. He pushed to his feet when I closed the door. For a while we only stared at each other until the pressure in my chest threatened to crush my ribcage. Why was I being so emotional about this? Romero crossed the room and gripped me by the hips, then he turned us around and led me backwards toward the bed until my calves bumped against it and we both fell back on the mattress.

Our hands roamed each other's bodies almost frantically, undressing and caressing. Who knew when we'd get the chance to feel each other again? It could be weeks. *Too long.* We needed to make the best of our last night together.

Tonight I wanted to be in control. I pushed Romero onto his back and he didn't resist. I straddled his hips and lowered myself onto his erection, feeling it slide into me all the way. I closed my eyes for a moment, releasing a low breath at the familiar feeling of fullness. Romero gripped my hips and started pushing upwards, driving himself deeply into me. I leaned forward onto my forearms so my face was above his and my hair surrounded us like a curtain, our own personal sanctuary from the outside world. "I'm going to miss you," I whispered as I rocked back and forth. "I'm going to miss this, *everything.*"

"You won't be gone long," he growled.

He sounded absolutely sure. I kissed him, moving even faster until we both came at the same time, but we weren't sated yet. We made love two more times that night as if we could stamp the sensations of our togetherness into our mind that way.

"I don't want to leave," I murmured afterwards as I lay in Romero's arms. "I want to fall asleep in your arms."

Romero reached for his alarm clock. "Then don't. We'll get up early so you can sneak back to your room without anyone noticing."

I smiled, and rested my cheek against his chest. It didn't take long for me to fall asleep with the sound of Romero's heartbeat like music in my ear.

***

The alarm woke us before sunrise and I quickly gathered my clothes in the dark room. Before I left, Romero pulled me against his chest and kissed me fiercely, then I slipped out and rushed back to my room. I caught a couple of hours of sleep before I really got up and prepared everything for my drive to the airport.

The hardest part about leaving was that I couldn't hug or kiss Romero when we said goodbye in the airport waiting hall. With a last glance, I walked away, trying to ignore the insistent worry that I wouldn't return.

***

When I landed in Chicago, my old bodyguard Mario was waiting for me. He wasn't the most talkative person so we didn't speak during the drive to my family home.

As I stepped up to the entrance door, my heart pounded in my chest like a drum. The last time I'd been here, the house had brimmed with sadness and death.

Mario opened the door for me and I stepped in. It wasn't as bad as it used to be but I definitely didn't feel at home here anymore. Was it my imagination or did the stench of disinfectant still linger in the corners?

"Where's my father?" I asked quickly before my mind conjured up more craziness.

"In his office. He wants to see you right away."

I doubted the reason for that was that he'd missed me. Mario headed off to take my luggage up to my room. I walked down the long corridor and knocked at Father's door, trying to ignore the way my stomach twisted with nerves.

"Come in," Father called.

I took a deep breath and slipped in. Fabi stood near the window. He had grown in the three months that I'd been gone and something about the way he held himself told me that wasn't the only change in him. The last few months seemed to have taken a toll on him. It would have been better if Fabi had been allowed to go to

Chicago with me for the summer, but naturally that had been out of the question.

Father sat behind his desk as usual. He didn't bother getting up to hug me. But Fabi walked up to me and I wrapped my arms around him before he could decide he was too cool for affection. He was taller than me. I leaned back to take a look at his face.

I knew something was wrong the moment I saw Fabi's expression. Recently Father had involved him more and more in the mob business, even though Fabi wouldn't turn 13 for several more weeks. Had something happened? He couldn't have been forced to kill someone already, right? The idea that my little brother might already be a killer turned my stomach into an icy pit.

"Sit," Father said with a nod toward the armchair in front of his desk. Fabi immediately freed himself of my embrace, but what worried me more was that he made sure to keep his eyes on my chin.

"It's good to see you back in Chicago. I trust Luca and Aria took good care of you?" Father asked.

No mention of Gianna, which wasn't a huge surprise.

I sank down on the chair across from him. "Yes, they did. It was lovely."

I tried to catch Fabi's gaze; he'd returned to his spot at the window where he was busy avoiding my eyes, his hands balled to fists at his side and his lips a thin white line in his angry face. My stomach tied itself into a knot.

Father tapped his fingers against the smooth wood of the desk. If I didn't know better, I'd say he looked almost ashamed. Fear gripped me. Again I darted a look at Fabiano but he was glaring at the floor.

The silence stretched between us until I was sure I'd suffocate. "You said to Luca that you wanted me here for a few parties?"

"That's part of the reason. You need to become part of our social circles again." Father paused, then he cleared his throat. He looked almost guilty. "Life must go on. Death is part of our existence but we must make sure that our family line stays strong."

Where was he going with this?

"I'm going to marry again."

I was torn between relief and shock. At least I wasn't in trouble but I couldn't believe, much less understand how he could be considering another marriage when Mother had been death for less than six months. "But—" I stopped myself. Nothing I could say would change a thing. It would only get me in trouble. "Who is she? Do I know her?"

There were a few widows in Father's age I knew but I wasn't sure if any of them were his type. Even thinking that made me feel guilty and I wasn't even the one considering replacing Mother.

Maybe Father was lonelier than he'd let on. I'd always thought he and Mother hadn't cared much for each other but maybe I'd been wrong. Maybe he had loved her in some twisted way. Maybe he hadn't been able to show it. Some people were like that.

Fabiano let out a low sound, drawing my eyes toward him, but he was still glowering at his feet. Which was probably for the best because Father gave him a look that sent a shiver down my back. I noticed a fading bruise on Fabi's left temple, and I couldn't help but wonder if there were more hidden beneath his clothing and if Father was responsible for all of them.

Father's fingers took up their tapping again. "Ramona Brasci."

I almost fell forward in my chair. "What?" I blurted. He had to be kidding. Ramona was only one year older than me. She could have been Father's daughter. She'd gone to school with me, for God's sake!

I peered at Fabiano again, needing him to tell me this was a joke, but his grimace was all the answer I needed. This was disgusting. Was this some kind of midlife crisis thing on Father's part? I couldn't even begin to understand how he could choose someone who could be his daughter.

"In turn," Father continued evenly. "You are going to marry her Father Benito Brasci."

And that's when my whole world shattered. I could see it right before my eyes. All the images of a future with Romero, of happiness and smiles, of sweet kisses and endless nights of lovemaking splintering into tiny pieces, and they were replaced by something horrendous and dark. Something people whispered about in hushed voices because they were worried the horrors might become reality if they spoke about them too loudly. Not in my darkest nightmare had I imagined that Father would marry me off to an old man like Benito Brasci. I didn't remember much about him, but I didn't have to. Everything about this was wrong.

I tried to speak but I was mute. I wondered when the first tears would fall. Right now, I still felt too numb.

"You're condemning Lily to a life of misery," Fabiano said the words I could only think. He sounded so...old. Like he'd become a man some time when I hadn't been looking. I wanted to give him a grateful smile but my face was frozen, all of me was. Was this really happening?

This morning I'd still kissed Romero and now I was supposed to marry Brasci.

"I'm making reasonable decisions. You don't understand it yet, but you will."

"No. I would never do something like that."

"You will do worse, believe me, Son." He sighed. "We all have to make sacrifices. That's life."

What kind of sacrifice was it to marry a young woman who could be his daughter? I was supposed to do the sacrificing.

I couldn't stop wondering when the tears would come but there wasn't even the trademark prickling yet. There was nothing. I was nothing. Again I tried to call up an image of Benito Brasci, but I came up empty. It didn't matter. He wasn't Romero.

"You'll meet him tomorrow. He and Ramona are coming over for dinner."

Maybe it could have been funny if it wasn't so terrible.

"Okay," I said simply. I sounded collected. Fabiano frowned at me, Father looked immensely pleased. I rose from my chair and crossed the room toward the door. "I'm going to bed. I had a long day."

"Aren't you going to join us for dinner?" Father asked, but he didn't sound like he cared.

"I'm not hungry," I said calmly.

"Then sleep well. Tomorrow is an exciting day for both of us."

My hand on the door handle stilled for an instant. A flicker of something, maybe anger, seized my body but then it was gone and I was numb again.

One foot in front of the other. One foot in front of the other. The mantra filled my head as I ascended the staircase. Steps thundered after me and then Fabiano was beside me. He grabbed my arm. He was as tall as me now. He was so grown. These thoughts repeated themselves in my mind. Maybe my brain had been broken by shock, or shut down because the reality of the situation was too much to bear.

"What the fuck is wrong with you, Lily?" he growled. His voice wasn't man yet, but not boy either.

"Wrong?" I asked.

"Yes, wrong," Fabiano muttered. He released me and I rubbed my arm. He was strong.

Was something wrong with me? Maybe that was the problem. I'd done many wrong things in the past. I'd slept with Romero, even though we weren't married. Maybe this was punishment for my sins. The pastor in our church would probably have said so.

"Why aren't you freaking out? Why did you just say okay? Do you even realize what you agreed to?"

I wasn't aware I'd agreed to anything. How could I have when nobody had ever asked me about my opinion? "Because there is nothing I can do."

"Bullshit," Fabi said, stomping his foot. Maybe not as grown up as I thought.

I almost smiled, if my face had been capable of movement. "When did you start swearing so much?"

"All the Made Men do."

"But you aren't one of them yet."

"But soon."

I nodded. That's what I'd feared. Father seemed keen on ruining both of our lives.

"And that doesn't even matter right now. You can't just accept this marriage. You have to do something."

"What? What can I do?" I asked with a hint of anger. That brief burst of emotion scared me because I preferred the numbness.

"Something," Fabiano said quietly, brown eyes pleading with me. "Anything. Don't just accept it."

"Then tell me what I can do. You are the future Made Man. Tell me."

Fabiano averted his gaze, guilt on his face.

I touched his shoulder. "There's nothing either of us can do."

"You could run like Gianna," Fabi burst out.

"She got caught."

"But you wouldn't."

"I would." I was nothing like Gianna. I wouldn't even last one month, probably not even a week. I wasn't a rebel. I didn't even want to leave this life behind. There was no way I would survive on my own for long.

But maybe I wouldn't have to be alone. Romero could come with me. He knew how to evade pursuers. Together we could make it.

"You're thinking about it, aren't you?" Fabi asked with a boyish grin.

"Remember where your loyalties are," I whispered. "This is betrayal. If Father finds out, you're going to be punished harshly."

"I'm not a Made Man yet."

"But as good as, you said it yourself. They will judge you as they would a Made Man, and that would mean death."

"Father needs an heir," Fabi said.

"Father will soon have a young bride who can give him plenty of children. Maybe he won't need you after all."

Fabi made a gagging sound. "It's like he's marrying you. It's sick."

I couldn't deny it. "Benito Brasci is older than Father, isn't he?"

"I don't know. He looks ancient."

"I should go up to my room," I said absent-mindedly. I needed to talk to Romero. Fabi didn't stop me as I walked up the remaining steps and headed for my room.

When the door closed after me, I feared for a moment that I'd actually burst into tears, but the stopper keeping my emotions in held fast.

I fumbled my mobile out of the bottom of my travel bag and dialed Romero's number. My hands shook and when Romero didn't pick up after the first two rings like he usually did, I could feel panic slip through the cracks in my numbness. He didn't know I'd call, but I couldn't help but worry that something had happened to him. Or that he'd found out about my engagement to Basci and didn't want anything to do with me. What if Luca had known all along? It was possible that Father had told him on the phone and Luca hadn't mentioned it because he knew Aria and Gianna would make a scene.

I was sent to voicemail and quickly hung up. I hadn't even put the phone away when the screen flashed with Romero's name. Taking a deep breath, I answered.

"Lily, are you okay? I was in a meeting and had the phone on mute."

I slumped against the wall at the sound of Romero's voice. It calmed me but at the same time it made me realize what I could lose if I had to marry Basci. "Father has chosen a husband for me," I said eventually. I sounded like I was talking about the weather, completely detached.

Silence followed on the other end. I couldn't even hear breathing. I didn't dare say anything, although I was bursting with fear and anxiety.

"Who is it?" Romero asked in a low voice. I wished I could see his face to get a hint about his emotions. He sounded as emotionless as I had.

"Benito Basci. You probably don't know him, but--"

Romero interrupted me. "I know him. I met him during a gathering last year."

"Oh," I said, then waited but again Romero was silent. Why was he so calm? Didn't he care that I was going to marry another man? Maybe this had always been a distraction for him. Maybe he'd never intended for us to have more than...what? An affair? I felt dirty just thinking about it. "He's much older than me."

"I know."

Of course Romero knew but I wasn't sure what else to say.

"I thought," I said hesitantly. "I thought we could..."

I didn't dare utter the words.

"You thought we could what?"

I closed my eyes. "I thought we could run away together." I cringed when the words had left my mouth. Could I sound any more pathetic and naïve?

"That would mean war between the Outfit and New York."

He said it matter-of-factly, like it had absolutely nothing to do with him. I hadn't thought of that but of course that would be the first thing that crossed Romero's mind. The Famiglia always came first.

I'd been stupid. Mother had always warned me that men promised you the world if they wanted something from you. Romero had been kind and loving, and I'd given him everything in turn. My body, my heart, every little thing I could give. I'd given it gladly and I didn't want to feel regret over a single thing, but it was hard.

I bit my lip, suddenly on the verge of crying. I could feel the floodgates open. It wouldn't be long now. "You're right," I croaked. "I--" I choked and quickly hung up. Then I hid the phone in my travel bag again and curled up on my bed, letting sobs wrack my body until my muscles hurt, until my throat hurt, until everything hurt, but nothing as much as my heart. Was this it? The end of every dream I had?

CHAPTER THIRTEEN

Romero

I stared at my phone. What the fuck was Scuderi thinking? I'd wanted to kill him so often in the past, now I wished I'd done it.

Nino came out of the meeting room and put a cigarette into his mouth. That guy grated on my fucking nerves. "Why the long face? Get yourself a nice long blowjob from one of the girls. That always puts a smile on my face."

I stormed toward him, gripped him by the collar and flung him against the wall. His head smashed against it and he dropped his stupid cigarette. "What the fuck, you asshole! Let me go!" he screamed like a fucking pussy.

I punched him in the stomach twice and he dropped to his knees. God, I wanted to fucking kill someone. I didn't even care whom. I hit him over and over again.

"Hey! What's going on here?" Luca growled. He gripped my arms and pulled them behind my back. "Romero what the hell are you doing? Calm the fuck down."

I relaxed in his hold and took a deep breath.

Matteo knelt beside Nino who was bleeding from a wound on his head and from his nose. I hadn't even realized I'd hit him in the face too. Aria joined us after a moment. Since she'd started working the books of the clubs, she was here quite often. She gave me a questioning look, then worry twisted her face.

"I'm going to kill you, you bastard," Nino snarled.

Matteo helped him to his feet. "You won't do anything. Go inside and have someone stitch up your head."

Nino staggered off, but not without sending me a death glare. As if I gave a fuck. Let him try to kill me. I'd wipe the fucking floor with his weak ass.

"Did something happen with Lily?" Aria asked fearfully, walking up to me.

"You can let me go now," I told Luca. He did and stepped back, his narrowed eyes flitting between his wife and me.

"Why would Romero know if something was wrong with Lily?" he asked carefully.

Aria didn't say anything, only looked at me. Maybe I should have been worried that Luca might find out, but I didn't give a shit about that either.

"Your father has arranged a marriage with Benito Brasci for her," I said in a low voice.

Aria gasped. "What? He never said anything that he was looking for a husband for her!" She glanced at Luca. "Or did he mention anything to you?"

Luca's expression was stone. "No, he hasn't. But right now I'm more concerned about the fact that Romero knows about this

206

before anyone else and that he almost kills one of my men because of it."

I leaned against the wall. I might as well tell him the truth. "Lily and I have been seeing each other during the summer."

Matteo let out a low whistle. For some reason it annoyed the crap out of me. I glared at him and almost lost my shit again when I saw his grin. What the fuck was so funny?

Luca got into my face. "Didn't you tell me not too long ago that you weren't interested in her? That there wouldn't be a fucking problem when she was around? I remember that conversation pretty damn well, and now you're fucking telling me that you were *seeing* Liliana behind my fucking back all summer?"

Aria touched Luca's arm and positioned herself halfway between us. "Luca, please don't get mad at Romero. He and Lily didn't mean any harm. They fell in love. It just happened."

"And you knew all along?" Luca muttered. "You knew and didn't tell me? Didn't we have a discussion about loyalty and trust when you helped Gianna run away?"

Aria blanched. "They are my sisters."

"And I'm your fucking husband."

"Luca, she didn't mean--" I began.

Luca jabbed his fingers against my chest. "You stay the fuck out of this. You're lucky I don't put a bullet into your head right this second for going against my orders."

"Hey, calm down Luca. Maybe it's not as bad as it sounds," Matteo said, trying to be the voice of reason, which was a joke in itself.

"Oh, I suspect it's exactly as bad as I think it is," Luca murmured. His eyes fixed me. "Just tell me this, will we be in trouble on Liliana's wedding night?"

I knew what he was asking.

"Lily won't marry that guy. Isn't he over fifty? It's ridiculous," Aria butted in.

"Over fifty and a nasty piece of shit," Matteo added.

Luca ignored them. His eyes bored into mine. "*Will* there be a fucking problem on her wedding night?"

"I slept with Lily," I said calmly.

Matteo let out another of his annoying whistles.

Luca cursed. He looked like he wanted to smash my head in with a sledgehammer. "Why couldn't you leave your dick in your pants? Couldn't you at least have drawn the line at actually fucking her?"

"I don't regret it," I said. "Now less than ever."

Luca took a step back from me as if he didn't trust himself this close to me. "This is a fucking mess. Do you realize what happens if Benito Brasci finds out his wife isn't a virgin? Scuderi will figure out it happened in New York and we'll be screwed."

"I don't think there will be a problem. I stood beside Brasci at the urinal once. That guy's cock is tiny. He can't possibly expect there to be any blood on the sheets with that small sausage. Liliana probably won't even notice his cock in her," Matteo joked.

I saw red. I lunged at him, my fist colliding with his jaw. But Matteo wasn't Nino. After my first hit, he blocked my second and pulled his knife. Mine was out too. We faced off, knives pointed at each other.

"Enough!" Luca roared, stepping between us and shoving us away from each other. "I'm going to put you down like rabid dogs if you don't get a grip on yourself right this second."

"He started it," Matteo said, never taking his eyes off me. We'd never fought against each other, and I wasn't sure I could beat him in a knife fight, but I wouldn't mind to find out.

"You provoked him," Aria said. "What you said was horrible."

Matteo rolled his eyes. "My God, I was trying to light the mood."

"You failed," Luca said coldly. "Now put your knives away. Both of you."

I sheathed my knife and Matteo did the same. I exhaled. "I shouldn't have punched you," I said eventually.

Matteo nodded. "I should keep my mouth shut now and then."

We shook hands and I leaned against the wall again. My legs felt heavy. I peered down at my phone. I needed to call Lily, to tell her I wouldn't give her up.

"But she's not pregnant, is she?" Luca asked after a moment.

I shook my head. We'd always been careful.

"Then maybe we'll get out of this unscathed. Brasci might not notice, and there are ways to fake blood stains on the sheets."

"She won't marry that man," I said.

Luca raised his eyebrows. "Oh, isn't she? Are you thinking about stopping Scuderi? Maybe kidnap Lily and marry her?"

I didn't say anything. I wanted to punch Luca too, but that would have definitely been the nail in my coffin.

"Luca, please. Can't you talk to my father?"

"Talk to him and tell him what?" Luca growled. "That my best soldier screwed his daughter and wants her for himself? That I broke my oath to protect Liliana and now she's lost her fucking honor? That will go over *fucking well*."

"No, but you could tell him that Gianna and I want our sister in New York with us and if he wouldn't maybe consider marrying her to someone from the Famiglia. You wouldn't have to tell him who right away. It would give us time to figure something out."

"I can't get involved. It's none of my business. And if your father has already promised Liliana to Brasci, he won't change his mind. It would make him look bad and offend Brasci."

210

"But we have to do something!" Aria exclaimed.

"I won't go into war over this!" Luca hissed.

I understood him. He had to consider only the Famiglia. But I didn't have to.

***

Liliana

I was woken by the ringing of a phone. Slowly my conversation with my Father and then Romero replayed in my mind. My eyes darted toward my travel bag in the walk-in closet, thinking and hoping it was Romero again before I remembered that it was on mute. Disappointment crashed down on me once more. I sat up, disoriented and exhausted from crying. The clock on the nightstand told me it was only 10pm. I walked toward my desk where the landline phone was and picked it up. It was Aria. She must have heard already. Had Father called her to tell her the good news?

I picked up. "Hi Aria," I rasped. There was no hiding that I'd been crying. Aria knew that voice.

"Oh, Lily. I just heard. I'm so sorry. I can't believe it."

"We're not going to let Father get away with it. We'll figure something out," Gianna shouted in the background. They were together, they had husbands they loved, and I'd be stuck here with an old man I would never be able to love. How could things have gone so horribly wrong?

"Did Father call you?" I asked, my voice regaining some of the emotionlessness I preferred.

"No, he didn't. We found out through Romero."

"He told you."

"Yes, he did," Aria said slowly. "He attacked one of the other soldiers who said something to him, so Luca had a word with him, and figured it out."

"Why did he attack that man?"

"What do you think? Because he doesn't want you to marry Basci," Aria said softly. "He's been trying to call you for the last hour but you didn't pick up. He almost went crazy over here. He wants to talk to you."

"He's there with you?"

"Yes. I'll hand him the phone now, okay?"

Fear corded up my throat. "Okay."

"Lily," Romero murmured into the phone. His voice was anything but detached now. I released a harsh breath and felt tears run down my face.

"Lily?"

I swallowed hard. "I thought you didn't want anything to do with me anymore now that I'm promised to someone else."

"No, never. I know I didn't react the way I should have. I...I was so angry when you told me your fucking Father wants to sell you off to that old bastard. I wanted to fly over there and kill him. I didn't want to let out my anger on you so I tried to push it back."

"Okay," I whispered.

"Do you still want to run away?"

Yes, more than anything else. "It would mean war. You said it yourself."

"I don't care. I would risk war for you."

"Is Luca there to hear you say that?"

"No, he isn't."

"He would kill you if he could hear you."

"Your sisters would risk war over you as well."

I didn't doubt it. Gianna, in particular, but even Aria who was the more reasonable would do anything to protect me, and that was what scared me so much. Fabiano would soon be in the midst of mob business. The war with the Russians had gotten worse in recent years, and I probably didn't even know half of it. If New York and Chicago started fighting each other again, this could cost the lives of many people I cared about.

"I have to meet him tomorrow."

"I don't want you alone with him, Lily."

"But what if he asks me and Father says 'yes'?"

"You are a honorable Italian girl, play that card. If I have to worry that you'll be alone with him I'll book the next flight and be there tomorrow. Fuck. I want to do just that and kill him."

I smiled slightly, wishing he could. I wanted nothing more than to have him with me, to feel his arms around me. "I'm not a honorable girl anymore. Maybe if I tell my father I can get out of this marriage."

"He might kill you. Your father has been very volatile since that thing with Gianna."

"Maybe that would be better than marrying that guy."

"Don't say something like that. We'll figure something out."

I nodded, even if he couldn't see it. I wanted to believe him. "I know," I said quietly.

"Aria is going to call your father tomorrow morning to get a feel for his resolve."

"I don't think she'll be able to talk him out of it. Does Luca know everything about us?"

"Yes, at least everything he needs to know to assess the situation."

My cheeks flamed, but Romero was right. We needed to tell Luca the truth if we wanted him to be able to do something. "Was he very angry?"

Romero was silent for a moment. "He wasn't happy. I punched Matteo, that didn't really help matters."

214

"You hit Matteo? Why? I thought Aria said you'd attacked another soldier."

"I did both," Romero admitted. "I just really lost it."

"Please don't get in trouble because of me. I don't want you to get hurt, promise me." There was another moment of silence, before he said, "I promise."

But I had a feeling it was a promise he wasn't sure he could keep. If he'd already attacked Matteo, the Famiglia's Consigliere, that wasn't a good sign.

"Call me after your meeting with Brasci tomorrow. I'll go crazy if I don't hear from you. And don't let him try anything. He's got absolutely no right. I'll fucking kill him if he puts a toe out of line, if he even looks at you the wrong way."

"Didn't you promise to stay out of trouble?" I joked half-heartedly.

"I'll try, but I'll be on edge tomorrow, that much is sure."

We talked about a few unimportant things before we said good-bye and hung up. I clutched the phone against my chest. Slowly I lay back on the bed. I was relieved that Romero still wanted me but I was also scared that he'd do something that would get him killed. Luca liked Romero a lot, but he was also Capo and needed to keep his men in line. If Romero did something that publicly hurt the Famiglia, Luca might not have a choice but to punish him severely. I wouldn't let that happen.

***

I barely slept more than two hours. I'd known that my first night in Chicago wouldn't be easy but I hadn't expected it to be this horrible.

There were dark shadows under my eyes and I didn't bother covering them up. Maybe Benito would decide not to marry me if I looked like a corpse. I put on jeans and a shirt before I made my way downstairs. Fabi and Father were already sitting at the table, eating breakfast. I wondered if they'd done the same when I was gone. "Since when are you awake this early on a Saturday?" I asked Fabi as I took the chair across from him.

"Only because he doesn't have school doesn't mean he should laze around," Father answered in Fabi's stead. Fabi stabbed at his fruit with his fork, looking like he wished it was Father.

"Is he getting inducted soon?"

Father set his coffee down. "You know very well that that's none of your business."

I curled my hands into fists under the table. My throat tightened at my next words. "When are Benito Brasci and his daughter going to arrive?"

"Around six. I already told you we'd have dinner with them." His eyes narrowed. "I hope you don't intend to wear that tonight. Take one of your cocktail dresses and let your hair down. That's how Benito prefers it."

I blinked a few times, too stunned for words. Fabi dropped his fork with a clang.

"And you should eat. I don't want you to faint again. Tonight is important," Father continued unimpressed.

I reached for a Danish and stuffed a few pieces into my mouth but I wasn't sure I could keep them down.

"Stop picking at your food, Liliana, for God's sake."

"Leave her alone!" Fabi shouted.

Father and I both froze.

"What did you just say?" Father asked in a dangerous voice.

Fabi glared back but then he lowered his eyes. "Why can't you leave her alone? I don't like how you treat her."

"I won't have you criticizing me, Fabiano. You better learn to keep your mouth shut or you'll be in major trouble once you're part of the Outfit. Understood?"

Fabi nodded, but his lips were a thin white line.

I forced the rest of my Danish down even though it tasted like nothing. Father picked up his newspaper and disappeared behind it.

Fabi and I didn't try to talk. And really what was there left to say?

CHAPTER FOURTEEN

Liliana

I chose the dress I'd worn to last year's Christmas party. It was more modest than my other dresses with a high cut collar and a hem that reached my knees. It was more fitted than I would have liked for the evening though. Like Father had said, I let my hair fall down to my shoulders, even though the idea of being attractive for Benito terrified me to no end. I decided to wear ballet flats since Father had said nothing about high heels.

"Liliana, what's taking you so long? Our guests will arrive any moment. Get down here!"

I took a deep breath and walked out of my room. Everything would be alright. If I got through today, Romero would figure out a way to get me out of this marriage. Everything would be alright. I repeated the words over and over again as I walked down the stairs, but my throat tightened anyway. Fabi was dressed in a proper dark blue suit and a tie, but his expression was that of a sulking teenager.

Father, too, wore a business suit but he almost always did. He scanned my outfit critically. "You should have chosen a different dress, but it'll have to do now. We don't have time for you to change again."

I paused on the stairs. Anger surged through me again, fiercer than before. The doorbell rang, preventing me from saying something that would have probably earned me a slap across the face. Father gave Fabi and me a warning look before he went to the door and opened it.

My fingers on the handrail tightened painfully.

"Benito, good to see you. Come in, come in. Dinner is ready for us. I've let our cook prepare a wonderful roast," Father said in an overly friendly manner that he only ever used with people of importance, definitely not with his family.

I had to stop myself from running up the stairs and hiding in my room. I wasn't a child anymore. I'd handle this situation with grace, and then I'd do my best to stop this marriage. There had to be a way.

But what if there wasn't?

I walked down the last few steps and stopped beside Fabi.

Father opened the door wider to let Brasci and his daughter in. I held my breath. And when my intended husband entered the entrance hall, revulsion overcame me.

He was tall and thin, with greying brown hair that was combed back the same way as Father's, but where Father's was full, Benito's had thinned and his scalp peeked through. His skin was tanned from too many hours on the tanning bed, and looked almost like leather. He looked old. His dark eyes settled on me and a grin twisted his lips.

Benito's gaze felt like slugs crawling over my skin, the way they traveled over every inch of my body, already marking me as his. I wanted to wipe it off like slime. My eyes slid over to the girl beside him, barely older than me and with a look of desperate resignation on her face. She wasn't better off than me. She'd marry my father. Our eyes met. Was there accusation in hers? Maybe she thought I was the reason for the deal between my father and her own. I couldn't even blame her. Everything about this felt so unfair.

Father motioned for me to come over to them. Even though every fiber of my being was against it, I crept toward them. Fabi was a couple of steps behind me. When I reached Father's side, he put a hand on my lower back and said with a proud smile, "This is my daughter Liliana."

Benito inclined his head but his eyes never ceased their staring. He wasn't doing anything obviously inappropriate but for some reason his gaze felt like it was invading my personal space. "It's a pleasure to meet you," he said, then he stepped up to me and kissed my cheeks. I froze but didn't push him away. Father would probably have killed me if I'd done that.

"And Fabiano," Benito said, facing my brother, who looked like he tasted something bitter.

Benito waved his daughter forward. "This is Maria."

Father greeted her with a kiss on the cheek too, and I almost threw up. Maria glanced my way again. She looked so...resigned. But when she faced my father again, she gave him a smile. It looked fake to me but Father seemed satisfied with her reaction. I could practically see his chest swelling with pride.

Father nodded toward the dining room. "Let's have dinner. It'll give us the chance to talk."

Father held out his hand for Maria to take and she did so without hesitation. I knew what was coming. But instead of taking my hand, Benito put his palm on my lower back. I almost flinched away from him but I forced myself to remain still. I couldn't muster up a smile though.

We walked into the dining room and when I finally sank down on my chair I almost cried from relief of being rid of Benito's touch. He sat beside me though. Father and Benito were soon immersed in conversation, which left Maria and me to sit in awkward silence. I could hardly ask her anything of importance with our fathers sitting right beside us. I escaped into my mind, but every so often my eyes drifted to the man beside me who smelled of cigar smoke.

All I could think about was that I wanted to be back in New York with Romero.

"Why don't you girls go sit on the sofa, so we can discuss business?" Father asked, tearing me out of my thoughts.

I rose from my chair and led Maria toward the living area. We sat down beside each other and another awkward silence began. I cleared my throat. "It's strange, isn't it, that we're sitting here with our fathers who are planning our marriages?"

Maria watched me cautiously. "They want what's best for us."

I almost snorted. She sounded like a parrot. Had her father put those words into her mouth? "Do you really believe that? You're going to marry a man who could be your father. How is that the best for you?"

Again her gaze darted toward our fathers. She was very well behaved, that much was sure. What worried me was how she'd gotten that careful. Was her father that strict? Violent maybe?

"I'm going to be the wife of the Consigliere. That's a good thing."

I gave up. She obviously wouldn't talk honestly with me, or she'd been brainwashed so well that she actually meant what she said. "Yes, that's certainly a great achievement." I didn't mean to snap at her but my nerves were too frayed to be considerate. But she didn't catch my sarcasm. She was too busy chancing looks toward our fathers.

Father stood from his chair. "Why don't you take a moment to talk to Benito, Liliana? And I'll talk to Maria."

That was the last thing I wanted. Benito strode toward me and panic started to set in. Where would we go? I didn't want to be alone with him. Romero's words flashed through my mind. I was a reputable Italian girl, at least as far as they knew. Father and Maria sat at the dining table together and Benito took a seat beside me on the sofa. At least I wouldn't be alone with him.

He even left a space between us but he was still too close for my taste. I could smell the cigars on his clothes and breath, and his knee was only about three inches from my knee. I could feel my vision tunneling. God, I wasn't getting a panic attack because he was sitting beside me, right? What would happen when he really married me? Then he'd do more than only sit beside me. I stared straight ahead, not sure what to do or say. I could feel him watching me.

"You are a very attractive girl," he said. He took my hand and lifted it to his lips. I couldn't even react, I was too shocked. When his lips brushed my skin, I wanted to sink into myself. I'd had many men kiss my hand at parties but for some reason, this was worse.

"Thank you," I choked out.

"Has your father told you the date of our wedding yet?"

There was a date? I'd found out about this only yesterday. How could there be a date already? I shook my head mutely.

"Four weeks from now. October 20th. Your father didn't want to wait and I agree. He'll marry Maria the week before our wedding."

I stared at him, then toward my father who was leering at Maria like she was a piece of candy he wanted to devour. I was going to be sick. Any moment now, my dinner would come up again.

"Liliana, are you listening?" There was a hint of impatience in Benito's tone and something less kind shone in his eyes.

I shivered. "I'm sorry. I was only surprised." Surprised? Surprised? God, surprise didn't even begin to describe my feelings. If there was already a date, how could Romero possibly convince my father to choose him as my husband instead? He couldn't. I wasn't naïve. Father would never agree to it. He wanted Maria and for him to get her, he needed to sell me off to Benito in turn.

Benito smiled but somehow that made him look even scarier. Maybe it was my imagination. "It's short-notice of course, but people won't want to miss our weddings so I'm confident that we'll pull off a grand feast."

I nodded. I clasped my wrist, feeling my pulse and surprised to find it at all. I felt so numb, I might as well have been dead.

Benito talked about guests we needed to invite and food we needed to serve but I couldn't focus. I needed to talk to Romero. Benito touched my knee and I jerked out of my thoughts.

"You're jumpy," he said accusingly. He didn't take his hand off my knee.

"I'm glad you're getting along so well," said Father as he came up to us from behind, Maria trailing a few steps after him like a good dog. I'd never been so glad to see my father. Benito removed his hand from my knee and I quickly got up. I needed to get away before I lost it.

Thankfully, Benito and his daughter left shortly after that.

Father looked incredibly satisfied when he closed the door after them. When he turned to me, his smile dropped. "Don't give me that look. Benito is an important man. He's one of our most influential Captains with a big number of loyal soldiers. To have him on our side is important."

"Can I fly back to New York so I can go wedding dress shopping with Aria?" I didn't mention Gianna, even though I felt bad about it, but I couldn't risk Father getting angry again. And I definitely didn't want to remind him of Gianna's flight.

Father laughed. "You can go shopping here. I won't let you leave Chicago again. There's too much to do, and I don't trust you not to do something stupid if I let you out of my sight. I know you and Gianna aren't too different. I won't let you ruin this. You will marry Benito."

Once I was back in my room, I dialed Romero's number with shaky fingers. He picked up after the first ring. "Are you okay?" he asked immediately.

"The wedding is in four weeks."

"Fuck," Romero growled. I could hear him hitting something and then the sound of something shattering. Romero had always seemed so in control. "Your father has lost his fucking mind. I won't allow it. I don't give a damn if he's Consigliere."

"Please calm down." Part of me relished in his fury because it showed how much he cared for me but the other part was terrified of the consequences he might face if he acted on his emotions.

"How can you be this calm, Lily? Do you realize what that means?"

"Of course," I whispered. "What about Aria and Luca? Can they do something?"

"I don't know. Aria's talking with your father right now."

"Good," I said half-heartedly, but I knew it was no use. Father had looked determined.

"Will you be allowed to return to New York?"

"No, Father doesn't want me to leave Chicago. He wants to keep an eye on me until the wedding."

"Damn it. I'm going to talk to Luca. We'll find a way."

"Okay," I whispered.

"I won't lose you Lily. I won't allow anyone to hurt you. I swear."

"I know."

"I'll call you once I've talked to Luca."

"Okay." I sounded like a broken record. I hung up and sat cross-legged on my bed. I wasn't sure how much time passed until Romero called again. I picked up at once. I was oddly calm.

"And?" I said.

Romero released a harsh breath, and I knew everything was over. A bone-deep sadness overcame me. "Your father will go through with this wedding. Aria tried to talk him out of it but he got really mad and accused her of trying to weaken the Outfit. He warned her not to get involved or he'd see that as an attack on the Outfit and advise Dante to cease relationships with us."

"So there's nothing to stop this wedding."

"I can fly over to Chicago tomorrow and get you. I doubt your father's men could stop me."

"And then?"

"Then we'd figure something out."

"Could we return to New York? Would Luca protect us?"

Romero was silent for a long time. "Luca won't risk war over this. We'd be on our own."

"Would that mean Luca would hunt us too?"

Romero sighed. "Lily, we could make it. I could keep us both safe."

I didn't doubt it, but what kind of life would that be? I'd never see Aria and Gianna again, never see Fabi again, never be able to return to New York or Chicago, and we'd always have to live in fear.

"Can I talk to Aria?"

"Of course. What's the matter, Lily? I thought you wanted us to run away together."

"I did. I do. But you love the Famiglia, and you and Luca are like brothers. You'd lose all that if you ran away."

"You are worth it."

I wasn't sure that was true. "Can I talk to Aria now?"

"Sure. We'll talk later again, okay?"

"Okay," I said.

Aria's voice sounded on the other end. "Oh Lily, this is such a mess. How are you?"

"I feel like I'm falling and there's nothing to stop my fall," I admitted.

"We won't let you fall, Lily. I'll convince Luca to change his mind. You are my sister. I won't let you be miserable for the rest of your life. If Luca loves me, he'll help you."

"He says he doesn't want to risk war. Does he think Dante will really start a war if I don't marry Benito?"

"If you run off to be with Romero, then Father will take that as an attack from the Famiglia and will convince Dante to retaliate. There will be war. Both Luca and Dante have to show strength. Their men expect it from them. Despite years of cooperation, New York and Chicago still don't like each other."

"If Romero decides to act on his own and take me away from Chicago, what would Luca do?"

"I don't know. He's really determined to avoid war with Chicago. To do that he would have to call Romero a traitor who acted without the permission of his Capo and in order to keep the Outfit happy, he'd have to hunt Romero and..." She trailed off.

"And kill him," I finished for her. "Could he do it? Could he really kill Romero?"

"I don't think he would do it," Aria said. "But he might hand him over to the Outfit."

"That would also mean Romero's death."

"I'll talk to Luca. If he loves me, he won't do it. Gianna will talk to Matteo as well. We will help you Lily, no matter what it takes. I don't care if it means war."

"Fabi will soon be part of the Outfit. He might have to fight against Romero, Luca and Matteo. Many will die, and the Russians might use their chance and kill even more of us."

"I don't care if the Russians take over parts of the city. This is all about money. I want us all to be happy."

"But could we be happy? What if Dante and the Outfit try to assassinate Luca? It's happened before when New York and Chicago were at war."

Aria was silent. She loved Luca. "It won't come to that."

"You don't know that." We were silent.

"Do you want me to give Romero the phone again?" Aria asked after a while.

"Yes." I could hear her move and then Romero was back on the other end.

"So have you and Aria talked everything through?"

"We did. Aria is going to talk to Luca again."

"He won't change his mind. And he's right to remain firm. He needs to think of the Famiglia," he said.

"I don't care about the Famiglia, but I care about you."

"Don't worry about me. I'll gladly die if it means saving you from Benito Brasci."

That was exactly what I feared. "Don't say that. My life isn't worth more than yours. Marrying him isn't a death sentence."

"Do you want to marry him now?" Romero asked tersely. He was so on edge. I wished I could touch him and calm him down.

"Of course not, but I don't want you to risk your life."

"There's no other way, Lily. But don't worry. I've done it before."

I knew he had, but this was different. We talked a couple more minutes before I promised to call him the next day for detailed plans about my escape.

When I'd hung up, I stared at the white wall across from my bed for a very long time as if it could give me the answers I needed.

The people I loved the most would risk everything to keep me safe, to save me from a loveless marriage, but at what cost?

Romero'd sounded as if he didn't care at all that he might lose everything. I knew he loved the Famiglia, was proud to be a part of it. He loved this life, but he'd have to leave it behind if he helped me escape this marriage. Luca wouldn't risk war. His people would mutiny. He'd have no choice but to give up Romero and hand him over to the Outfit. Aria might destroy her marriage if she tried to blackmail Luca into helping me. He'd forgiven her once for betraying him, but would he do it again?

Could I risk everyone's happiness for my own?

Someone hammered against my door and then Father stepped in without warning. I stood immediately. His expression was thunderous. "What did you tell your sister? Why are she and Luca trying to get involved in our family? Did you really think they could make me change my mind about your wedding?"

"They want to help because they're worried about me."

"I don't care!" he roared. "You are going to marry Benito, end of story."

"I can't," I said desperately.

"You can and you will."

"I'm not a virgin anymore. If you don't want people to find out you can't let me marry Benito!" I blurted.

Father stormed toward me, gripped my arms and pushed me against the wall. The back of my head rang from the impact.

"What did you say?" he snarled.

I gaped up into his menacing face.

He shook me hard until my vision turned blurry. Suddenly Fabi raced into the room. He tore at Father's arm, trying to free me, but Father lashed out. Fabi landed on the floor, his face flashing with pain.

"Go back to your room, boy. *Now*, or I swear I'll make you regret it."

My arms hurt from Father's grip, but I gave Fabi a small nod. I wanted him to leave. He didn't need to get into trouble because of me. Fabi struggled to his feet and after a moment of hesitation, he limped out of my room. When he was out of view, Father turned back around to me.

I quivered.

"Tell me the truth."

I couldn't talk. I regretted ever having mentioned anything. Father really looked as if he wanted to kill me.

He slapped me hard across the face but didn't release me. "Who was it? Who turned you into a little whore? Someone from the Famiglia, wasn't it?"

Tears burned in my eyes but I didn't cry. I couldn't tell Father the truth. "No," I said quickly. "I met him in a club, it's no one you know."

"I don't believe a fucking word you say, you disgusting slut. And it doesn't matter. You will marry Benito and you'll scream like a little scared virgin in your wedding night so he doesn't doubt your innocence. I swear, if you ruin this for me, I'll break every bone in your body." He let me go and stepped back, eyes hateful. "And if you try to get out of this wedding, and maybe even ask your sisters for help, believe me, war between the Outfit and the Famiglia is only the beginning. I'll personally hunt you and your sisters down, and then I'll figure out who fucked you and skin that asshole alive. Do you understand?"

I gave a jerky nod. Father looked like he wanted to spit on me. Instead he turned on his heel and walked out.

I slumped to the ground. Everything was really over now. I couldn't allow Father to hurt everyone I loved only because I wanted to get out of my wedding with Benito. The image of Father's hateful eyes seemed burned into my brain.

If I married Benito, the Outfit and Famiglia would keep working together. Fabi would be safer, everyone would be safer. I'd be able to see my sisters and Fabi at least occasionally and Romero could keep working for Luca. He'd get over me and find someone else.

And I? Maybe things wouldn't be so bad. I didn't even know Benito. Maybe he wasn't a horrible guy. And it wasn't like I hadn't gotten a taste of happiness. Being with Romero had been amazing. It was something I'd never regret and would always cherish. It was time to do the right thing. Maria was accepting her fate. So many girls had before me. I should too, if only to keep my loved ones safe.

Once I'd made up my mind, I felt relief, then deep sadness. I lied down but sleep wouldn't come. I remembered the longing in Mother's eyes before her death and couldn't help but wonder if the same look would be in my eyes one day.

***

Romero

I'd have never thought I'd ever consider going against the Famiglia, but I could *not* watch Lily getting married to that man. She was mine and I didn't care what I'd have to do to keep it that way. Luca had been eying me almost all day yesterday. He'd never looked at me with true suspicion in his eyes before. I had to admit it hurt to know he didn't trust me anymore, and worse that he had every right to be wary of me. I'd go against his direct orders, break my oath, and betray the people who'd been as close, maybe even closer than my own family. When I came to Luca's and Aria's penthouse that morning, I saw In Luca's gaze that he knew he'd lost me. Another Capo might have eliminated me right then to prevent worse. Aria gave me an encouraging smile but I didn't miss that Luca left without kissing her. That never happened and was a fucking bad sign.

As soon as I could I called Lily. The phone rang almost two dozen times before I gave up. Aria shot me a worried look. "Maybe she's still having breakfast with Fabi and Father."

I waited a couple of minutes before I tried again. If she didn't answer this time, I'd book a fucking flight to Chicago today and get her. To my relief, Lily picked up after the third ring.

"Where were you? I tried to call you before. Are you okay?"

"I'm fine." The detachment in her tone made me pause. It felt like there was a barrier between us that had nothing to do with our physical separation.

"I've been thinking about the best way to go about it and I think I should fly over to you as soon as possible. Luca is getting more and more suspicious, so we need to act quickly."

"I don't think we should do it."

"Do what?" I asked carefully.

"Run away."

"I know you don't want to leave your sisters, but maybe Luca will take us in later. Aria might change his mind."

"No," she said firmly. "I mean I don't want you to come here and take me away. I'm going to stay."

I couldn't believe what I'd heard. "What are you saying? That you want to marry Benito? I don't believe that for one second. He could be your father."

"But he's an important man. He has many soldiers who follow him."

"Since when do you care about something like that?"

"I've always cared about it. I enjoyed our time together Romero but we have to be reasonable. It could never work out between us. You are a soldier and I have a duty to fulfill as the daughter of a Consigliere. We all have to do things we don't want to do."

"What the fuck did your father do? This doesn't sound like you, Lily."

"Romero, please. Don't make this harder than it is. You have your responsibilities to Luca. I don't want you to break your oath."

"I don't care about my oath."

"But you should!" she said angrily. "I don't want you to come here. It's over between us Romero. I'm going to do the right thing and marry Benito. And you should do the right thing and follow Luca's orders."

Suddenly I was angry. "So what was this between us? An adventure for the summer? Curiosity how it would be to fuck a common soldier?"

Lily sucked in a deep breath and I regretted my harsh words, but I was too proud to take them back or apologize. "We can't talk again," she said quietly. Was she crying? "We should forget what happened."

"Don't worry, I will," I said, then I hung up. I flung my phone away. "Fuck!"

Aria rushed toward me, alarmed. "What's wrong? Is it Lily?"

"She wants to go through with marrying Brasci."

Aria froze. "She said that?"

I nodded. I headed for the kitchen. I needed a cup of coffee. Aria hurried after me. "What else did she say?"

"Not much. Only that Benito is a good catch and that we should both do our duty. Fuck that."

"She doesn't mean it, Romero. She loves you. She probably only wants to protect us."

I wasn't sure anymore. And even if Aria was right, maybe Lily had a point. I'd devoted my life to the Famiglia. I shouldn't abandon my oath only because of a woman. I was a Made Man and my priority should always be my job.

CHAPTER FIFTEEN

Liliana

Aria called me thirty minutes after my call with Romero, trying to talk me out of my plan to marry Benito. But she was already fighting with Luca because of me. I wouldn't allow her to really put her marriage at risk for my own selfish reasons. I would marry Benito and try to make the best out of it.

The next few weeks passed in a blur of wedding dress shopping with Valentina, choosing flowers and the menu, calling important guests to invite them personally. I only saw Benito on two occasions and there wasn't time for more than a few exchanged words and a kiss on the cheek. That and the fact that I was too busy to be worried, I almost managed to forget that I was actually preparing my wedding to a man I could hardly stand. But reality set in on the day of Father's wedding to Maria. He hadn't talked to me since I'd told him I wasn't a virgin, except on the few occasions when we had to pretend for Benito or other people.

While Gianna and Matteo would arrive later to attend my wedding only, Aria and Luca were also invited to Father's feast of course, and that meant Romero was with them. I'd hoped he'd decide to stay in New York, not because I didn't want to see him but because I was scared of facing him, of being confronted with what I was losing.

Luckily, they were all coming directly to church because their plane arrived so late; that meant there was a chance of me being able to avoid an encounter with Romero.

I sat in the front row, Benito beside me. He didn't touch me in any way, thank God, because it would have been improper before our marriage, but every time Aria or Gianna looked my way I felt like I was doing something indecent by sitting next to a man I didn't even want to marry.

I wasn't sure where Romero was sitting. Since he wasn't family, probably somewhere in the back of the church. After the service we headed toward the hotel where the wedding celebration would take place. I managed to get through dinner without seeing Romero, but later into the evening when I was dancing with Benito I spotted him at the other end of the room. He was watching me. Suddenly the other dancers around me faded into the background. Shame washed over me. I wanted to push Benito away. I wanted to cross the room and fling myself at Romero, wanted to tell him that I needed him. I had to look away. When the song ended, I excused myself and quickly left the dance floor. I hurried toward the exit. I needed to get away from this for a moment before I lost it.

Once the door closed after me and I found myself in the hallway of the hotel, I could breathe easier. I didn't stop though. I didn't want to come across guests returning from the bathroom or heading in that direction. I wanted to be alone.

I turned two corners before I stopped and leaned against the wall, my chest heaving. In two days we'd be celebrating my wedding. Panic flooded me. I squeezed my eyes shut.

Soft footfalls made me turn and my gaze fell on Romero. He stood a few feet from me, watching me with an expression that felt like a stab to the heart. Despite everything I'd gone through and despite my best intention to mute my feelings for him, they seemed louder than ever. Romero looked irresistible in his dark suite.

"What are you doing here?" I whispered.

"I hated seeing you with him. It's wrong and you know it."

I did. Every fiber in my being fought Benito's closeness, but I couldn't tell Romero that.

He took a step closer to me, his dark eyes burning into my own.

"We shouldn't be here alone," I said feebly, but I wasn't trying to leave. I didn't want to.

He took another step closer, every move so lithe and graceful, and yet dangerous. I wanted to fly into his arms. I wanted to do more than that. I stayed where I was. Romero bridged the remaining distance between us and braced one arm above my head, his gaze hungry and possessive.

"Do you want me to leave?"

Say 'Yes'. If Father found us here, he'd kill Romero on the spot, and as distracted as Romero was at the moment, my father might actually succeed.

I released a shuddering breath. Romero bent down and kissed me, and then I was lost. I raked my hands through his hair and down his back. He kissed me harder. His hands cupped my butt and then he lifted me up. I wrapped my legs around his waist, so the skirt of my cocktail dress rode up but I didn't care. Romero's erection was hot against my opening despite the fabric of my panties and of his pants between us. I ground myself against him desperately. I was already so aroused. I'd missed this. I'd missed *him.*

I knew someone might come down this corridor and find us, but I couldn't stop. Romero pressed me against the wall and held me with only one arm. His other hand cupped my breast through my dress, making me moan into his mouth and my nipples harden. Romero groaned. He thrust against me, rubbing his erection against my panty-clad heat.

"I need you," I gasped against his mouth. Romero stroked his palm down my side, then slipped it between my legs and pushed a finger under the fabric of my panties. He found me wet and aching. I shivered at the feel of his touch.

"Fuck. You are so wet, Lily." He pushed a finger into me and I arched off the wall with a gasp. Only he had that effect one me.

241

He removed his finger again and opened his zipper. My core tightened with anticipation and need. I heard the rip of a condom package and then his tip pressed against my opening and he started to slide into me. My walls yielded to his hot length until he'd sheathed himself completely in me. We peered into each other's eyes. This felt so right. Why did it have to feel so right?

"You feel so fucking good, Lily. And so fucking tight, good God."

Our lips found each other again. It had been too long. Romero thrust into me, driving me higher up against the wall. I moaned when he hit a spot deep inside of me. "We have to be quiet," he murmured in a low voice, then his mouth swallowed my next sound. I wrapped my arms even tighter around his neck. It felt like we were one, inseparable.

I dug my heels into his butt, driving him deeper into me. Pleasure surged through me and I came apart. Romero kept pounding into me until his own orgasm hit him. We clung to each other, still united. I kissed the side of his neck. His familiar scent flooded my nose and I closed my eyes. I wanted to stay like this forever.

Distant sound of laughter dragged me back into the realm of reality. Romero pulled out of me. I loosened my hold on him and let my legs slide down until my feet hit the ground. I couldn't even look up at him as I straightened my skirt. Romero threw the condom into a nearby bin before he returned to me. Neither of us said anything.

From the corner of my eye, I saw him reaching for my cheek. I backed away. Bracing myself, I lifted my gaze. "This was a mistake," I whispered.

Shock crossed Romero's face, then it became emotionless. "A mistake."

"I'm going to marry Benito soon. We can't do this again."

Romero gave a terse nod, then he turned on his heel and walked off. I had to resist the urge to run after him. I waited a couple more minutes before I headed toward the restroom. I needed to clean up before I returned to the party or people would realize something had happened. To my relief, there was no one in the restroom when I stepped in. I checked my reflection. My hair was all over the place and my make-up needed touching up. Sweat trickled down my back. But worse than that was the telltale prickling in my eyes. I couldn't cry now. That would ruin everything. I took a few deep breaths through my nose before I started to redo my make-up. When I left the restroom twenty minutes later, I looked like nothing had happened, but my insides were twisting. I'd thought I'd made peace with my marriage to Benito, had hoped my feelings for Romero had lessened, but now I realized that was far from being true.

The moment I stepped onto the dance floor, Luca was there and asked me for a dance. I knew he wanted more than that. He steered us toward a part of the dance floor where there weren't as many dancers before he started to talk quietly. "You are still going through with this marriage? You and Romero were gone for a while."

"Yes. I will marry Benito, don't worry," I said tiredly. I couldn't even blame Luca for being so insensitive. He'd invited me into his home and taken care of me, and I'd paid him back by making one of soldiers break his oath.

"You don't have to stay married for him forever," Luca said casually.

"Father would never agree to a divorce." Father would kill me before that ever happened.

"There are other ways out of a marriage than divorce. Sometimes people die."

"He's not that old."

Luca cocked an eyebrow. "Sometimes people die anyway."

Was he really suggesting that I should kill Benito? "Why can't he die before my wedding?"

"That would look suspicious. Wait a few months. The time will pass quickly, trust me."

I wanted to believe him but months sharing a bed with Benito, of having him inside of me like Romero had just been sounded like hell.

"Romero won't want me anymore then."

Luca remained silent. He knew it to be true. Why would Romero still want me after I'd spent months sleeping with another guy? I was already disgusted by the thought, how much worse would it be for him? "There are good men in the Outfit too. You'll find new happiness. You're doing the right thing by marrying Benito. You're preventing war and you're protecting Romero from himself. That's a brave thing to do."

I nodded, but I wanted to cry. Luca and I returned to our table. Aria tried to talk to me again but she gave up when I barely said anything. I needed to survive this day somehow and then my wedding, and the months thereafter, and then maybe I'd get another chance at happiness. I searched the room until my eyes settled on Romero. He was pointedly not looking at me. I loved him, loved him so much it hurt. I knew there would be no happiness for me without him.

***

Aria and Gianna helped me with my dress. It was white of course, with a veil that trailed after me. I wore my hair open because Benito had wanted me to.

"You look beautiful," Aria said from behind me.

I checked my reflection but I could only see the look of utter despair in my eyes. I'd need the veil to hide if from the world. Gianna and Aria didn't know about my last conversation with

Father, and it was better that way. If they knew how much he'd scared me, they'd take me away despite the risk for their own lives.

"This is crap," Gianna muttered. She touched my shoulder. "Lily get the hell away from here. Let us help you. What's the use of being married to the Capo and the Consigliere of the Famiglia if we can't force them to start a war for our little sister? You're going to be miserable."

"Luca said I could get rid of Benito in a few months when it won't look suspicious anymore."

Gianna snorted. "Oh sure, and what until then? My God, could Luca be any more of a jerk?"

Aria didn't say anything, which was a sign in itself. She usually always tried to defend Luca.

"Are you and Luca still fighting?" I asked.

She shrugged. "I wouldn't call it fighting. We're basically ignoring each other. He's angry at me for keeping you and Romero a secret from him, and I'm mad at him for making you marry Brasci."

"He isn't making me, Aria. Father is. Luca's acting like a Capo should. I'm not his responsibility but the Famiglia is."

"Good God, Romero has really rubbed off on you. Please tell me you don't really believe what you just said," Gianna said.

"I won't have you all risk everything for me."

Gianna touched her forehead in exasperation. "We want to risk it for you. But you have to let us."

246

Even if I said 'yes' now, what could they do? Both Luca and Matteo wouldn't help us, not when they were surrounded by Outfit soldiers. This would be suicide. And Romero? He would do it without hesitation and get himself killed. Father's words flash in my mind again. No, I had to go through with this. It was the only option.

Someone knocked and a moment later Maria poked her head in. She was one of my bridesmaids, even though we still weren't talking much. "You need to come out now."

She disappeared before I had time to say something.

"I can't believe Father is married to her," Gianna said. "I don't like her but I still feel sorry for her. Father is a bastard."

I barely listened. My vision was turning gray. Fear filled my bloodstream, made me want to bolt. But I held my head high and lowered my veil over my face. "We should go now."

"Lily," Aria began but I didn't give her the time to finish whatever she wanted to say. I hurried toward the door and opened it, startled to find Father right in front of it. I hadn't expected him to wait for me here. I knew he'd lead me to the altar but fathers usually waited in the ante-room. Maybe he'd worried I'd run off in the last minute.

"There you are. Hurry," he said. He slanted a hard look at Gianna when she and Aria walked by but didn't say anything. He held out his arm for me. An image of him with Maria popped into my head and I wanted to throw up. I put my hand on his forearm and let him lead me toward the main part of the church, even

247

though every fiber of my being wanted to get away from him. Inside the church music was already playing. Before we entered, Father leaned down to me. "You better convince Benito you're a virgin or he'll beat you to death, and if he doesn't I will." He didn't wait for my reply. We went through the double doors and every pair of eyes turned toward us.

My feet felt like lead as I walked toward the altar. Benito waited for me at the end of it, a proud grin on his face, as if he could finally present his catch to everyone. Despite the risk, my eyes searched the crowd until they settled on Romero. He leaned against the wall on the right, an unreadable expression on his face. I tried to catch his gaze, even though it would have made this walk even harder but Romero didn't even glance my way. He was completely focused on Aria, playing the part as her bodyguard.

I returned my attention to the front, hoping no one had noticed the detour my gaze had taken.

In the spot where my mother should have been was Maria, hunched shoulders, pale skin, sad eyes; maybe she thought nobody was looking because this was the first time she hadn't put on a brave face. This was a taste of what I would look like soon enough. I peered up at Father. He on the other hand seemed rejuvenated, as if the marriage to a barely twenty-year old had allowed him to drop a few of his own years. Didn't he miss Mother at all? She should have been at his side for my wedding. My eyes sought Romero again. I couldn't seem to stop. And Romero should have been the one waiting at the altar for me. We reached the end of the aisle and

248

Father handed me over to Benito. Old-man fingers curled around my hand, sweaty and too firm. Father lifted my veil and for a moment I was worried my disgust and unhappiness were plain as day but from the look on Benito's face, he didn't seem to notice or care. I didn't listen to the priest as he started his sermon. It took everything I had to stop myself from peering over my shoulder, seeking out Romero one more time.

While the priest and the gathered guests waited for my 'I do', I considered saying 'no' for a brief moment. This was my last chance, the last exit before I was forever stuck on a highway to unhappiness, or at least until I figured out a way to get rid of my husband. Was I even capable of something like that? I couldn't even smash a fly when it bothered me.

Just say 'no'. I wondered how people would react if I refused to marry Benito?

Benito would be furious, and so would Father. But my sisters and Romero, they would understand, would probably fight everyone else to protect me. Benito cleared his throat beside me and I realized how long I'd been saying nothing. I quickly said what everyone expected even when the words tasted like acid. "Yes, I do."

"You may kiss the bride."

Benito grasped my waist. I stiffened but I didn't push him away. His rough lips pressed against mine. I could taste cigars. I pulled my head away and turned to our guests with a forced smile. Benito shot me a disapproving look but I ignored him. If he knew how much restraint it had taken not to shove him away, he wouldn't be mad at me for ending our kiss a bit too soon.

Taking my hand, he steered me down the aisle. My eyes darted toward Romero but he was gone. I searched the entire church, not finding him. He probably hated me now that he'd seen me kiss Benito and didn't want anything to do with me. Would I ever see him again?

Romero

I should have never come to Chicago. Watching Lily stride down the aisle toward Benito, I felt like someone was squashing my heart under a boot. I wanted nothing more than to stick my knife into Benito's eye very slowly, see the light leave him, hear his last labored breath. I wanted to skin him alive, wanted to give him more pain than any man had ever endured.

I forced my eyes away from Lily and focused on Aria as I was supposed to do. She looked back at me and gave me an understanding smile. I didn't react. I shut off my emotions like I'd learned to do in the first few years after my initiation when seeing people get killed or tortured still bothered me.

"You may kiss the bride."

My eyes shot toward the front of the church where Benito *fucking* Brasci had put his hands on Lily's waist and was practically dragging her toward his body. I saw red. I wanted to kill him. I pushed away from the wall, turned around and walked out of the church. I didn't run like I wanted. I moved slowly, as if nothing was wrong. Fuck, what a fucking lie. Everything was wrong. The woman that was supposed to be mine had just married some old bastard.

I headed straight toward our rental car. I'd wait there until it was time to drive to Brasci's mansion for the feast.

***

Luca hardly left my fucking side at the wedding party. He probably worried I was going to lose my shit on everyone. He wasn't wrong. Every time I glanced toward Lily and Benito, something snapped in my brain. I couldn't stop imagining pulling my gun and putting a bullet in Benito's head, and then one in Scuderi's head for good measure. If I was lucky, they wouldn't stop me quick enough.

Aria came toward me after dinner. I wasn't sure if I could take her pity, but I wasn't going to send her away. She was only trying to be kind. "You don't have to stay, you know? Luca is here for my protection. This must be hard for you. Why don't you go ahead and find yourself a hotel? I'm sure you don't want to spend the night under the same roof with Benito."

Tonight. So far I'd managed not to think about the wedding night too much. "No. I'm fine. I can handle this."

Aria hesitated as if she wanted to say more but then she headed back to Luca.

When the party drew to an end, I could feel myself getting more and more agitated. And then what I'd been dreading happened. Benito and Lily rose from their chairs to head to the master bedroom for their first night together. A crowd followed them, cheering and making suggestions of what should happen tonight. My pulse quickened and my fingers longed to reach beneath my vest.

I trailed after them, though I knew it was the last thing I should do. I had always prided myself on my control but I could feel it trickling through my fingers.

I knew I'd said to Lily that I would accept her marriage. She had told me she didn't want me. As a soldier of the New York Famiglia it was my duty to put them first. Wanting Lily could mean war. No, it would lead to fucking war. Dante Cavallaro was a calculating man but his soldiers had been waiting for a chance to tear into us again. I'd seen it in many of their eyes today. Things between us had gone steeply downhill in the past few years. The honeymoon phase of our union had waned off quickly after Luca's and Aria's wedding, and now this was a marriage of convenience, a marriage both the Famiglia and the Outfit wanted out of. The smallest infraction would be enough to blow up everything.

Without realizing it I'd followed the other guests into the lobby. I spotted Lily's dark blond locks at the top of the steps, next to Benito's bald head, and a crowd of other men around them. And then my feet started moving, my hand going for my gun, my temples pounding with anger. I had to push through the crowd, and ignored the mumbles of protest. I couldn't let that fucker Benito have her. Lily was mine, and would always be mine. If that meant a fucking war, then so be it. I'd spend until the end of my days hunting Russians, and Taiwanese and Outfit bastards if that meant I could keep her.

I sped up and then Luca was suddenly in front of me. I ground to a halt, breathing hard. I had half a mind to punch him, but I fought the urge. If I made a scene surrounded by so many people, I could screw up everything. Luca grabbed me by the shoulder and steered me into an empty corridor. He pushed me against the wall, making my ears ring, then he released me.

"Goddammit!" He snarled and gripped my shoulder again. "She's not yours. She's a married woman now."

"She never wanted any of this," I said harshly and shook Luca's hand off. "It should have been me next to her at the altar."

"But it wasn't. It's too late Romero. This is Chicago. We won't start a fucking war because you can't keep it in your pants."

I got straight into his face. "This is much more than that and you know it."

"I don't care, Romero. You watched Liliana walk down that aisle and now you have to accept the consequences. She did her duty and so should you. Go to your room and get some sleep. Don't do anything stupid."

Luca was Capo. It was his job to look out for the best of the Famiglia, but right then I wanted to kill him. I'd never wanted to kill my Capo. "Yes, Boss."

Luca grabbed my arm. "I mean it. This is a direct order. I won't have war over this. I've warned you about how this would end a long time ago, but you didn't listen."

"I won't do anything," I gritted out. Even I wasn't sure if it was the truth, or if I was lying. I hadn't made up my mind yet.

CHAPTER SIXTEEN

Liliana

When people started to call for Benito and me to retire to his room, I felt the blood leave my face. Benito didn't waste any time though. He took my hand and pulled me to my feet, then before I knew it we were heading toward our room.

His palm stuck to the thin material of my wedding dress. It was sweaty and heavy and too warm. Slowly it traveled lower until it rested on my butt. I suppressed a shudder. I wanted to push his hand away, push him away but he was my husband and soon enough he'd touch me there without the protection of fabric, he would touch me everywhere, would see every inch of skin that was supposed to be Romero's only.

Sickness washed over me, and I almost threw up. Sheer power of will kept my wedding dinner in my stomach. I glimpsed over my shoulder, even though I'd promised myself I wouldn't do it. My eyes searched the crowd for Romero but he wasn't there. Part of me was glad that he didn't have to witness Benito pawing me, but the other, the bigger part, was disappointed. That silly part had hoped that he'd somehow stop this. Of course that would have only got him killed. They would have shot him on the spot and then war would have broken out. Many people would have died, maybe even Fabi, Aria and Gianna. It was a good thing that he'd kept his oath, that he hadn't interfered and let me do what was expected of me.

I turned back around and realized that we'd already arrived in front of our room for the night. Benito opened the door and half shoved me into the bedroom. I froze in the middle of the room, listening to the sound of the door closing and Benito's steps. "You're a real beauty," he said, his voice already thick with desire. "I wanted to be alone with you all evening. If it hadn't looked rude, I'd have taken you to our room hours ago."

Bile clogged my throat. I didn't dare move from fear of vomiting onto my shoes. He gripped my arms and turned me around to him, then before I could even gather my bearings his mouth pressed against mine. I gasped, and he used the chance to thrust his tongue past my lips. He tasted of the cigars he'd smoked with the other men, and it made me feel even sicker. His tongue was everywhere. He didn't give me the chance to do anything. God, this was horrible. My hands grasped his shoulders, fingers digging into his suit, and I shoved as hard as I could, but his arms wrapped around my waist, pulling me even tighter, giving me no chance to escape. His breathing was quick and excited. He was so eager.

I didn't want this. I squeezed my eyes shut, fighting back tears and desperately trying to imagine it was Romero kissing me, but everything about this felt wrong. The clumsy hands on my waist, the taste of him, the way he moved his tongue like a dying slug.

Ripping away from him, I drew in a few desperate breaths. His taste lingered on my tongue. I wanted to rinse my mouth to get rid of it.

Benito stepped in front of me again and leaned close. "Don't worry, sweetheart. I'm going to take good care of you. I'm going to make you a woman. You'll never forget this night."

I knew I'd never forget it. I'd probably have nightmares about it for the rest of my life. Mother's last words, the look in her eyes filled my mind. How could I have let it come this far?

"No, I can't." I took a step back. I needed to get away, out of this room, needed to find Romero and tell him that I couldn't survive this marriage, that I wanted only him, that he'd always been the one I wanted and would do so till the day I died. I was being selfish, I knew. But I didn't care about causing a war anymore if the alternative meant having to spend my life being touched by Benito. Maybe Luca could handle the situation. He was a good Capo. He could prevent war. Right?

Benito's expression tightened, that sugary sweet smile being replaced by something more leery and hungry.

Fear settled like a weight in my stomach. He grabbed my arms too tightly, making me wince. "You are my wife and you will do what's expected of you."

"No, please. I'm not ready. I need more time." Time to figure out a way out of this without getting everyone killed. There had to be a way where nobody got hurt.

Benito chuckled. "Oh, don't try this bullshit with me, sweety. I've been jerking off to the image of your perfect perky ass for weeks now. Tonight I want to bury my cock in it. Nothing in this world will stop me, not even your big puppy dog eyes."

I opened my mouth for another attempt at begging but Benito pushed me backward. I cried out in surprise.

My heel caught in the hem of my wedding dress and then I was falling. I braced myself for the impact, instead I landed on something soft and bouncy: the bed. How could I have been this close to it?

I tried to scramble off immediately but didn't get the chance. Benito leaned over me, his knees between my legs, pinning my dress beneath him. I was stuck. I struggled, but my legs were tied down by the fabric. And I panicked. Panicked like I'd never had before, not even when I saw the torture scene in the basement.

Benito lowered his face down to mine and then he kissed me again. I turned my head to the side so he slobbered all over my cheek. His fingers clutched my chin, forcing me to face him. His cigar breath washed over me and his chapped lips were too close. His eyes narrowed to slits. "Listen, sweetheart. We can do this the easy or the hard way. For your sake, I hope you work with me. I don't give a shit either way. I like it rough."

He meant it. He'd force himself on me if I kept up the struggling, I could see it in his eyes. I couldn't expect any kindness from my husband tonight. Tears and pleading wouldn't change his mind.

I willed myself to relax beneath him. He smiled in a condescending way and shifted his body, finally giving my dress free. He pressed up against me, his mouth wet on my throat. He licked his way down to my collarbone. I tried to imagine it was Romero and when that didn't work, I tried to stop thinking about him altogether. Tried to be empty and numb, tried to cast my mind to another place and time, away from my husband who would have his way with me, no matter what I wanted. Benito shoved my skirt up and slipped his hand up my calf. He grunted appreciatively and pressed his body even closer against mine. I could feel how much this excited him. Whenever I'd felt Romero's erection, I'd been excited, but this? Oh god. I couldn't do this. But he was my husband and I was his wife. I'd chosen this way to protect everyone who wanted to help me. This was my duty, not only to him but to my family, to the Outfit. It was the fate of many women. They had survived and so could I.

I hated the sounds my husband made, the smell that wasn't Romero's, the way his clumsy fingers tugged at my dress. He was my husband. His hand traveled up to my knee.

My husband.

Then up to my thigh.

My husband. My husband. My husband.

His hand reached the edge of my panties and I couldn't take it anymore. I lay my palms against his chest and pushed him off me. I wasn't sure where I took the strength from. Benito had at least seventy pounds on me, but he lost his balance and fell to his side. I leaped off the bed but my dress was slowing me down. I staggered toward the door, arms extended. My fingers were mere inches from the doorknob when Benito caught up with me. His fingers bruised my forearm with their grip, and he flung me back toward the center of the room. I couldn't gain my footage quick enough and fell forward, hipbones colliding with the desk in the corner. I screamed out from pain. Tears burned in my eyes.

Benito pressed up behind me as I was bent forward and his erection dug into my butt. "Tonight, doll, you are mine."

And there it was, right in front of me. I barely noticed Benito's hands squeezing my breasts through the fabric. My eyes were fixed on the gleaming silver letter opener. Benito squeezed again, harder, probably angry because of my lack of reaction. I gripped the letter opener. It felt good in my hand, cold and hard. My husband tore at the edge of my corset. I tightened my grip on the opener and jabbed my arm backward as hard as I could. Benito stumbled away with a gurgling gasp, giving me free. I whirled around. The letter opener stuck out of his right side. Blood soaked the white fabric of his shirt. I must have hit him really hard, maybe even injured him seriously. I'd never done something like that.

My lips parted in shock. I'd really plunged a knife into my husband's stomach. His wide eyes stared. "You bitch, I--" He gasped and dropped to his knees. His ugly beetle eyes grew even wider as he rasped in pain.

I stumbled away from him. What if he called for help? What if someone saw what I'd done? I'd stabbed *my own* husband. They would kill me for that, and even if they didn't, Benito surely would beat me to death if he survived the wound.

There was only one thing I could do, only one person who could help me and I wasn't even sure if he still would after everything I'd put him through. After what I'd said and what he had to witness today. Maybe he wasn't even in Chicago anymore. Maybe he'd already taken the next flight back to New York to get as far away from me as possible.

I rushed toward my bag, ripped it open and fumbled for my phone. With shaking fingers I keyed in the number I knew by heart. Benito seemed still dazed but he had gotten up on his elbows. He was gasping for breath, obviously trying to find his voice to scream for help. What if he came toward me? Could I finish what I'd started?

A new wave of panic hit me hard.

After the first ring, Romero's familiar voice rang out. "Lily?"

I'd never felt more relieved in my life. He hadn't ignored my call. Maybe, just maybe, he didn't hate me.

"Please help me," I whispered, voice hoarse with tears. They were streaming down my face. It wasn't because I'd just stabbed someone with a letter opener, I felt no regret over that.

"I'm coming. Where are you?"

"Bedroom."

"Don't hang up," he ordered. I wouldn't have. I could hear him moving, could hear his calm breathing, and it calmed me in turn. Romero would be here soon and then everything would be all right.

After everything that had happened, he still rushed to help me.

Less than two minutes later, there was a knock. He must have been close or it would have taken him much longer to reach the bedroom. For a couple of seconds, I wasn't sure if I could even move. My legs felt numb.

"Lily, you have to open the door. It's locked. If I break it down, people will be up here in no time."

That was all it took. I crossed the room in a few steps and opened the door. My heart was beating in my throat, and only when I saw Romero's worried face did I dare to lower the phone from my ear and hang up. I felt safe now, even though I knew I was far from it. We both were in grave danger if anyone found us like that. By calling Romero, I'd put him in harm's way. How could I do that to someone I loved? Hadn't I gone through with this marriage exactly to protect Romero?

Romero eyes wandered over my half-open corset, my disheveled hair and ripped skirt, and his face flashed with fury. He stepped into the room, closed the door and cupped my face. "Are you okay? Did he hurt you?"

I shook my head, which I realized a moment later, could be taken as an answer to either question. "I stabbed him. I couldn't bear his touch. I didn't want his hands on me. I..." Romero pulled me against him, my cheek pressed against his strong chest. I listened to the sound of his pounding heart. Outside he looked calm but his heart betrayed him. "I didn't sleep with him. I couldn't."

"He's still alive," he murmured after a moment before he pulled back. Deprived of his warmth, I wrapped my arms around myself. Romero advanced on my husband whose eyes were darting between Romero and me like he was watching a tennis match. His breathing rattled in his chest, but he'd dragged himself closer to the desk and was reaching for his phone. Romero stood over him, then calmly pushed his arm back down to the ground.

Benito fell onto his side with a pained gasp. He reminded me of a beetle who was trapped on his back, its legs helplessly pedaling above its body. I didn't feel any pity though.

"You," Benito snarled, then started coughing. Blood speckled his lips. "Did your Capo set this up? Chicago will make him pay tenfold. Dante won't let you make a fool out of me and everyone else."

"You aren't important enough for Luca to give a shit about you," Romero said coldly. He had the same expression I'd seen when he'd watched the Russians getting tortured in the basement.

I shivered.

Realization settled on Benito's face as his eyes swiveled from Romero to me. "You and her." His mouth pulled into a nasty grimace, spittle clinging to his lips. "You nasty whore let him fuck you. You--"

He never got the chance to finish his sentence. Romero stepped up to Benito, jerked him up by his collar and then in one practiced motion he pulled his knife and plunged it in an upward angle between my husband's ribs, silencing his rattling breath. Without even blinking, Romero let go of Benito, who fell to his side, lifeless.

CHAPTER SEVENTEEN

Liliana

Romero had just killed a member of the Outfit for me. Our eyes met, and cold fear spread in my chest like fog. Romero wiped his knife clean on my husband's pant leg before he sheathed it in its holder.

My throat constricted as I walked toward him. "This means war."

"We can come up with a story. I'll pretend I've lost my mind. I've been lusting for you forever but you were never interested in me and today I snapped, and barged into your bedroom and attacked your husband, who tried to defend himself with the letter opener, which I then used to stab him. We can make it look like I tried to rape you so nobody suspects you were involved. Nobody would doubt it the way you look." He stroked my cheek. "The bastard died too quickly for how he treated you."

I couldn't believe he was suggesting something like that. It was bad enough that I'd dragged him into this at all. I wouldn't make him look like a disgusting rapist to save my own hide. "I won't pretend you tried to rape me. You are the only man I want to be with."

Romero bridged the distance between us again and wrapped me in a tight embrace. His smell, his warmth, the way my body perfectly fit against his; this felt right. My eyes found Benito on the ground. I'd tried to be his wife and failed, but I couldn't be sad about it. I'd never wanted this, and he'd known it from the start. He would have forced himself on me, maybe that didn't deserve a death sentence but he lived in a world where death was almost always the punishment. His eyes were still open and it seemed they were staring straight through me. The longer I stared at him, the worse their look seemed to get. I shivered violently.

Romero pushed me gently away. "Don't look at him." He walked toward the body and turned Benito so he was facing the ground, and no longer me. And just like that I felt better. He was still dead, but at least he wasn't looking at me with that reproachful expression anymore.

I stumbled toward the bed and sank down. My legs were too shaky to hold me. Romero stood for a moment before he joined me. He brushed his thumb over my cheek, catching a few stray tears. I hadn't even noticed I'd started crying again. "He's dead now. He can't hurt you ever again," he said roughly. "Nobody will ever hurt you again. I won't allow it."

"If you confess to murdering Benito, you'll be killed and then you won't be around to protect me from anything." Maybe it was a low move to play the guilt card but I couldn't let Romero take the blame.

Romero's gaze settled on Benito and the puddle of blood slowly spreading around him, turning the beige carpet into a sea of red. "We can't cover this up. Even if we got him out of the house without anyone noticing, we could never get the blood out of the carpet. People would suspect something. Someone will have to take the blame for this."

I buried my face in my hands, desperation clawing through my insides. "I should have let him have me. I should have endured it like so many other woman before me. But I had to act like a selfish bitch."

"No," Romero said sharply, wedging a finger below my chin and tilting my face up. "I'm glad you stabbed him. I'm glad he's dead. I'm glad he didn't get what he doesn't deserve. You are way too good and beautiful for this bastard."

I leaned forward and kissed Romero. I would have deepened the kiss, despite everything, would have lost myself in Romero as I always did, but he was more reasonable than I and pulled away. "I have to call Luca. As his soldier, I need to confess to him at least, and then it's up to him to decide what happens next."

"And what if he decides to kill you so he can keep the peace with Chicago?" I asked quietly. "You know how angry he was when he found out about us. Even Aria couldn't convince him to risk war for me."

For a long time Romero merely looked at me, then he picked up his phone and lifted it to his ear. "Then I'll accept his judgment."

"No," I said suddenly. I shoved his phone away. "Let me call Aria. She can reason with Luca. He listens to her."

Romero smiled sadly. "This is something even Aria can't do anything about. Luca is Capo and if he needs to make decisions that protect the Famiglia, he won't let Aria mess with his mind. You said it yourself. He refused to listen to Aria."

"Please."

"I need to do this. I can't hide behind you or Aria like a coward." He raised the phone again and this time I didn't stop him. He was right. Luca would probably be pissed if I tried to use Aria to manipulate him.

I held my breath as I waited for Luca to pick up.

"Luca, I need you to come to Benito's room." I heard Luca's raised voice on the other end but couldn't make out what he said. It didn't sound nice. "Yes, I'm there. You should hurry."

"Damn it!" Luca growled loud enough for me to hear, then he hung up. Romero lowered his phone slowly and put it back into his pocket.

I took his hand, needing to convince myself that he was really there.

Romero glared at Benito's body but he didn't try to tell me things would be okay. I was glad he didn't try to lie to me. I rested my cheek against Romero's shoulder.

There was a soft knock. I straightened, but my grip on Romero's hand tightened. I didn't want to let him go. Once Luca saw what had happened, I might never get the chance to touch Romero's hand again, at least not while it was still warm. I shuddered when I remembered Mother's lifeless corpse. I wouldn't allow that to happen to Romero.

Romero kissed my forehead, then he untangled himself from my grip and got up. I rose too, my eyes darting to Benito. Anger for him welled up in me. If he'd never stepped into my life, then I could have been happy. But Father would probably have found another horrible husband for me. Fear corded up my throat as I watched Romero push down the handle and open the door. What if Luca really decided to kill Romero as punishment?

Romero didn't open the door all the way, so Aria had to slip in. She sucked in a harsh breath at the sight of my dead husband, then she rushed over to me and clutched my shoulders, but my eyes were frozen on Luca who had walked in after her. His gaze settled on Benito, on the letter opener still stuck in his side and on the hole in the shirt where Romero's knife had gone in. Romero closed the door noiselessly but didn't move away. I wished he'd bring some distance between himself and Luca. It was a ridiculous notion. It wouldn't protect him.

"My God, Lily," Aria said shrilly. I couldn't remember the last time she'd sounded so scared. I met her gaze.

"What happened? Are you okay?" she asked. She ran her hands over my arms, her eyes lingering on my ripped skirt.

I didn't reply. Luca had started moving toward the body and knelt beside it, scanning the scene without saying a single word. His

269

face was stone. This was it. Suddenly I was sure that Romero and I wouldn't find Luca's mercy today. Maybe Aria would manage to convince Luca to protect me, but Romero wouldn't be so lucky. I knew I wouldn't be able to watch him die.

Luca raised his head very slowly and fixed me with a look that turned my blood to ice. "What happened here?"

I glanced at Romero. Did he want me to tell the truth? Or should I lie? There had to be a story that wouldn't make Luca angry enough to want to kill us.

Luca straightened. "I want the fucking truth!"

"Luca," Aria scolded. "Lily is obviously in shock. Give her a moment."

"We don't have a fucking moment. We have a dead Outfit member in a room with us. Things will get ugly very soon."

Aria squeezed my shoulder lightly. "Lily, are you okay?"

"I'm fine," I said. "He didn't have time to hurt me."

She pursed her lips but didn't argue.

"Enough," Luca said harshly. He turned to Romero. "I want answers. Remember your oath."

Romero looked like a man resigned to his fate. It scared me senseless. "I always do."

Luca jabbed a finger toward the dead body. "That doesn't look like it. Or are you saying that Liliana did this alone?"

"Liliana is innocent," Romero said firmly. He never called me Liliana. What was he trying to do? "Benito was still alive when I arrived. She'd stabbed him with the letter opener because he attacked her. It was self-defense on her part."

"Self-defense?" Luca muttered. His grey eyes fixed me. "What did he do?"

"He tried to force himself on her," Romero said for me.

"I didn't ask you!" Luca growled. Aria let go of me and walked toward him and put a hand on his arm. He ignored her completely as he said, "And if he tried to consummate the marriage, nobody in this fucking house will see it as self-defense. Benito had a fucking right on her body. He was her husband for god's sake!"

Romero took a step forward but stopped himself.

"You can't be serious," Aria said, eyes imploring.

"You know the rules, Aria. I'm stating the facts," Luca said in a much calmer voice.

Aria always had that effect on him. "I don't care. A husband doesn't have the right to rape his wife. Everyone in this house should agree on that!"

I shivered. The events of the evening were catching up with me. I just wanted to lie down in Romero's arms and forget everything. Romero came over to me and wrapped an arm around my shoulder.

Luca narrowed his eyes. "I told you this would end in disaster. So let me guess, Liliana stabbed her husband, called you and you finished the fucking job to have her for yourself."

"Yes," Romero said. "And to protect her. If he'd survived he would have blamed Liliana and she would have been punished harshly by the Outfit."

Luca let out a dark chuckle. "And now she won't? They will put her on trial and they will not only punish her harshly. They will also accuse us of having set this up and then there will be a fucking bloodbath. Dante is a cold fish but he needs to show strength. He will proclaim war in no time. All because you can't control your dick and your heart."

"As if you could do it. You'd take down anyone who'd try to take Aria away from you," Romero said.

"But Aria is my wife. That's a huge difference."

"If it was up to me, Lily would have been my wife for months."

I stared at him in surprise. He'd never mentioned marrying me. My heart swelled with happiness, only to turn to stone at the sight of Luca's expression. "Someone is going to pay for this," he said darkly. He paused. "As Capo of the New York Famiglia I need to put the blame on Liliana and hope Dante buys it and doesn't start a war."

That would mean my certain death. Maybe Dante wouldn't give the orders himself but he would have to submit me to my father's judgment and I didn't expect any mercy from him. He hated Gianna for what she'd done and that wasn't nearly as horrendous as my crime.

"You can't do that," Aria whispered. Her knuckles were turning white from her tight grip on his forearm.

Romero let go of me and walked a few steps toward the center of the room where he got down on his knees and held out his arms wide. "I'm going to take the full blame for this. Tell them I lost my mind and ran after Liliana because I've been wanting her for months. I killed Benito when he tried to defend Lily and himself, but before I could rape her, you noticed I was missing and went in search of me. Then there won't be war between the Outfit and New York, and Lily will get the chance at a new life."

"If that's the story we want them to believe, there's something missing," Luca said.

Romero nodded. He met Luca's gaze straight on. "I will put my life down for this. Shoot me."

I staggered forward. "No!" Aria, too, screamed the same word.

Luca and Romero ignored us, locked in a silent staring contest. I stepped between them. I didn't care if that went against some secret mafia rule. I walked toward Luca. From the corner of my eye I saw Romero getting up. He looked like he was worried about me getting close to Luca but I wasn't worried for me. If Luca killed Romero because of me that would be the end of me. I'd never be able to live with myself.

"Please," I whispered, peering up into Luca's emotionless face. "Please don't kill him. I'll do anything, just please don't. I can't live without him." Tears started streaming down my face.

Romero put his hands on my shoulders and pulled me back against him. "Lily, don't. I'm a soldier of the Famiglia. I broke my oath to always put the Famiglia first, and I have to accept the due punishment."

"I don't care about any oaths. I don't want to lose you," I said as I turned in his grip.

Aria lay her palms flat against Luca's chest. "Please, Luca, don't punish Romero for protecting someone he loved. He and Lily belong together. I beg you." She said the last in the barest whisper. I wanted to hug her, but I was scared to move. She and Luca were gazing at each other and I didn't want to break their silent understanding, especially if it saved Romero's life. I glanced up at Romero. He looked so calm, nothing like someone whose life could end any moment.

Luca finally tore his eyes away from my sister and gently removed her hands from his chest. "I can't base my decisions on feelings. I'm Capo and have to make decisions that benefit my Famiglia."

Romero nodded, then he walked past me and stood across from Luca. I began shaking, completely terrified. Aria's wide eyes settled on me.

"You are my best soldier. The Famiglia needs you, and I don't trust anyone with Aria as I do with you," Luca said. He put a hand on Romero's shoulder. "War has been inevitable for a while. I won't end your life to postpone it for a few fucking months. We'll stand together."

I almost sagged with relief. Aria rushed over to me and hugged me tightly. My moment of euphoria was short-lived however.

"Of course, we might not get out of this house with our lives," Luca added. "We're surrounded by the enemy now."

"Most guests are either drunk or asleep. We could try to sneak out. By the time they notice Benito's missing tomorrow morning, we'll be back in New York," Romero said. A flicker of relief showed on his face. I wanted to be in his arms but he and Luca needed to deal with our dilemma, a dilemma I'd started. What if we really didn't get out alive? The Outfit outnumbered us greatly. This was their territory and we were thousands of miles away from reinforcement.

"I'll have to call Matteo and Gianna. They need to come here so we can figure out the best way to get out of this house," Luca said, already raising his phone to his ear.

Romero strode over to me and smoothed the crease between my brows. I pressed up against him. Aria headed for Luca, giving us space.

"I was so scared," I whispered.

Romero buried his face in my hair. "I know."

"Weren't you? It was your life on the line."

"My life has been on the line since I've become a Made Man. I've grown used to it. The one thing that fucking scared me today was when I had to watch you walk toward your wedding night with that asshole Benito. I wanted to kill him then. I've wanted to kill him every day since I found out you were forced to marry him. I'm glad that I finally did."

"Me too," I said, then rose to my tiptoes and kissed his lips.

"Damn it. Matteo isn't picking up his fucking phone."

"Do you think something happened to them?" Aria asked.

Romero let out a small laugh, and exchanged a look with Luca.

"The only thing happening is that he's probably fucking your sister's brains out right now and ignores his fucking phone," Luca said.

I wrinkled my nose. Of course I knew my sisters had sex, I just didn't want to be reminded of it, or worse: imagine it. "Can't we go over to their room?"

Luca shook his head. "It's farther away from the back entrance." He dialed again. "Damn it!"

"We should carry Benito into the bathroom and cover the blood stain in the carpet with something. That way if someone walks in tomorrow morning, it might buy us a bit more time."

Luca shoved his phone into his pocket, then gripped Benito by the feet while Romero took the arms. I shuddered as I watched them carry the corpse into the adjoining bathroom. My husband was like a sack of flour in their hold.

"You should get out of your wedding dress and wear something more sensible," Aria suggested softly. She touched my arm lightly, drawing my eyes away from the dead body. After a moment, I nodded. Luca and Romero came back out of the bathroom and discussed how best to go about our flight.

I grabbed jeans and a pullover from my bag in the corner, before heading toward the bathroom to change in peace, but froze in the doorway. Benito was sprawled out in the bathtub. I didn't want to be alone with a dead man. Bile traveled up my throat.

"Hey," Romero said gently, coming up behind me. "Do you want me to come with you?"

I nodded merely and finally stepped into the bathroom. Romero entered after me. I quickly got out of my dress with his help. "Somehow I always imagined it would be different when I'd help you out of your wedding dress," he murmured.

I laughed breathlessly. I dropped the dress unceremoniously on the ground. For me it was only a symbol for the worst day of my life. I wasn't sad to be rid of it. Maybe one day I'd get the chance to have another wedding, one I'd want, with a husband I loved. I changed into my other clothes.

Romero picked the dress up, and for a crazy moment I thought he wanted to keep it for our own future wedding. "What are you doing?"

"I want to cover the blood stain in the bedroom with it. Nobody will get suspicious if your wedding dress lies on the floor after your wedding night." He headed out of the room and set the dress down on the ground.

Luca nodded. "Good. Now let's get going. I don't want to risk staying here a moment longer than absolutely necessary." He held out his hand for Aria, who took it. I suspected the tension between them would be over after tonight. The way they looked at each other gave me hope that Luca would forgive her for her secrecy. After pulling his gun, he opened the door and peered out into the corridor.

"Stay close to me," Romero told me, drawing his own gun and grasping my hand with his free one.

Luca gave a curt nod, then pushed the door open wider and stepped out, Aria a step behind him. Romero led me after them. Nobody said anything. The long corridor was empty but from below you could hear scattered laughter and music from the party. The smell of smoke travelled up. Immediately I was reminded of Benito's breath and the taste of his tongue in my mouth. I shoved the thought out of my mind.

I needed to focus. I really hoped none of the guests would decide to head our way. Luca or Romero would have to shoot them. What if it was someone I knew? I didn't even want to think about it. Aria glanced over her shoulder at me as Luca pulled her along. The same worry I felt was reflected on her face.

CHAPTER EIGHTEEN

Liliana

Romero and Luca showed only determination and vigilance as they led us through the house. Eventually we arrived in front of Gianna's and Matteo's door. Luca knocked lightly, but I could tell from the thunderous look in his eyes that he'd have loved to take the door down if it weren't for the risk of getting overheard. Again nobody reacted and I was starting to freak out, when after another louder knock the door finally opened. Matteo appeared in the gap, hair ruffled and only dressed in boxer-shorts; they looked like he might have put them on the wrong way in his hurry and there was a bulge hidden beneath them. I drew my eyes away.

"Didn't you get the hint that I didn't want to be interrupted when I didn't answer your fucking call," Matteo muttered, then his eyes settled on Romero and me, and he grimaced. "I have a fucking bad feeling."

Luca shoved Matteo's shoulder. "For fuck's sake, Matteo, pick up when I call you. You need to get dressed. We have to leave now."

"What's wrong?" Gianna asked, coming up behind Matteo in a satin bathrobe. Her lips were red and swollen. There was really no doubt what they'd been doing before we arrived. Her gaze darted from Aria to me. "Shit, something bad happened, right? Did the asshole hurt you?" She slipped past Matteo despite his and Luca's protests and hugged me.

"He's dead," I whispered.

"Good," she said without hesitation. She patted Romero's shoulder. "You did it, didn't you?"

Romero smiled tightly. "Yeah, which brings us to the reason why we need to hurry."

"Romero is right. We need to get out of this house before someone realizes that the groom is dead," Luca said impatiently.

"I'd have bet everything that I'd be the one to start a war between the Outfit and the Famiglia. Kudos to you, Romero, for proving me wrong for once," Matteo said grinning.

"I would have bet that too," Romero said.

Luca sighed. "I hate to interrupt your chitchat but we need to get the fuck going."

Matteo nodded and motioned for Gianna to get into their room. The rest of us followed and waited while Matteo and Gianna got dressed. Every time I heard voices, I jumped, half-expecting Father or Dante to rip open the door and shoot us all on the spot. Romero brushed a few strands that had fallen over my eyes away from my face. The look in his eyes made me realize that it was worth it. Love was worth risking it all. I just wished I hadn't dragged others into danger with me. Five minutes later, the six of us left the room and continued our journey through the house. The sounds of the party had dwindled further, which meant more people could be walking back to their rooms and potentially cross our paths, but so far we'd been lucky.

We took the second staircase in the back of the house down to the first floor and headed for the door that led to the underground garage. Most houses in this area had them because outside space was limited. There was the sound of steps from the corridor to the left of the door. Romero pulled me to a stop and pointed his gun ahead. Both Matteo and Luca did the same. My pulse pounded in my temples. They had silencers on their barrels but a shooting always made some noise, and I really didn't want to have more blood on my hands.

Someone turned the corner into our hallway and I clutched at Romero's arm to stop him from shooting. It was Fabiano. He jerked to a stop with his own gun pointed at us. I didn't even know he wore a gun, especially to my wedding. He was too young for this. His eyes scanned our small group, his dark brows drawing together in suspicion. He was still in his festive vest and trousers. What was going on here?

Aria put her hand on Luca's arm with the gun but he didn't lower it, neither did Matteo despite Gianna's urgent whispering.

"Don't hurt him," I pleaded. Romero didn't take his eyes off my brother but he lightly squeezed my hand in response.

"What's going on here?" Fabiano asked firmly, standing even taller than usual and trying to look like a man. With the gun and that serious expression he almost managed to look like more than a teenage boy.

"Put that gun down," Luca ordered.

Fabiano laughed but it sounded nervous. "No way. I want to know what's going on." His eyes moved from Aria to Gianna then to me, and finally settled on Romero's hand, which was clutching mine.

"Why are you even running around with a gun? Shouldn't you be in bed?" Aria asked and was about to take a step toward our brother but Luca pulled her back.

"I have guard duties," Fabiano said with a hint of pride.

"But you aren't inducted yet," I said, confused. I would have noticed if he'd started the process, right? Fabi had always told me everything. It had been us against the rest after Gianna and Aria had moved to New York.

"I started the induction process a few weeks ago. This is my first task," Fabi said. The hand with his gun was shaking slightly. If I noticed it, Romero, Luca and Matteo definitely had. I wasn't sure it was a good thing because his nervousness made them realize he was still a kid, or a bad thing because it made him an easy target in their eyes.

"Father gave it to you because he thought it would be an easy first job, right? Nothing bad ever happens at weddings," I tried to joke.

Fabi didn't even crack a smile, neither did anyone else. I exchanged a look with Aria and Gianna. We had to escape, that much was clear, but we couldn't risk Fabi getting hurt.

"He gave me the job because he knew I was responsible and capable," Fabi said, sounding like Father's personal parrot. My chest tightened. What if Fabi really didn't let us go? The way he pointed his gun at us, he appeared absolutely determined. Had he changed so much?

"You don't really think you can kill all three of us, do you?" Matteo asked with a twisted grin.

Gianna shot him a glower. "Shut up, Matteo."

Fabi shifted on his feet but his face remained hard. When had he learned to wear a poker face like that? "I can try," Fabi said.

"Fabiano," Luca said calmly. "They are your sisters. Do you really want to risk them getting hurt?"

"Why is Lily here? Why isn't she with her husband? I want to know what's going on. Why are you trying to take her with you? She's part of the Outfit, not of New York."

"I can't stay here, Fabi. Do you remember how you told me I shouldn't marry Benito? That it wasn't right?"

"That's been a long time ago, and you said yes to him today. Where is he anyway?"

I glanced at Romero. Something in my expression must have given it away.

"You killed him, didn't you?" Fabi accused, his narrowed eyes switching between Matteo, Romero and Luca. "Was this some kind of trick to weaken the Outfit? Father always said you'd stab us in the back one day." He raised his gun a bit higher.

Aria tried to move toward him again, but Luca practically shoved her behind him.

"He's my brother!" she hissed.

"He's a soldier of the Outfit."

"Fabi," I said. "The Famiglia didn't try to weaken the Outfit. This isn't about power. It's all my fault. Benito tried to hurt me and I stabbed him. That's why I need to leave. Father would punish me, maybe even kill me."

Fabi's eyes widened, making him look younger at once. "You killed your husband?"

Romero's hand around mine tightened, but the hand with his gun was steady. He hadn't moved it at all. It was still pointed straight at Fabi's head. If he killed my brother...I couldn't even finish the thought.

"I didn't know what else to do," I said. I decided not to mention that Benito had still been very much alive when Romero plunged his knife into his heart. That would have complicated things even further.

"What about you and him?" Fabi nodded toward Romero. "I'm not stupid. There's something going on between you."

285

There was no denying it, and I had a feeling that Fabi would get angry if I tried to lie to him. Matteo had inched closer to Fabi while we'd been talking. I wasn't sure what he planned to do but knowing Matteo it wouldn't end well.

"We've been together for a while. You know I never wanted to marry Benito but Father didn't give me a choice."

"So you want to leave Chicago and the Outfit for New York like Gianna and Aria," Fabi said.

"I have to," I said.

"You could come with us," Aria suggested. Realizing her mistake, she peered up at Luca, who would have to accept Fabi into the Famiglia.

"You could become part of the Famiglia," he said immediately.

Fabi shook his head. "Father needs me. I'm part of the Outfit. I made an oath."

"If you're not fully inducted yet, it's not as binding," Matteo said, which was not quite a lie, but really, he'd be treated like a traitor if he ran off anyway and the punishment would be the same.

Fabi glared. "I won't betray the Outfit."

"Then you'll have to stop us from leaving," Luca said simply. "And we won't let you. There will be blood, and you will die."

I stiffened and was about to say something but Romero gave a small shake of his head.

"I'm a good shot," Fabi said indignantly.

"I believe you. But are you better than all three of us? Do you really want your sister Lily to be punished? If you force her to stay, you sign her death warrant."

Conflict showed on Fabi's face. "If I let you leave, and someone finds out, they will kill me too. I could die an honest death if I tried to stop you."

Luca nodded. "You could, and they would sing your praise, but you'd be dead all the same. Do you want to die today?"

Fabi didn't say anything but he'd lowered his gun a few inches.

"Nobody has to find out that you let us leave. You could have tried to stop us but we were too many," Romero said suddenly.

"They will think I was scared and ran away, and that's why you escaped."

Luca gave Romero a small nod. "Not if you got wounded. We could shoot you in the arm. This was meant as an easy first job, nobody expects you to be capable of stopping the best fighters of New York. They won't hold it against you if you got shot."

"You want to shoot my brother?" Aria asked incredulously.

"What if you injure him seriously?" I added.

"I could hit the zit on his chin if I wanted to, I think I can manage to hit an unproblematic spot on his arm," Matteo said with his shark-grin. "And we're taking a risk by not just killing him, so an arm wound is really nothing."

"So what do you say, Fabiano?" Luca asked quickly before Matteo could say more. None of the men had lowered their guns yet.

Fabi nodded slowly and aimed his weapon at the ground. "Okay. But I will have to call for help. I can't wait more than a few minutes or they'll get suspicious."

"A few minutes should be enough for us to drive away," Luca said. "They will follow us once they figure out what's going on but five minutes will bring enough distance between us and them. Dante isn't someone who likes fighting in the open, so I doubt he'll send his men on a wild car chase. He'll attack us later, once he's figured out the best way to hurt us."

My stomach tightened. All because of me. How selfish could a person be to let others risk so much for her?

Romero gave me an encouraging smile, but for once it didn't manage to cheer me up. "War with the Outfit was inevitable. Things have gotten worse by the day."

Luca looked over to us. "That's true. If it weren't for Aria and Gianna, Matteo and I wouldn't even have come to Chicago for the wedding."

That might have been the case, but Benito's death would put fuel into the fire. Things would get very ugly now.

"Let's do this now," Matteo urged. "We're wasting time."

"I think we should move our shooting to the garage. Maybe that will buy us additional time. People won't hear your scream as easily," Romero suggested.

Together we headed for the door and down a flight of stairs into the underground garage. It wasn't as big as the one I'd seen in New York. Despite our decision to work together, none of the men had put their guns back into their holder yet. When we stopped close to our two rental cars, I slipped out of Romero's grasp and walked up to Fabi. I didn't miss the way, Romero tensed and raised his gun, but I trusted Fabi. Maybe he was on his way to becoming a soldier of the Outfit, but he was also my little brother. That wouldn't change. I hugged him and after a moment he wrapped his arms around me. In the last year, he'd avoided public displays of affection because he'd tried to act cool, but it felt good to have him close, especially since I didn't know when I'd get another chance to see him.

"I'm sorry for getting you into trouble," I whispered. "I wished things were different."

"I never liked Benito," Fabi said only. "Father shouldn't have married you off to that guy."

Suddenly Gianna and Aria were there too, and took their turns embracing us.

"We have to go now," Luca reminded us.

I pulled away from Fabi and returned to Romero. He motioned for me to get into the car, while Aria and Gianna got

289

into the other. I watched as they tried to figure out the best way to fake a shooting. Eventually Fabi fired two muffled shots, and then it was Romero's and Matteo's turn. When Matteo's bullet, sliced through Fabi's upper arm, I winced. My brother dropped his gun and fell to his knees, his face scrunched up in pain. Nothing about that was fake. Romero rushed toward our car and slid behind the steering wheel before flooring the gas. Luca pressed the button that made the garage doors slide open. Most guests had parked in the driveway so I worried that the sound would draw attention to our flight even before Fabi started screaming. I doubted anyone had heard the silenced shots through the thick ceiling of the underground garage. Romero steered our car up the slope and down the driveway. Matteo was behind the steering wheel of the other car and close behind us. We raced down the driveway, past a couple of drunk guests who sat on one of the marble benches on the side. My heart stuttered in my chest, but there was no time for worry. I clutched the seat as we drove off the premises at dizzying speed. I glanced through the rearview mirror, but the only car behind us was the one with my sisters and their husbands. "Nobody is following us," I said.

"Give it a moment. Most of them are drunk and it'll take a while for them to figure out what's going on, but someone will be sober enough to chase us," Romero said.

He looked calm about it. This wasn't something new to him, even if the circumstances that had led to us being here were, but

Romero had been a Made Man for a long time. This wasn't his first chase and it wouldn't be his last.

I squeezed my eyes shut, trying to come to terms with everything that had happened in the last twenty-four hours. I'd walked down the aisle toward a husband I hated, a husband the man I loved had killed for me. Romero linked our fingers and my eyes shot open. Despite our speed, he was driving with only one hand. He'd stashed his gun in the compartment between our seats. I gave him a grateful smile. "When we're back in New York, what happens then?"

"You move in with me." He paused. "Unless you'd rather stay with one of your sisters."

I shook my head. "I don't want to be away from you again."

Romero brought my hand to his lips and kissed it gently, but then his eyes darted to the side mirror and he tensed. He let go of me and grabbed his gun.

I peered over my shoulder. Three cars were chasing us. I sank deeper into my seat and folded my hands, sending a quick prayer above. I wasn't particularly religious but it seemed like the only thing I could do. So far not a single shot had been fired from either side and it made me wonder if the Outfit had set a trap somewhere. "Why aren't they shooting?"

"This is a residential area and Dante doesn't like to draw attention to the Outfit. I assume he gave orders to wait until we're

291

out of the city limits, which will be any minute now. We're crossing over to an industrial area."

He was right. Once the family homes were replaced by storage facilities, the Outfit cars closed in and started firing. Since Matteo was close behind us with the other rental car, Romero didn't get a clear shot at our pursuers, but I could see Luca shooting bullet after bullet through the open passenger window. I couldn't see Aria and Gianna; they were probably crouched on the backseat so they didn't get hit by bullets.

What if we didn't get away? What if all of our lives ended here?

One of the bullets tore through the tyre of one of our pursuers. The car spun around and stopped. But the other two cars closed in. I couldn't even see their license tag anymore.

I wasn't sure how long they chased us but I knew at one point either Matteo or Romero would make a mistake and lose control of their car.

Suddenly both cars slowed and then they did a u-turn.

"Why have they stopped following us?"

"Dante's orders, I assume. I told you, he is a very cautious man. He'll wait for a better opportunity to make us pay. This is too risky for his taste," Romero said.

I exhaled. I knew it was far from over. From what I knew of Dante, Romero was right, but I was simply glad that tonight we'd all get away unscathed. We'd figure out the rest tomorrow. I glanced at Romero again. I couldn't believe I'd finally be allowed to be with him. Except for two toilet breaks, we didn't stop on our drive to New York and then we barely spoke. When the skyline of New York finally rose up outside of the car, relief flooded me. For some reason the city already felt like home and I knew we'd be safer here. This was Luca's city. It wouldn't be easy for Dante to attack us here.

CHAPTER NINETEEN

Romero

After more than fourteen hours on the road, we arrived at Luca's penthouse. Lily had fallen asleep a couple of times during our drive but she'd startled awake almost instantly. She was probably having nightmares about Benito. I was so fucking glad that I'd killed him. When I'd walked into the master bedroom and seen Benito with a letter opener in his body, I'd wanted to scream with joy. I knew the next few weeks and months, maybe even years, would be hard on the Famiglia, and for each of us. Dante would retaliate with everything he had.

I parked the car in the underground garage and got out. Lily could hardly stand on her own feet from exhaustion but she put on a brave face. I wanted nothing more than to take her home with me, but first Luca, Matteo and I needed to have a talk without the risk of an Outfit attack.

When we stepped into the penthouse, Aria and Gianna led Lily toward the sofa. A protest lay on the tip of my tongue. I still felt very protective of her after almost losing her and wanted her at my side at all times, but it would have been ridiculous to say something. She was still in the same room as me. Her longing gaze in my direction when she sat down between her sisters told me that Lily felt the same way.

"We have to call everyone in for a meeting. They need to know that the truce between the Outfit and us is no longer in effect. I don't want anyone to walk into a trap because they thought they could trust an Outfit bastard," Luca said. I could tell that he was still pissed at me, and he had every right to be. That he hadn't killed me was a bigger sign of his friendship than I'd ever hoped for.

"Some people might not be happy with Liliana and you," Matteo said. "They probably won't act on their anger but I'd be careful if I were you."

"Don't worry. And if someone lays a finger on Lily, I'll rip their throat out."

"I think you have done enough damage for a while," Luca said tightly. "And nobody will try to hurt Liliana. She's now part of the Famiglia and under my protection. I assume you're going to marry her?"

I had never asked her but I wanted her to be my wife. "If she says yes, then I'll marry her."

"After all the drama of today, she better marry you," Matteo muttered. He leaned against the dining table and yawned widely.

"I'll ask her soon enough."

Luca raised his hand. "This isn't our main concern right now. We have to double security measures. We didn't only kidnap Scuderi's daughter, we killed a Captain with a loyal following of soldiers. There will be blood to pay."

I chanced another look at Lily. The Outfit might try to kill her. Knowing her Father, he'd probably do it himself. He'd have to go through me if he tried to hurt her.

Liliana

After two hours in Luca's apartment, we were finally at Romero's place. I'd never been there and I was curious despite my exhaustion. I could tell that Romero was tense but I wasn't sure why. Maybe he regretted everything that had happened? Or maybe he was only worried about what was to come.

Romero unlocked his door and opened the door wide for me. I walked past him into a long hallway. Family photos in pretty silver frames decorated the walls. I promised myself to take a closer look at them when my eyes didn't fall shut anymore. Several doors branched off of the hallway. Romero led me toward the last one on the right. A master bedroom waited behind it but we didn't stop there. We had been on the road for hours and I'd been awake for more than twenty-four hours. It was already past noon but I wanted to sleep.

I could still smell Benito on me though; his blood, his sweat, his body odor. It made me sick. Romero opened the door to the adjoining bathroom. I quickly shimmied out of my clothes and stepped into the glass shower. Romero watched me silently, an unreadable look on his face. He looked exhausted. When the warm water streamed down my body, I felt some of the tension leave my limbs.

"Do you want to be alone?" Romero asked after a moment. He sounded...uncertain. That wasn't something I was used to from him. Maybe I needed to take into consideration that he needed some time to work through everything.

I shook my head. "I want you to join me."

Romero got out of his clothes. I didn't try to hide my admiration as I watched him. I loved Romero's body. I loved everything about him. I moved to the side so he could step into the shower with me. I slipped my arms around his waist and pressed my cheek against his chest as the water poured down on us. I'd missed the feel of his skin against mine. I squeezed my eyes shut. So much had happened and so much was still to come.

"Things will get really bad for Luca and the Famiglia now, won't they?"

Romero stroked my back. "The union between the Famiglia and the Outfit was bound to break at some point. I'd rather have it over something as important as you than over money or politics. You are worth a war."

"I'm not sure Luca agrees. He's probably already regretting taking me to New York."

"I know Luca. He doesn't regret his decision. Once he's made up his mind, he stands by his decision. And this wasn't only for you. It was also for Aria and Gianna. They want you to be happy."

I tilted my head up and smiled up at him. His body shielded me from the water. Romero lowered his head and kissed my forehead, then my lips. We didn't deepen the kiss, instead we finished showering quickly. Romero stepped out first and took a towel. He wrapped it around me and gently started drying my body. I relaxed under his gentle ministrations. The last bit of tension slid out of me. After he was done with me, I took a towel out of the shelf and dried Romero in turn. He closed his eyes when I massaged his shoulders. "How do you feel?" I asked softly. I knew men, and Made Men in particular, didn't like to talk about their feelings, especially sadness or fear.

He looked at me. "Tired."

"No, I mean because you had to kill Benito for me. Are you okay?"

Romero let out a humorless laugh. He took my hand and led me back into the bedroom. He sank down on the bed and pulled me between his legs, then made me sit down on one of them. "He hasn't been my first and he won't be my last, but I enjoyed his death more than the others, and I don't regret it. I'd do it again and enjoy it just as much."

Romero

298

It was the truth and now that Lily and I would start living together, she needed to know it, needed to know every dark part of me. I searched her eyes for a sign of revulsion but there was none. She kissed my cheek before resting her head on my shoulder. Her fingers traced my chest lightly. That and the feel of her firm butt on my thigh stirred my cock, but now wasn't the time to follow that urge. Not too long ago Lily had to fight off her new husband, had to stab him and watch him die. She needed time to recover. I stood and lifted Lily into my arm, then carried her around the bed and lay her down. She kept her hands wrapped around my neck and didn't let go even as I tried to straighten. "Lily," I said quietly. "You need to rest."

She shook her head and pulled me down on top of her. I braced myself on my elbows so I didn't crush her under my weight. Lily wrapped her legs around my hips and dug her heels into my lower back, pressing me down.

I didn't resist. Slowly I lowered myself until our bodies were flush against each other and my cock pressed against her pussy. She raised her head to claim my mouth for a kiss. I stared into her eyes, they were soft and filled with longing. I wasn't sure how could I have ever believed that Lily didn't want me. Her eyes showed her love for me as plain as day.

"I need you," she murmured, lifting her hips a few inches and making my tip glide over her lower lips. I let out a small hiss at the sensation. She was wet and warm. She always felt so fucking inviting. I didn't need to be asked twice. I always wanted her. I quickly put on a condom, cupped her head and eased into her slowly, and as I did I realized just how much I needed it too. She was tighter than usual, maybe from tension and exhaustion, and I made sure to be careful.

I made love to her slowly. This wasn't about getting off, about being consumed by desire and lust, this was something to show us everything was okay. A few days ago I'd thought I would lose her forever and now she was mine.

Between soft moans she told me she loved me. I kissed her lips. I'd never been the overly emotional type but I never got tired of her saying those words. "I love you too," I said quietly. It still felt strange to admit it to someone.

When we lay in each other's arms afterward, I felt a deep, all-encompassing peace I'd never felt before.

***

I woke at sunrise but Lily wasn't there. I jerked upright, reaching for my gun on the nightstand, as usual expecting the worst. But Lily was there at the window, looking out. I didn't have floor to ceiling windows like Luca's penthouse, but they weren't exactly small. But Lily had grown up as the daughter of a Consigliere. She'd had the best of everything all her life.

I swung my legs out of bed and walked toward her.

"It's not as grand as you're used to. Your family's townhouse and Aria's penthouse are much bigger than my apartment. You're going to be the wife of a mere soldier."

Lily jumped slightly, then she peered over her shoulder at me.

"Do you really think I care about things like that? When I lived in a huge house and had more money than I could possibly spend I was never happy, but when I'm with you I am."

"Still, this will be a big change for you," I said. I wasn't exactly poor but she wouldn't be able to afford as much as she had done before.

Lily turned to me fully and touched my cheeks. "I want only you, Romero. I don't care about money." She motioned around. "And this is a gorgeous place. Most people would be happy to live here. I love it."

That was why I knew Lily was the one.

The sun finally peeked over the surrounding skyscrapers. "Look," I said, pointing out toward the city.

Lily turned around in my arms, her back pressed against my chest, as we watched the sunrise. I wanted to enjoy this moment of peace and quiet, because I knew there wouldn't be many more moments like that today. The Famiglia was at war with the Outfit now.

"I'm worried about Fabi. I wished there was a way to find out if he's alright. What if Dante and Father didn't believe his story? I could never forgive myself if something happened to him because of me."

"I'll figure out a way to get information, but I'm sure he's fine. He's your father's only son. Even if your father is unhappy with him, Fabi won't be punished too hard."

"He's married to a young woman now. He could produce a new heir," she said bitterly.

"Let me call Luca and see if he knows anything," I told her and untangled myself from her. Luca would probably be awake already, if he'd gone to bed at all.

Luca picked up after the second call. "Did you kill another Outfit member?" It was mostly said in a joking way, but I could hear the strain in his voice.

"No. Have you heard anything? Did Dante try to contact you?"

"He didn't. He only sent me an email through one of his men that our cooperation is terminated."

"He didn't even contact you himself, or at least through his Consigliere?" I asked. That was a blatant show of disrespect and showed how bad the situation really was.

"I don't think Scuderi is very keen on talking to me right now," Luca said wryly.

Lily came up to me, an anxious look on her face.

"I suppose not," I said. "Listen Luca, Lily is really worried about her brother. Do you have any way of finding out if he's okay?"

"Aria has been trying to get in contact with Valentina but so far she hasn't had any luck. She'll try again later. You and Lily should come over anyway. We have a lot to discuss and the women can spend time together."

"Alright. We'll be there soon." I hung up.

"And?" Lily asked hopefully.

"Luca doesn't have any information about your brother yet, but he and Aria are trying to contact Valentina."

"Do you really think Val will react to Aria's calls? She's Dante's wife and now that there's war between New York and Chicago, she'd risk a lot by getting into contact with Aria."

Romero touched my cheek. "We'll find out about your brother, Lily, I promise."

We showered quickly before we headed for Aria's apartment. When we stepped into the penthouse, Gianna and Matteo were already there despite it being only seven in the morning. The scent of freshly made coffee greeted me and Danishes waited on the kitchen counter. My sisters were standing and talking and I steered toward them while Romero walked up to Luca and Matteo who sat on the stools at the kitchen island.

Aria put her arm around me. "How are you Lily?"

"Okay. I didn't sleep much but I'm just happy to be here with you and Romero."

"Of course, you are," Gianna said. "I'm so glad Romero got rid of that sick bastard Benito."

An image of Benito's blood covered body popped into my head but I pushed it aside. I didn't want to think of him anymore. He wasn't part of my life anymore.

Aria handed me a cup of coffee. "Here, you look like you need it. And you should eat something."

"Mother hen mode active," Gianna teased but then she too fixed me with a worried look. "And? How was your first night with Romero?"

"Gianna," Aria warned. "Lily has gone through a lot."

"It's okay. I loved spending the night in Romero's arms without being afraid of getting caught. For the first time we could watch the sunset together."

"I'm so glad you are happy," Aria said.

I nodded. "But I can't stop worrying about Fabi. I want to know if he's okay."

"I've left two voicemails on Val's phone. I really hope she'll call me back."

"Even if she does," Matteo said. "We don't know her motives. She might be doing it on Dante's orders and be looking for information."

"Val wouldn't do that," Aria said uncertainly.

"She's the wife of the Boss. The Outfit is with where her loyalties lie. You are part of the Famiglia and that makes you the enemy," Luca said.

I glanced at Romero. All this because I loved a man I wasn't supposed to love, and because I wanted to be with him. Was I a selfish bitch? Romero met my gaze. I wished I could say I wouldn't do it again but looking at him now, I knew I'd stab Benito again to save myself from a horrible marriage and be with the guy I was supposed to spend my life with.

I was a selfish bitch.

"Hey," Aria said gently. "Don't look so sad."

I turned back to her. "You and Val got along so well. I know you talked on the phone often and now you can't because of the mess I caused."

"You are my sister Lily, and seeing you happy and having you in New York with us is more important than my friendship with Val. And maybe Luca can negotiate another truce with Dante. Dante is a pragmatic man."

"Not as long as your father is Consigliere. It would be like a slap in the face for your father if Dante didn't seek revenge," Romero said.

"I hate this revenge crap," Gianna muttered. Matteo stood from his stool, went over to her and pulled her against him with a grin. "I know you do, but it's how things are."

Gianna rolled her eyes but let Matteo kiss her. In the past that would have sent a stab of envy through me, but now I walked over to Romero and leaned against him. His arm came around my shoulder and he kissed my temple. "We've been at war with the Outfit before. We'll handle this."

"I don't want people to die because of me."

"Romero is right. We will get through this. And I don't think Dante will kill one of ours. The Russian threat is still too strong. He can't risk his soldiers' lives in a war with us."

"Nor can we," added Matteo.

A phone rang, making us all jump. Aria snatched her phone off the counter and peered down at the screen, then she raised her head with wide eyes. "It's Val."

Luca got up. "Don't let anything slip that Fabi helped us and be careful."

Aria nodded, then she lifted her phone to her ear. "Hello?" She paused. "I'm so glad you called. Can you talk?" Aria listened for a few seconds, her expression dropping. "I know. I only wanted to ask about Fabi. He got shot when he tried to stop us and I'm just so worried about him. He's so young. He shouldn't have been involved in this. Can you tell me how he's doing?"

Aria released a breath. "So he's okay? He'll be able to use his arm like he used to?"

I slumped against Romero in relief, but at Aria's next words I tensed again. "Is he in huge trouble because he wasn't able to stop us?" Aria nodded, then gave us a thumbs-up. She was silent for a long time after that, listening to Val.

"Okay, I will tell him. Thank you so much, Val. I won't forget it. I hope our men figure something out soon. I'll miss talking to you. Bye."

"So?" I asked, the moment she had hung up.

"Father and Dante seem to believe Fabi's story. Nobody blames him for letting us get away. He didn't have enough experience for the job. Only because of Father's insistence did he get it in the first place."

Luca looked like a blood-hound on a trail. "Did she say anything else? About Dante's plans and his mood?"

"He's furious," Aria said with a shrug. "But he wanted Val to give you a message," she told Luca, her eyes flitting to me.

Romero became still beside me. I had a feeling I knew what kind of message.

"If we send Lily back today, they might consider not retaliating."

Romero pushed himself off the stool. "She won't go back."

Luca narrowed his eyes but then he took a deep breath. "Of course not. Dante knows we won't agree to that offer. That's why he made it."

Romero rubbed my arm lightly and brought his mouth down to my ear. "Nobody will take you away from me. I'll fight a million wars if it means I can keep you."

***

Two days had passed but they might as well have been a lifetime. Romero had been busy and I'd spent most of my time with my sisters. But tonight Romero wanted us to have dinner together alone in his, no, *our* apartment. He'd ordered food at his favorite Italian place and spread it all out on the dining table in his huge kitchen.

A few minutes into the dinner, Romero set down his fork. "Luca made me Captain."

"Really? That's wonderful!" I could see how much this meant to him. I'd never gotten the feeling that he was unhappy as Aria's bodyguard but of course it was a big deal if you got promoted, especially because the mob was a place where people usually took over their father's position. "What business are you going to get?"

"I'll be taking over a few clubs in Harlem. The old Captain has cancer and needs to retire, but he's got only daughters so Luca decided to give me his businesses. I'll be making more money for us."

I smiled. "You know I don't care about that. I'm just happy for you because you deserve it."

Romero grimaced. "Some people don't think so after I caused war with the Outfit."

"I thought the majority was eager to stop cooperating with Chicago?"

"Those think I deserve to be Captain," he said in amusement.

"So who will be guarding Aria?"

"That's a bit of a problem. Sandro will guard Aria and Gianna for now. But that won't be enough especially when you're with them often. He can't protect all three of you, but we'll figure something out."

When we were done with desert, Romero got up and walked around the table toward me. I watched him in confusion. Did he look nervous?

Without warning, Romero dropped to his knees right in front of me and pulled a small satin box from his pants pocket. I froze as he held it out to me and opened it, revealing a beautiful diamond ring. Of course I'd hoped we'd marry soon. It was expected in our world but I hadn't expected Romero to have bought a ring already. He hadn't wasted any time, that was for sure!

"I know you've been through a lot and your last wedding experience was horrible, but I hope you give it another chance. I want to be the husband you deserve. I want to make you happy and love you, if you let me. Will you marry me?"

I flung myself into his arms, my knees colliding with the hard floor but I hardly felt it. "God yes." I kissed him fiercely.

Romero grinned when he pulled back. We didn't get up from the floor. As long as I was in Romero's arms I didn't care where I was. "I understand if you want to wait a bit before you marry me. You're probably not in the mood to plan another wedding."

I shook my head quickly. "This is a wedding I want to plan. This time I will enjoy it. I can take Aria and Gianna wedding dress shopping with me and actually be excited about it."

He chuckled. "But I want you to meet my family first. That way we can tell them the good news."

"Oh, sure," I said slowly. I was excited to meet Romero's family but I was also worried that they wouldn't like me.

***

The next day Romero took me to his family. His mother lived with her new husband and Romero's three sisters in a modest apartment not too far from us. I shouldn't have worried that they wouldn't like me. They were kind, humble people. I knew his two oldest sisters already from my birthday party many years ago but we'd grown and his oldest sister Tamara had already started college. Something I'd never considered because I knew Father wouldn't approve of it.

Dinner in my family had always been a formal affair, with my Father sitting at the end of the table and with everyone on their best behavior, well except for Gianna perhaps. But this was easy-going and fun. We talked and laughed all evening, and when Romero told them that we were going to marry, they hugged me and were actually happy. Nobody looked at me strangely because I'd married Benito less than a week ago.

I knew right then that I would be happy in this new life, not just because of Romero's love, but because of my sisters and my new family. That wouldn't stop me from missing Fabi but I had to trust that he would find his own happiness one day even if we'd never see each other again.

Epilogue

<u>Liliana</u>

I'd waited for this moment for a long time, had imagined it so often that it felt almost like a deja-vu. When a few weeks ago at my wedding to Benito, there had been only anxiety, sadness and fear, I now felt like I could fly. Happiness and euphoria buzzed in my body. I couldn't wait for the party to be over so Romero could undress me and make love to me over and over again. The only thing missing for a perfect day was Fabi. I hadn't seen him since my wedding night and I wasn't sure if I ever would. I didn't even know if he was alright. If he'd gotten in trouble for getting shot and letting us get away.

Romero lifted me into his arms under the excited cheers of our guests. I couldn't help but laugh. I'd never felt lighter, as if any moment I would soar up into the night sky. I risked a glance up, wondering if Mother was watching. I'd done what she'd wanted. I'd risked happiness, and it was worth it. Romero kissed my cheek, drawing my attention back to him. Our eyes met and my heart swelled with love. He started walking toward our room, and this time I couldn't wait to arrive, to be alone with my husband, to have him to myself for the night. This was how it was supposed to be. Every women should be happy on her wedding day, should feel safe in the arms of her husband, should have the right to marry for love and not because someone decided her match for her.

I pressed my face into the crook of his neck, smiling to myself. From the corner of my eyes, I caught sight of my sisters and her husbands. Aria beamed at me, and Gianna wiggled her eyebrows. I stifled a laugh. Romero brushed his lips across my ear. "I can't wait to undress you and kiss every inch of your silky skin."

Desire rushed through me. "Hurry," I whispered.

Romero chuckled but he did actually speed up. He opened the door to our bedroom with his elbow, then kicked the door shut before crossing the room toward the bed and setting me down.

"God, you're so damn beautiful. I can't believe you're finally mine."

"I've always been yours."

Romero cupped my cheek and kissed me fiercely before his hands started their work on my dress, slowly uncovering inch by inch of my body. He kissed every new spot, but not the places I wanted him to. When I lay before him in my corset and panties, his eyes traced my body with hunger and reverence. I loved that look. It made me feel like the most beautiful girl in the world. He let his fingers glide over my ankles then up my calves and thighs until he'd reached my panties. I lifted my hips. Romero let out a low laugh and kissed my hipbone, then licked the spot. "Romero, please." He hooked his fingers under my panties and slid them down. When he came back up, he parted my legs and closed his mouth over my folds. I exhaled. With slow strokes of his tongue Romero drove me higher and when he slipped a finger into me, pleasure rolled over me. My toes curled and my butt lifted off the bed but Romero kept up his pleasuring until I couldn't take it anymore and pushed his head away, laughing and gasping.

"Your first orgasm as my wife," Romero said with a self-satisfied grin as he crawled up until he hovered over me.

"I hope not the last," I teased.

"Are you saying you're not done yet?" He slipped a finger into me again and moved it slowly.

I shook my head.

Romero pulled his finger out and unlaced my corset, laying my breasts bare. He sucked one of my nipples into his mouth as he eased his finger into me again.

It felt so good, and I could feel myself getting close, but I needed to feel Romero inside of me. "I need you inside of me," I begged.

Romero didn't waste any time. He climbed out of bed and quickly undressed. His cock was already hard and glistening. He moved between my legs. I closed my hand around his shaft, enjoying its firmness and heat. I stroked a few times before I guided it toward my entrance. When the tip brushed my opening, I relaxed against the pillows. Romero started moving into me slowly. I could feel every inch of him until he finally filled me completely. I wrapped my fingers around Romero's neck and pulled him down to me for a kiss. I loved kissing him, the way his stubble lightly scratched my lip, his taste, everything. I never got enough.

Romero moved in a slow rhythm, sliding almost all the way out, only to drive his cock all the way into me again. "Caress yourself," he ordered in a low murmur.

I didn't hesitated. I sneaked my arm between our bodies and my fingers found my clit. I started to draw small circles. My fingertips brushed Romero's cock occasionally and it drove me even higher.

"Yes, baby, come for me," Romero rasped. His kissed my neck and one of his hands grasped my leg and hooked it over his hip. I caressed myself even faster and when Romero pushed into me again, I shattered. My body arched off the bed. Romero groaned, his pushes coming harder and faster and then I felt him release into me.

I trembled from the aftershocks of my orgasm. Romero buried his face against my neck and I ran my hands through his hair and down his back. After a moment, he rolled off me and onto his back, pulling me with him so I half lay on his chest. I raked my fingers through his chest hair and listened to his fast heartbeat.

"I can't believe you're finally mine. Nobody can take you away from me now," Romero pressed a kiss to the top of my head. I smiled, sated and happy. Briefly, my thoughts drifted to Fabi, wondering what he was doing now. Without him and my sisters, I wouldn't be lying beside Romero right now. They'd risked so much for my happiness, so had Romero. I would always be grateful for what they'd done. I'd try to make their sacrifices worth it, I'd try to live life to the fullest.

I turned around and Romero wrapped his arms around me from behind. It was late and I was exhausted. Eventually Romero drifted off to sleep. I loved listening to him sleep beside me. It always set me as ease.

Romero's even breathing fanned over my naked shoulder. I couldn't fall asleep even though I was sated and exhausted. I slipped out under Romero's arm and slipped out of bed. I grabbed a bathrobe and put it on before I made my way toward the door and walked out onto the balcony, which had a beautiful view over the premises and the ocean. Tomorrow we'd return to New York and then our life as a married couple would really start. I watched the night sky. The stars were always brighter out of the city, and yet there were always a couple of stars that shone the brightest. As a small kid I used to think they represented people who had died and who were watching over us as stars. I'd stopped believing in that a long time ago. Still I couldn't help but wonder if somewhere somehow Mother was watching me. Would she be happy for me? Maybe even proud? I would never find out, but I'd kept my promise to her. I'd risked everything for love and happiness. I glanced over my shoulder at Romero's sleeping form, then with a last glimpse at the stars, I returned into the bed and snuggled against him. He wrapped his arm around me. "You were gone," he mumbled.

"I needed fresh air," I said softly.

"I'm glad you're back."

"I love you," I whispered.

Romero's arms tightened around me and he kissed my temple. "And I love you." Maybe things wouldn't always be easy in the future, but I knew I'd never regret taking this risk. Love was worth every risk.

Books in the

Born in Blood Mafia Chronicles:

Bound by Honor

(Aria & Luca)

Bound by Duty

(Valentina & Dante)

Bound by Hatred

(Gianna & Matteo)

Bound By Temptation

(Liliana & Romero)

Bound By Vengeance

Other Books by Cora Reilly

Voyeur Extraordinaire

Lover Extraordinaire (2015)

<>

Not Meant To Be Broken

About the Author

Cora Reilly is the author of erotic romance and New Adult novels. She lives in Germany with too many pets and only one husband. She's a lover of good vegetarian food, wine and books, and she wants nothing more than to travel the world.